1

THE STRANGER

The man groaned and tried to move as he slowly regained consciousness. He felt nauseous. His head throbbed, and he couldn't understand where he was or how he'd come to be there. Blinking several times he still couldn't see a thing. *Was he blind?*

A low drone pounded like a bell clapper inside his skull, the pain clearing his thinking enough to realise he was trapped with no space to move. His legs were tucked up to his chest and sweat seeped from his pores. His prison cell jolted, and bit by bit the pieces fell into place. The noise and the movement were familiar. He was in a moving vehicle. He lifted his hand and hit metal. The boot of a car.

He fought back the urge to vomit and panic rose in his chest, making it hard to breathe. The stranger. He'd met the man in the car park behind a bar. The guy was looking to buy some product. He hadn't seemed like a cop. The opposite, although it was hard to tell with undercover guys these days. That's all he could recall from their brief meeting. Anything which transpired after that was lost in the fuzzy haze.

The car slowed to a stop and the man thumped against the boot lid with his fist. The noise echoed back like the sound of a sledgehammer, but he kept making a racket, praying someone would hear. Voices grew louder and he hit the metal so hard he felt blood trickling down his hand. The car moved away and he realised the voices came from a talk show playing on the car's radio. The driver had turned it up.

The ride continued along what the man sensed were smaller roads. He couldn't hear the surrounding traffic of a motorway, and didn't feel the stop and go of city streets. Depending on what his imagination concocted about what lay ahead, the man vacillated between wishing they'd hurry up and get there, and praying for more time to come up with a plan.

His best defence had always been his quick wit, and on the few occasions he'd been unable to avoid a physical confrontation, he'd got his arse kicked every time. But the man had a bad feeling a simple arse-kicking wasn't what awaited him this time. The stranger could have taken care of that behind the bar. No one would have batted an eye in Little Havana, which wasn't known for being one of Miami's safer neighbourhoods. The locals knew to keep their noses out of other people's business.

As the fog lifted from his brain, the man focused on what he could do to escape. He'd heard somewhere that newer cars had emergency boot openers inside so people couldn't be trapped. He fumbled around the interior, hunting for a switch or a handle. He found nothing within his reach, which wasn't very far considering how his frame was crushed into the limited space. He quickly gave up, thinking if the clunky ride was any indication, the vehicle wasn't a newer model.

The car slowed, turned, and continued slowly down an unpaved road, the tyres crunching on a loose gravel surface. He knew they had to be close now and the man readied himself for the only option he had left. He'd feign being unconscious when the boot opened, then make a sudden strike, hoping he could stun the stranger long enough to get out and run.

Finally coming to a complete stop, the driver turned off the ignition and all fell silent for a few moments. The car rocked as a door

BURNING SOMMER

NORA SOMMER CARIBBEAN SUSPENSE - BOOK FOUR

NICHOLAS HARVEY

HarveyBooks

Printed in the United States of America

First Printing, 2023

ISBN: (978-1-959627-16-6)

Cover design: Covered by Melinda

Cover model: Lucinda Gray

Mermaid illustration: Tracie Cotta

Editor: Andrew Chapman at Prepare to Publish

Proofreader: Gretchen Douglas

Author photograph: Lift Your Eyes Photography

This is a work of fiction. Names, characters, businesses, places, events and incidents are either the products of the author's imagination or used in a fictitious manner unless noted otherwise. Any resemblance to actual persons, living or dead, or actual events is purely coincidental. Lisa O'Neill, Tony Lunders and Max Jones names are used with permission in a fictional manner.

DEDICATION

This book is for my incredible wife, Cheryl.
I'm thankful every day for her love, support, and patience.
Loving me certainly requires an abundance of patience!

opened, then the man heard crunching footsteps approaching the back of the vehicle. He readied himself as best he could as a key scraped in the lock, followed by the clunk of the barrel turning.

When the boot lid swung open, the man was instantly blinded by the blazing Florida sunshine. He tightly closed his eyes and rolled onto his back thrashing the air above him with his fists. He hit nothing except the metal of the boot lid and more blood weeped from new cuts.

"What the fuck..." he began but a beefy hand reached down and lifted him from the boot before he could finish his sentence.

The man wound up to swing again but instead of landing a punch, his head shot back as the stranger beat him to it. A fierce pain shot through his left cheek, and he fought to stay conscious as the stranger's rough grasp rolled him out of the boot and dropped him to the ground. The man groaned and curled up to protect himself.

Grabbing the man's shirt collar, the stranger pulled him to his stumbling feet and led him to the driver's side of the car. The man could now see it was an old Buick, Pontiac, or other indistinct shitbox from the nineties. The door was open, and the stranger shoved him into the torn and stained, cloth-covered driver's seat.

They were parked down a dirt and gravel trail, which the man guessed to be in the Everglades. He could see a narrow canal of water beyond a white car parked nearby. For a second, the man considered calling for help, but he decided the car had to be staged there. The stranger wouldn't have gone to all this trouble to bring him to a spot where other people were around. Which meant what?

"What the fuck do you want with me, man?" he gasped.

Instead of answering, the stranger, a burly man who looked sixty but carried himself like a forty-year-old boxer, punched the man in the side of the head. His head swam in a fog of disorientation, only vaguely aware of vomiting down his own chest.

When the man came to once more, his head was hurting so badly, he thought the stranger might still be punching him. He pulled his hands to cradle his head but they wouldn't move and a searing pain came from both wrists. His vision cleared enough to see he was fastened to the steering wheel by hose clamps, blood oozing from the edges of the metal bands.

He searched his woozy mind for any clues as to who the hell this stranger could be. He hadn't had even the tiniest spark of recognition upon meeting him in the car park, and he was still baffled having seen him again. The stranger had a life-worn face with deep wrinkles around his eyes and the scars of a fighter blemishing his lightly tanned skin.

The man heard movement in the back of the car and smelled the pungent aroma of petrol. The stranger reappeared by the man's side and knelt down. His eyes were cold blue, blank gateways to a soul robbed of all empathy.

"What have I done to you?" the man muttered.

He'd spent his life on the wrong side of the law, but he'd always been just a petty criminal. Nothing serious or big time. He peddled dope, for fuck's sake. Pot, a few pills, nothing hardcore. He'd steered clear of the heavy stuff so he'd avoid the drug lords and crazies who owned their sections of town and regularly waged wars with each other. He was just a bit player in the ugly world of illegal narcotics which people frowned upon, then turned around and bought from him.

Was this some bullshit small-time turf war? He'd never seen this guy before and besides he remembered the stranger had an accent when he'd spoken at the car park. Not the usual East Coast or Hispanic accent — some foreign crap the ladies liked to hear.

The stranger reached into the footwell and squirted petrol sparingly from a squeeze bottle around the man's feet. He ran a line of petrol alongside the seat, then stood, reached over, and did the same along the centre of the car. He then tossed the empty bottle into the footwell. The man tried to kick it out the open door but only succeeded in bouncing it around and covering his trainers in more petrol.

"Fuck, man! Are you going to burn me?" the man spluttered in desperation, kicking his feet and wrenching his hands against the hose clamps.

The steering wheel flexed and creaked but wouldn't budge. Blood rolled freely from the cuts in the man's wrists and the pain joined the almost certain concussion from the blows in making him dizzy.

The stranger walked slowly around the car, opening the other doors and winding down each window an inch. He closed each door before moving to the next, finishing with the driver's window, where he knelt down once more, looking around the interior as though the other human being wasn't even there.

"C'mon, man, what do you want from me? You want my turf, man? Let's make a deal. This is fucking crazy; you can't just light me up, man!"

The stranger looked at him, his penetrating stare gouging a hole into his mind until it reached a place deep inside. A hidden crevice where long ago the man had shoved a memory. An unfortunate prank. A mistake of youth.

Surely it couldn't have anything to do with that? he asked himself. Could it? He closed his eyes, dragging the memory from its long-hidden grave, regret, guilt, and the filth of his past spilling aside as the thought became clearer. He opened his eyes and looked at the stranger, but the stranger was no longer looking at him. He was striking a match, and dropping it into the footwell.

"No! You fucking maniac!" the man screamed.

The stranger slowly closed the door and nudged it latched with his knee. He strolled to the front of the old car and looked through the windscreen, his expression unwavering.

The man shuddered in fear as flames licked at his feet. He pulled his legs tightly under the seat, but the petrol on his shoes had already lit. Desperately, he kicked and shoved until he'd knocked the trainers from his feet and shuffled them to the front of the footwell.

The sweltering Florida sun had kept the interior of the car at close to forty degrees centigrade, even with the doors open, but now the man could feel the intensity of the fire beginning to surround him. The carefully placed petrol formed a ring around him, and the fuel quickly lit like a fuse. He could feel the back of the seat getting scorching hot and the floor carpets ignited, searing his ankles and bare legs below his shorts.

The man screamed in terror, desperately pulling and tugging at the steering wheel. The pain in his wrists was nothing now compared to the flesh being burnt from his body as his socks caught fire. He heard a whomp behind him and knew the back of the seat had now caught. Smoke billowed in swirls above his head as the fire sucked air through the top of the windows to fuel its rage.

Pulling himself away from the flames licking his back, the man looked out of the windscreen. The stranger hadn't moved. He stared back without a hint of emotion on his face, watching the man burn to death before him.

2

LOLLYPOPS AND REGGAE

Six weeks later

Edvard looked at me from across the deck in the warm light of pre-dawn. He tilted his head to one side in the jerky, fast motion typical of lizards and birds.

"Come here," I urged, which won a head tilt to the opposite side, but no motion towards me.

We'd been playing this game for months now. He knew I had lettuce for him, which was alluring enough for him to come out of the woods before the sun rose to warm his body, but he still didn't trust me. Instinct, I guessed. His iguana brain, wrapped inside his tough blue-grey skin which looked like a spiny overcoat draped over his flesh, couldn't bring itself to approach a larger creature.

"Breakfast," I said, wiggling the green leaf near the deck in front of my wooden chair.

He blinked, tilted his head once more, and took two steps towards me. I tossed the lettuce leaf so that it landed halfway between us. He raised a foot in readiness to flee but decided to hold his ground.

"You're not very smart and you're definitely not good looking, so I'd risk it if I were you," I told him and sat back in the chair. It didn't seem like a stretch of the imagination to figure out why the indigenous blue iguanas were working towards extinction.

I looked out to the Caribbean Sea where glassy water lapped against the ironshore coastline just ten metres from my shack. The dark veil of night was lifting, revealing another calm day with little more than a gentle wisp of a breeze. Perfect conditions to freedive the reef and my hand fell to the fins resting against my chair.

Edvard had taken a small step closer to the prize and I knew if I rose from my seat he'd bolt. Leaving my fins where they were, I picked up my coffee cup from the arm of the chair instead and took another sip. What was left was lukewarm but still tasted good.

In a manic rush, the iguana decided to make his move, wiggling forward, grabbing the lettuce, and swinging his long tail to retreat to the far side of the deck.

"You're welcome," I muttered after him.

Movement in the shack caught my eye and a face appeared in the upper glass of the back door. A pretty, dark face with a mass of frizzy hair. I nodded, indicating it was clear for Jazzy to come outside. She carefully opened the door and looked for the iguana. Edvard looked her way but was now slowly munching his break-fast and didn't seem bothered.

"Did he take it from you?" Jazzy asked in a sleepy voice.

I shook my head. "He's an idiot."

Jazzy handed me my mobile phone then sat down in the other seat. "It bin buzzing," she said.

I looked at the screen. I had two missed calls and a voicemail. "*Dritt,*" I mumbled. The calls were from the West Bay station which couldn't mean anything good was going on. I put the phone down on the arm of the chair.

"You're up early," I said, taking another sip of coffee.

Jazzy squinted at me. "Dat ting buzzin' woke me up."

I kept it on silent overnight, but Jazzy was a light sleeper. Living on the streets would do that to you. She was still only fourteen and

I was providing her a temporary foster home until a permanent placement could be found. We were six months into that arrangement, and I knew she would be happy if temporary turned into long term. Most days I'd be fine with that too. Until she played up, and then the whole situation was a pain in my arse I could do without. Besides, I wasn't even twenty-one myself; what did I know about raising a teenager?

I looked back to the water where the crisp early light shimmered on the ripples. Perfect freediving weather and I wouldn't get to go out. It was Edvard's fault. If he hadn't screwed around, I'd have been in the ocean by now and Jazzy would have had no one to hand the mobile to. I returned my attention to the phone and reluctantly played the voicemail.

"Hey dere Nora, we got a situation needs your help, right quick," the local-accented voice of Station Sergeant Redburn explained. "Call me back soon as you get dis."

I sighed. Maybe it would be something exciting, an interesting case to deal with, but a niggling feeling told me it wasn't.

"What dat be about?" Jazzy asked.

I shrugged my shoulders.

"Can you still take me to da bus?"

"Take your bike," I replied, knowing Jazzy hated riding the bicycle I'd bought her. It wasn't actually riding the bike she hated; it was dealing with it the rest of the day. She was paranoid about it being stolen, which was based on the fact she'd nicked quite a few bicycles in her time. According to her, the lock wasn't an adequate deterrent.

I could probably still drop her off, but I didn't want her to think it was a given every time she asked. Calling the sergeant's direct line, I waited for him to answer.

"Nora, you on your way in?"

"No."

"Did you get my message?" he said sternly.

"*Ja.*"

There was a pause. I knew he was now replaying the message

he'd left in his own mind. He'd figure out in a second that he'd asked me to call him back.

"Right den, well, get here right now."

"Okay. Fifteen minutes."

"Actually," Redburn said quickly before I hung up, "go straight to George Town hospital. Dat's where dey need you."

"What about Jacob?" I asked, wondering how I'd meet up with my partner for our daily shift.

"I ain't talked to him. S'pose you'll meet him here when you done in town."

"Call him and tell him to be at the station in fifteen minutes," I said, remembering to add "sir" a few moments later.

"Fine. Just hurry up."

"Sir?"

"Yes?"

"What's this about?"

"Some girl we can't understand nuttin' about what she's trying to say," he said impatiently. "She talks like you. We need to know what on earth she's sayin'."

With that the sergeant hung up.

"Can you take me to the bus?" Jazzy asked.

I stood up, grabbing my empty cup and unused fins. "Be ready in ten minutes and I'll take you to school."

"All the way to school?" Jazzy queried excitedly. She wasn't keen on the bus ride either.

"If you're ready in ten minutes. If not, you're on your own."

Jazzy shot inside the shack and began flinging clothes around in a fury to get ready.

Seventeen minutes after I'd returned the phone call, I parked my old CJ-7 Jeep around the side of the little West Bay police station and Jazzy led me inside. She liked Clara, the constable who worked the reception desk most days, but she'd forgotten we were about an hour early for the day shift starting. Clara kept a stash of sweets behind the counter and liked to spoil Jazzy. She tolerated me.

Sergeant Redburn was waiting in the lobby, but there was no sign of Jacob. I knew he'd need more than fifteen minutes to organise himself, explain what was going on to his wife, and fend off a million questions from his kids.

Redburn tossed me the keys to a patrol car. "Jacob's on his way."

I caught the keys, nodded and turned for the door, pausing to see where Jazzy had got to. Redburn was looking at her suspiciously and Jazzy had a sly grin on her face as she skipped across the lobby to follow me outside. We walked towards the patrol cars lined up along the fence and I held my hand out. Jazzy giggled and dropped a lollypop into my palm.

"Orange?" I said, frowning. "I like the purple ones."

"Jeez," Jazzy groaned, popping her lollypop in her mouth. "I didn't have time to be choosy."

I opened the car and started the ignition, letting the engine warm and the interior cool down. I didn't much care for sweets, but I sucked on the lollypop regardless. I needed to know where and when Jazzy exercised her pilfering skills, so she needed to think I was okay with a lollypop here and there. Besides, it made me laugh that she'd managed it literally under the nose of the sergeant.

After a few minutes, Jacob pulled into the car park. I could see he was already frazzled. Jacob hated not knowing what was going on and hated surprises even more.

"I'll get in da back," Jazzy offered.

"Stay up front," I replied, and she took her hand off the handle.

Jacob jogged over, beads of sweat already dribbling down his forehead. He saw Jazzy sitting up front and his brow creased another step, but he opened the back door and got in.

"What's all dis panic about?" he asked as he plonked himself down in the cage.

"Dunno," I replied.

"Good mornin', Jacob," Jazzy said politely.

"Mornin', Miss Holder," Jacob replied.

"Would you like a lollypop?" Jazzy asked.

"Oh, sure ting," Jacob said, and I stifled a smile as Jazzy squeezed a lollypop around the edge of the steel mesh. "Miss Clara was generous dis mornin', huh?"

"She was," Jazzy replied, and I subtly shook my head as I pulled out onto West Church Street and headed towards the dual carriageway and George Town.

"We droppin' you at school?" Jacob asked.

"You are," I replied before Jazzy had a chance to.

"I am?" Jacob mumbled around his lollypop.

"I need to get straight to the hospital," I explained. "You can drop me and take her to school."

"Da sergeant said someting about da hospital," Jacob said leaning forward in the back seat and holding the mesh with his fingers. "So what's dat all about, den?"

"Don't know until we get there," I said, and Jacob slumped back into the seat with a grunt.

I pointed to the switches and Jazzy flicked on the lights and siren with glee. I grinned again. It wasn't too long ago she'd have been in danger of involuntarily riding in the back of a police car and dreading the sound of a police siren.

Handing her my mobile, she connected the Bluetooth and played a reggae version of a well-known tune as I sped down the hard shoulder of the bypass, zipping by the stop-and-go commuter traffic.

3

A PIN ON A MAP

I hate hospitals. There's never an enjoyable reason to visit one. Some would argue that babies are a wonderful reason, but I disagree. Babies come with pain, a hefty bill, and too many people are having them who have no business reproducing.

Perhaps I'm biased, as I have no intention of producing offspring. To me, throwing a child into the world is a bit like conscription. They have no choice in the matter, a few end up having a great time, but most tolerate it at best, and too many are just miserable. I don't want to do that to my own flesh and blood.

I was wondering what or who I was supposed to ask for at the emergency room reception desk when the nurse pointed to a hallway and told me, "Down there."

Maybe my uniform was a giveaway. I walked down the hall and saw Detective Whittaker standing outside a room, talking to a another copper. I recognised the man as Constable Dexley from the West Bay station.

"Hey," I greeted them both.

"Good morning, Nora," Whittaker replied in his lightly island-tinted accent.

He was neatly dressed as usual in a sport coat and crisp white shirt. Roy Whittaker was my mentor, and a man I owed for giving my life a direction and purpose after too many tragedies and challenges. I was unofficially in detective training until I became twenty-one and had two years on the job. If I didn't screw it up by the time I reached those two landmarks, I'd be fast-tracked through the official channels. Meanwhile, I worked my constable shifts and squeezed in extra cases as he saw fit.

"I was just getting up to speed," Whittaker continued. "But I believe you were called in to see if you can understand this young lady."

He nodded at the doorway into the hospital room, and I took a step forward to see. A young woman lay in the bed asleep. She had sharp features, blonde hair, and an IV in her arm which hung from a saline bag on a stand.

"What's wrong with her?" I asked.

"We found her at five dis mornin'," Dexley said. "Wearing nuttin' but undies and a tank top. No shoes, no purse, no ID. She was sitting on da wall by da cemetery opposite da fire station in West Bay. Can't understand a word she bin mumbling on about, but she didn't look so good, so we brought her here. Stoned if you ask me."

Whittaker and I shared a glance.

"Tox screen?" I asked.

"Not back yet," Dexley replied.

"Can I wake her?" I asked.

"Nurse say it should be okay as long as we don't get her all fussed up," Dexley replied.

I walked into the room and Whittaker followed me.

"I'm knockin' off if dat's all right wit you, Detective?" Dexley asked, remaining in the hallway.

Whittaker turned to him and paused for a moment. "We'll need your report," he said.

Dexley clenched his teeth. He was clearly hoping to get some sleep first. "Yes, sir," he replied, and disappeared down the hallway.

I looked at the woman, or maybe girl; she looked younger up close. Dark circles shadowed her eyes, and her hair was a mess. She had a small cut on her lip and a red mark on her cheek.

I rested a hand on her shoulder and gently shook her. "Wake up," I said softly.

She stirred and her limbs all curled up as though she were protecting herself.

"It's okay, you're safe."

Her eyes shot open and glared at me. "*Farðu frá mér!*"

I held my hands up. "*Det er greit, det er greit. Du er på sykehus.*" I told her in my native Norwegian, letting her know she was okay and in a hospital. It was a long shot as I hadn't understood anything she'd said.

"*Hvar er ég?*" she muttered, her eyes darting around the room.

A nurse came rushing in. A short, round, fair-skinned woman with a face which looked like it usually beamed. Except she wasn't smiling now.

"Don't be getting her all riled up now. We just got her to sleep," the nurse said, then turned to me, her expression breaking into its naturally friendly form. "Oh, you must be the Scandinavian constable they talked about."

The nurse had an American accent I hadn't expected.

"*Ja,*" I replied. "But she's not Scandinavian."

"She looks like you, all blonde and pretty, with those features," she said, touching her own nose.

I took a deep breath. Most people outside Europe had no idea where all the different countries were. Americans especially. They had enough trouble keeping up with their own states.

"I think she's Nordic, but not Scandinavian," I explained.

"Oh," the nurse muttered, clearly none the wiser.

I returned my attention to the young woman, who'd nodded off again but was restlessly moving, her eyelids twitching. I took out my mobile and searched for an online translator. I couldn't speak much Swedish, Danish or Finnish, but she hadn't sounded like any of them to me. I made my best guess and shook her shoulder again.

This time, her eyes opened more slowly and fought to focus on me.

"*Ertu íslenskur?*" I asked.

She immediately perked up, reaching for and grabbing my arm, letting out a string of words I couldn't follow.

"I think she's Icelandic," I said.

"Oh," the nurse said again.

I guessed she couldn't pinpoint Iceland on an unmarked map if her life depended on it. But there again, I had no idea where Kansas was. Or why Kansas and Arkansas were pronounced completely differently.

"I'm not sure we have an Icelandic translator on the island," Whittaker said from behind me.

I took the young woman's hand and set it back on the bed. Using my mobile I typed quickly then spoke the words as best I could. "*Þú ert öruggur. Þú ert á sjúkrahúsi.*"

She subtly nodded and drifted off again.

"She hasn't uttered a word in English yet," the nurse commented.

"We won't need a translator," I said, putting my mobile in my pocket. "She'll speak English."

"She's stoned is my guess," the nurse added. "Maybe she'll make more sense when whatever it was she took works its way out of her system."

I waited while the nurse finished fussing around the bed and started towards the door. She paused. "I wish I'd learned another language."

"Icelandic would be useful right about now," Whittaker said with a good-humoured smile.

The nurse laughed. "Spanish. I think I'd like to speak Spanish. Then I could understand what they're saying on those Mexican daytime soaps with all the dishy men," she added, and left the room still laughing.

"If they found her at five, who knows how long she'd been

wandering about," Whittaker said as we both looked at the young woman.

"Not very long if she's taken what we think it is," I replied, "judging by how out of it she still is."

Whittaker nodded and we both left the room, walking down the hall past rooms with mostly empty beds. A few had patients being attended to. In one a man was groaning and complaining loudly. He sounded drunk.

At the front desk, Whittaker asked if the tox screen was back for the unidentified woman. The nurse hit a few keys then nodded.

"Looks like it is. Just came in two minutes ago. Let me buzz the doctor on duty for you."

"Just show it to us," I said impatiently. "We know what we're looking for."

The nurse looked me over. "That's not how we do things, miss."

I wanted to explain how little I cared about her bullshit procedures when we potentially had far bigger problems on our hands, but I reminded myself Whittaker was standing next to me.

"We'll wait for the doctor in the patient's room," Whittaker said. "Thank you."

I followed him back down the hall. The drunk guy had quietened down, reduced to slurred grumbles, so if the duty doctor had been attending to him, I hoped we'd be their next port of call. The young woman appeared to have settled into a deeper sleep and didn't stir as we entered. We sat down in the only two visitor chairs in the room.

My mobile buzzed and I checked the text. It was Jacob; he was parked outside the emergency room wondering what to do. I replied for him to wait there. I hoped I wouldn't be here much longer.

Whittaker also sent a text as we waited.

"Immigration?" I asked.

He nodded.

I thought about my own next steps and texted Jacob again, asking him to start working on CCTV from the West Bay fire station. They had a couple of cameras out front covering their fore-court off West Bay Road. With a bit of luck, the cameras also caught the cemetery across the street.

A tall, slender man with a closely trimmed beard and perfectly styled hair walked into the room. He nodded to Whittaker, then looked me over with mild curiosity as he moved to the computer terminal on a rolling cart near the bed.

"I'm Doctor Emery," he said with a hint of the island accent. "I wasn't here when this patient was admitted, but I believe we have a preliminary tox report my predecessor ordered."

He clicked on the keyboard and brought the report up on the screen.

"She has alcohol in her system. Over the limit to drive, but not excessive. She wasn't intoxicated by social standards."

"By alcohol," I pointed out, and the doctor turned to me.

"Correct."

His eyes wandered from my face to my figure before returning to the computer.

"Huh," he said after a few moments, and looked at Whittaker. "What do you know about this young lady, Detective?"

Whittaker shook his head. "Nothing. We believe she's Icelandic, but she was found without ID or room key. She was barely clothed."

"Rohypnol?" I asked.

Emery nodded. "Yes. More than a prescribed dose would be. Not that anyone in their right mind prescribes Rohypnol anymore."

We all looked at the young woman sleeping soundly in the bed. I gritted my teeth. In all likelihood she faced an evil hangover, followed by the shock of knowing events took place that she had no memory of.

"Am I to assume this isn't the first case lately?" Emery asked.

"We had another incident ten days ago. Tourist from England," Whittaker replied, rubbing his forehead. "She couldn't even remember where she'd gone after leaving her hotel. About six hours of her life missing."

My fingers tightened around the handle of the computer cart. "Better have a rape kit ready for when she wakes."

"She has to give us permission," Emery pointed out.

"The English girl got on the next plane available and flew home," Whittaker said. "Refused a test."

"Call me when she wakes up," I said. "I'll talk to this one."

Whittaker's phone buzzed and after a quick glance at the screen he held it for me to see.

"That's her," I said, looking at the passport photo of a pretty, smiling young woman. "Elín Árnadóttir. Eighteen years old. On holiday from Iceland."

4

BIKINIS, BEADS, AND BRIGHTON

2009

Allie couldn't believe her eyes. She'd grown up surrounded by fast food restaurants, all-night convenience stores, and many other flashy American imports to Europe, but before her was a sight she couldn't have imagined. A parade of cars was driving slowly along the road by the beach with young people perched, hanging, and sprawled over every available seat and surface area.

Pick-up trucks packed with a dozen people in the bed. Convertibles with bodies protruding like too many straws stuffed into a glass on a diner table. The guys all wore board shorts and no shirts, the girls, bikinis of varying shapes and sizes, some of which matched the varying shapes and sizes of the girls. Many not. Most of the people were tanned, but the newbies from colder climes glowed red like the neon signs dotting the waterfront shops and restaurants.

Music played from every car and business, the sounds clashing in a constantly changing mash-up of raucous noise. The dance track playing on the stereo of Allie's ride, a Jeep, was swamped by bigger amplifiers, and the driver, Bruce, turned it off.

"Crazy, huh?" he said, turning to Allie in the back seat.

"Barmy," she said, although her soft English voice was lost to the acoustic chaos.

The top was already down on Bruce's Jeep, and the other occupants peeled off their T-shirts as Bruce joined the endless line of vehicles edging along A1A. To their right, she knew pale yellow sand stretched from the road to the Atlantic Ocean, but hardly any of it was visible. Instead, the beach was smothered in a sea of youthful humanity, crowded in large groups that milled, swayed, and played.

She'd smothered herself in sunblock before leaving the Miami motel that morning in readiness for a day at the seaside but was intimidated to remove her shirt. The two-piece she'd bought in London before the trip was daringly scant and she'd felt bold in front of the mirror of the changing room. Now, surrounded by a swarm of perfectly tanned and toned bodies, she wished she'd packed a more conservative one-piece.

Allie had thought about going to a tanning salon before the trip, but her friends back home would have laughed at her. Tanning beds were for the rich and ridiculously vain. Now she wished she'd told them to sod off and paid for a few sessions.

Rachel stood up in the passenger seat and hung on to the top of the windscreen frame. She wore a skimpy little black bikini, the top of which she impressively filled out, making Allie wonder if she'd had a boob job. Her hips and bum were so slender they made the woman's chest seem disproportionate, but who had breast augmentation surgery at age nineteen? Maybe they were real, she concluded, glancing down at her own nicely balanced but far less conspicuous cleavage.

With a deep breath, she peeled off her T-shirt, and Ozzy, or Alfred as his American friends called him, sitting next to her in the back seat looked her over approvingly. The visual appreciation made her feel a little better, but she reminded herself he'd been drinking beer since they'd left Miami and would probably letch at a naked cat by now. His head had been on a swivel since they'd arrived in Fort Lauderdale.

Besides, they were just friends, and had been since they'd been in middle school. Allie didn't plan on spoiling that in a drunken lapse, and the lyrics to the Dave Matthews Band's 'Say Goodbye' sprang to mind.

She couldn't call him Alfred, despite him and the other two insisting. Apparently, they'd been enthralled with *The Dark Knight*, the movie hit of 2008, and come up with their nicknames after seeing the Batman film multiple times. Allie couldn't even remember the real names of Ozzy's friends in the front, as they hadn't been used since she was first introduced.

Bruce and Rachel seemed like a perfect couple, straight out of one of those American college movies. Beautiful people with perfect bodies and from what she'd gathered in the past few days since her arrival, plenty of family money back home in Georgia.

"The coppers don't care about the drinking and seatbelts and stuff?" Allie shouted to be heard, realising she still had her seatbelt on.

Bruce turned around again. "Hell no. But this is tame. Years ago, the city clamped down on everything, saying Spring Break had gotten out of control."

"Bloody hell, this is tame?"

Bruce laughed. "So I'm told. But just wait until tonight. Things really get going when the sun goes down."

Rachel was writhing to the music, still standing on the passenger seat, although Allie had no idea which of the numerous beats she was moving to. She turned and squealed a loud "Woohoo!"

"Isn't this the best, Allie?" Rachel asked, beer spilling from the fresh bottle of Corona she'd just been handed. "We gotta give this girl her Batman name, baby," she said, turning her attention to her boyfriend.

"The Joker feels most appropriate," Allie said, and Ozzy laughed.

He was now perched on the back of the rear seat, with an arm looped around the roll cage of the Jeep, a fresh beer dangling from his hand. Allie undid her seatbelt and moved up next to him. She thought she'd feel unsafe and exposed, but they couldn't have been going more than four or five miles per hour, so it was more of a relief to feel the breeze on her skin. The temperature was low eighties, but the sky was perfectly clear and the midday sun intense.

Rachel cackled like a drunken hyena, "The Joker she is then! That's fucking hilarious!"

Ozzy chuckled and leaned towards Allie. She thought he was being amorous but realised he was just getting a better view of Rachel's boobs jiggling as she bounced around to the mystery rhythm.

'Come over for a holiday,' his email had said, 'we'll hang out at the beach with some friends of mine from uni.' Ozzy had been a quiet, well-mannered lad throughout school, and his move to America had been spurred by his parents' divorce and subsequently his father's job change. Allie had not been prepared for this overwhelming cultural shift, or for Ozzy's apparent ease into the lifestyle.

She wasn't appalled or shocked, she decided, more surprised. She enjoyed a drink with her friends as much as the next uni student, but this all seemed like a scene from a Hollywood movie. Although she had to admit the number of dishy-looking blokes around the place was impressive.

Allie had broken up with her first love a few months before, and while she missed having somebody to be close to, she was certain all that Spring Break in Fort Lauderdale offered was as many temporary relationships as a girl chose to pursue. That wasn't her scene, but the party atmosphere was beginning to loosen her up, and she reached into the cooler for a Corona.

Ozzy held up his bottle and clinked against hers with a big smile. "That's the spirit, Allie."

A large crowd milled down the edge of the road, cheering loudly and waving their arms in the air. It was mainly guys, bare chested with strings of brightly coloured beads around their necks. Several girls were with them in skimpy bathing suits. They had even more beads around their necks.

Before Allie could fathom what was happening the crowd erupted into louder cheers, all looking at the Jeep. Bruce and Ozzy whooped and screamed as strings of beads landed inside the Jeep, thrown by the men in the crowd. It was then that Allie realised Rachel was waving her bikini top in the air and shaking her naked breasts for the crowd to see.

Rachel turned to Allie in the back as she refastened her top. "Your turn, Joker! Shake your money makers, baby!"

Allie felt her cheeks flush and her knees go weak. All eyes were now on her, expectantly waiting for her to flash them, including all three people in the Jeep.

"Go for it, Allie," Ozzy yelled, laughing. "You'll never see these people ever again!"

"Let your hair down," Rachel encouraged. "This is Spring Break!"

"Off, off, off," the crowd began yelling, and Allie felt like the whole beachfront was staring and taunting her.

The group had paused, waiting eagerly with beads in hand. She fought back a feeling of dread, grabbed the underside of her bikini with both hands, and quickly lifted the cups. The crowd erupted in cheers and strings of beads rained down. Along with the clicking of pictures from several of the fancy new iPhones.

As quickly as she'd flashed her chest, she pulled the bikini back down and made sure it was securely back in place. Appeased, the crowd moved on and more cheers echoed around the waterfront as other willing participants earned their beads.

Allie felt a conflicting mixture of embarrassment and excitement. Her mother would be mortified if she knew what had just transpired, but the thrill of doing something so daring and out of character was surprisingly exhilarating. Maybe it was her father's genes. She had no way of knowing, as she had no recollection of her father and knew little about him.

"Now you're getting in the spirit of Spring Break," Ozzy enthused. "And it's not like it's the first time I've seen you topless," he added with a laugh.

Allie took a swig of beer and wondered what her friend was talking about. She couldn't think of a time he would ever have seen her naked.

"What do you mean?" she asked, frowning.

Ozzy leaned closer, his beer breath washing over her still-blushing face. "That time at the beach in Brighton when I held your towel," he said with a grin. "I swore I didn't look. But I admit it now you just flashed 'em to half of Florida. I sneaked a bit of a look."

Allie smacked him across the arm, and he burst out laughing. "Perv."

"Hey," he retorted, "You can't blame a bloke for having a peek." He raised his eyebrows a few times. "Mighty nice I must say."

Allie's face blushed all over again and her arms instinctively closed in around her chest. In the front seat, Rachel was lifting her top once again as another large group encircled the car. This time, Allie slid from the seat back, dropping to the seat itself where she pulled her knees up to her chest and ducked as strings of beads landed everywhere.

Once was enough. In her mind, she'd already let her hair down and had a story to take home and tell her friends, if they'd even believe her. She wished she had one of those newer mobiles with a camera so she could capture some of the chaotic festivities. She'd brought a small pocket camera, but it was in her rucksack, which was buried under luggage in the back, and no way was she leaving the Jeep amongst the drunken crowd.

And then Bruce's words came back to her, "Wait until tonight. Things really get going when the sun goes down." Allie had no idea what he could possibly mean, but a knot formed in her stomach at the thought. She was already overwhelmed.

5

THE HANDBOOK

Present Day

Jacob knew about date rape drugs from television shows and movies, but the idea that a drug like that was being used on the island was hard for him to accept. The concept was completely foreign in his mind. A big city problem, not the kind of thing we'd come across on Grand Cayman.

He was right, for the most part, but I doubted this was the first time Rohypnol or one of its derivatives had been used on some unsuspecting tourist. We'd have never known about the English girl if she hadn't asked for help finding her hotel. Suspected of intoxication, she'd been made to take a urine test.

How many young women had been taken advantage of in the past and not reported it? Shame, confusion, denial were all strong motivations to get on the plane home and pretend it never happened. Whoever was behind these attacks was smart, picking on tourists who wouldn't stay around long.

Driving north, Jacob finally broke the silence in the car. "You tink da Iceland girl been… you know…" he asked, struggling to say the word out loud.

"Raped," I replied bluntly. It was an ugly word, appropriate for one of the ugliest crimes humans commit on each other. "Yes, but we won't know for sure unless she allows the doctors to give her an exam."

"They didn't check her… you know…" he said, pointing a finger in the vague direction of my crotch.

I frowned at him. "Jacob, you're a policeman. There are terms to use for all this."

It was hard to tell with his dark skin, but I was sure he blushed. "I know, I know. I just get a little messed up talkin' about da lady's private tings."

He turned into the fire station car park and came to a stop. I opened the passenger door but paused when I felt his hand on my arm.

"Nora," he said, barely above a whisper.

I dropped back into the seat and looked at my partner. His eyes were damp, and his lip quivered ever so slightly.

"You've bin through dese tings, haven't you?" he said, his voice tentative and unsure.

He took his hand from my arm as though I might be offended or bothered by his touch. I nodded. Jacob knew enough about my troubled past to piece together a correct conclusion. I wasn't keen on talking about most things in life, as generally it all seemed pointless jabbering, but I cared even less to discuss the sexual abuse I'd endured.

He nodded in return and held my stare. A tear escaped his eye, making a circuitous route down the features of his face.

"I survived," I said. "It's okay."

I wasn't sure why I used the word *okay*, as nothing about my own situation had been *okay* and I couldn't imagine it ever would be. But for once I told someone what I thought they needed to hear instead of the cold, hard truth. Jacob was a lovely man with a warm heart. I'd never considered whether he cared for me or not.

He'd found me difficult to deal with when we were first partners, but it was something I didn't think about anymore. We were
partners. We watched out for each other, fussed and laughed as
people who spent so much time in close proximity usually do.

The look on his face told me how much he really cared for me,
and my own reaction meant I felt the same for him. In part it made
me uncomfortable. I wasn't good at being close to people. It never
turned out well, and I realised with a knot in my stomach that I was
currently accumulating a small list of 'relationships'. It was
baffling. I considered myself quite unlikeable.

It also felt nice to have humans around me who accepted me
despite my cold and distancing exterior.

"*Takk*," I said, so Jacob didn't feel the need to say anything
more. His lip had quivered again which threatened more words
and we'd surpassed my limit for mushy shit. I quickly got out of
the car and walked to the fire station office.

I didn't know their names, but I recognised several of the firemen
on duty. We'd met over time at the scenes of a mixture of tragedies
and false alarms, and they all seemed to remember me, nodding or
saying hello. A tall, lean, blonde Norwegian in a Royal Cayman
Islands Police Service uniform tended to get noticed.
Unfortunately.

"I need your CCTV footage from last night," I said to a man
behind one of the desks who looked in charge. "From the cameras
out front," I clarified. "My partner called."

"Aye, he did," the fireman replied with a Scottish accent. "I put
what we had on a thumb drive for you," he said, handing me a
small USB stick. "Is it about that wee girl that you're interested?"

"You looked at the footage?" I asked, which of course they had a
right to do. It was their CCTV after all. "Was there anyone else in
the shot?" I added, figuring he might save me some time.

"Just the girl is all I saw. Stumbles into view from the north and
sits down against the wall by the cemetery. I wrote the timestamps

here for you," he said, handing me a Post-it note. "Bit before five, she gets up and sits on the wall. One of yours comes by shortly after."

"Okay, thanks," I said, looking at the badge pinned to his chest. "Malky?"

The man smiled. "Pronounced Mal-kee," he said, correcting my poor attempt. "Short for Malcolm."

I nodded. "Well, thank you for the help, Malky."

The others bid me farewell as I left the office, and I hoped I wouldn't see them again anytime soon. They seemed like a great bunch of guys, but I'd prefer people weren't trapped in crashed cars or in buildings on fire.

Jacob was back to his normal self by the time I returned to the car, and I told him to take us to Foster's market. As he drove us the half a kilometre north, I put the thumb drive into our dashboard-mounted laptop and found the timecode Malky had given me. Jacob was parked in time to watch the CCTV footage with me.

A combination of a nearby streetlight and the floodlights from the fire station made it easy to see Elín enter the picture. Now we needed to track down how she came to be there.

"Your turn," I said to Jacob, and he started to get out of the car.

"Coffee?" he asked.

I eagerly handed him my long since empty travel mug. "Something for breakfast too," I said, realising I'd skipped food with the rush to leave the house. It was gone 9:00am and my stomach was complaining.

While Jacob went in search of CCTV from the market's exterior cameras, I ran backwards through the footage we had, looking for vehicles. At four-something in the morning, traffic was scarce, but four cars and one van went by in the thirty minutes prior to Elín showing up. She walked there from the north, but that didn't rule out her being dropped from a car arriving from either direction. Of course, it was possible she'd stumbled there from the beach or a house nearby; we had no idea.

My mobile rang and seeing it was Whittaker, I answered through the car's hands-free system.

"Sir."

"Hi, Nora. Any luck with CCTV?"

"We have the fire station footage. She was alone. Jacob's inside Foster's now seeing what they have, and I've got five vehicles passing the cemetery before Elín arrived. We'll compare them to Foster's footage."

"I don't suppose you can you see any registration plates?"

"No. Hard to see the occupants too, but maybe with some work we could."

"Okay, keep me posted," he said. "She was staying at The Locale Hotel on Seven Mile Beach, and as far as we can tell she was here alone. Immigration has her entering by herself, and the hotel have no record of anyone else sharing the room."

"Have her family been contacted?" I asked, hoping they hadn't yet. I imagined her family would be devastated; at least I hoped they would. It would be even sadder to think she had no one to go home to, or no one who cared. Assuming she had loved ones, they'd be devastated whether they were told this morning or later today, and later today they'd get far more answers to the questions they'd undoubtedly ask.

"She listed a family contact on her immigration paperwork, but we haven't tried calling them yet," Whittaker replied.

"I think it's best to wait, sir."

"I do too. For now, anyway. Call me if you get anything useful from the CCTV," Whittaker concluded. "I'm meeting the hotel manager at ten to look through her room."

"I can be there by ten, sir," I said keenly.

I wasn't sure why I wanted to see her belongings, but it felt important. I knew I was already becoming too attached to the case, which wasn't a good thing. Probably high on the list in the detective training handbook would be don't get personally involved, but I hadn't learnt how to do that yet.

How do you care about a case yet not give a shit about the

victims involved? Ambition, I supposed, was one way. If I was driven by success, promotions, and accolades perhaps, but I couldn't care less about any of that. Some cases were easy when they involved *drittsekker* screwing over *drittsekker*, like a drug dealer knifing another drug dealer, but in my mind Elín was truly a victim.

That was probably on the same detective handbook list. Don't assume anyone is guilty or innocent until proven so. Usually, I leaned towards being suspicious of everyone, but in this case, I was sure Elín had been sexually abused, and I can't think of a single reason why anyone deserved to be subjected to that torture.

It was 9:47am when Jacob finally returned with another thumb drive in hand along with coffee and a paper bag containing something I probably shouldn't be eating for breakfast.

"*Takk*," I said, quickly taking them all from him. "Drive us to The Locale Hotel."

Fuck the handbook. I needed to see Elín's things.

6

NORMAL

I waited in the hotel lobby for a few minutes until Whittaker arrived. Jacob stayed in the car to begin hunting through the new CCTV footage. The camera was well back from the road, but there were streetlights so we should be able to match the colour and shape of a vehicle to the fire station recording. Or spot the girl if she walked by.

After a quick word with the lady at reception, a maintenance man guided us to the room and let us in.

"We'll close the door when we're done," Whittaker told the man, who reluctantly left us be.

We both slipped on nitrile gloves and shoe covers. The hotel was relatively new, taking over an existing building which had been built as offices and retail space which never happened. It stretched along West Bay Road, behind Seven Mile Beach but an older, larger property sat between The Locale and the water.

The room itself was a modern design with two queen beds, a funky lounge seat thing under the window and a desk extending from exotic-looking wood wainscotting. As I'm Scandinavian, I guess I'm supposed to like the Ikea vibe, but to me it was sterile. No framed pictures on the walls, no island feel, just harsh, crisp lines. On the other hand, I was glad it wasn't the bamboo and parrots crap most places insisted was a touch of the islands.

To our right, a barn-hung wooden door led into a blindingly white bathroom which was where I chose to begin searching. A glass held a single toothbrush and a tube of toothpaste next to the raised, dished sink — the type which looked fancy but splashed water all over you when you tried washing your face.

Elín's toiletries bag was minimalist. An eyeliner and lipstick were the only make-up; deodorant, nail clippers and file, hairbrush, moisturiser, and hand sanitiser. The final item was a blister pack of birth control pills. In the shower were small bottles of shampoo and conditioner, although the hotel provided them via a dispenser mounted on the wall, and a razor.

Everything else in the bathroom belonged to or was supplied by the hotel. I stepped out of the bathroom to a small kitchenette arrangement on the opposite wall. It too had a sink, but a more practical one, with a neat drying rack, pod-style coffee maker, microwave, and waist-high refrigerator.

The room hadn't been cleaned for the day yet, and I noticed several used pods in the rubbish bin. I opened the fridge and found a six-pack of diet soda with one can missing, and a pizza box with two slices left of what appeared to be a vegetarian topping pizza.

"Anything useful?" Whittaker asked from across the room.

"Not yet," I replied, and walked to the first bed. Neither had been slept in, but the closest one to me had slightly ruffled covers and the pillows stacked. She'd lain on the bed and probably read a book, or used her laptop computer, both of which sat on the bedside table.

"Have you looked in here?" I asked, pointing to the bedside table.

"No, go ahead," Whittaker replied, meticulously sifting through a suitcase on the other bed.

I stepped closer. The laptop was a small, travel-sized Mac and the book looked like a post-apocalyptic novel judging by the cover. It was by someone called AG Riddle and was in English. I opened the drawer and found the one thing I hadn't expected. A bottle of prescription pills.

I wondered why a doctor would prescribe Rohypnol to an eighteen-year-old as its only real use anymore was for acute insomnia. It pretty much turned even the worst sleeper into a zombie. I grabbed the bottle and read the label, letting out a long sigh. The pills were Naproxen, and while I didn't know what Naproxen was actually for, I knew it wasn't the drug found in her system.

I quickly searched on my mobile and discovered Naproxen is an anti-inflammatory drug used to treat pain, menstrual cramps, inflammatory diseases such as rheumatoid arthritis, gout and fever. Maybe it would be better if she was on prescribed Rohypnol, then perhaps she'd been innocently wandering the streets in a haze without anyone else involved. But life doesn't tend to be that kind.

"Some pills," I told Whittaker as I slid the drawer closed. "But just anti-inflammatories."

"Nothing much in here, either," he replied, placing the few clothes Elín hadn't unpacked back into the suitcase. "The usual clothes and bathing suits I'd expect from a young lady on holiday. Nothing outrageous or out of the ordinary."

I wondered exactly what Roy Whittaker would consider outrageous, but then my idea of dressing up was putting on my police uniform, so what did I know? I was in leggings, flip-flops and T-shirts the rest of the time. Or a wetsuit.

Whittaker looked around the room. "What did we learn?"

I thought for a moment, used to the detective's little tests he liked to give me. They're annoying, but made me think things through.

"Nothing here to suggest anyone else has been in the room, or any problem began here. If she was on the island for more than a holiday, it's been well hidden," I said, pausing briefly. "She appears organised, tidy, and understands English."

I noticed Whittaker's brow tighten slightly. "The book is in English," I explained, and he nodded.

"Do you find it strange she's here alone?" Whittaker asked.

I shrugged my shoulders. "No. Plenty of young people travel by themselves."

"I get that if they're taking a train around Europe, or backpacking, or even staying at a dive resort where they'll meet other people," he continued. "But Grand Cayman isn't the cheapest destination; even rooms off the waterfront like this place are expensive. It strikes me as slightly odd a young woman would come here alone without more of a reason than sitting on a sandy beach. I know we are blessed with one of the best beaches in the world, but she could stay twice as long or spend half the price by going to Mexico. So why here?"

I chewed his comment over for a moment. It was possible she had a friend or family member here on the island or came here before and loved the place. A thought occurred to me, and I picked up the phone by the bed, dialling zero on speakerphone.

"Front desk... oh," the woman said, presumably noticing the room number she was being called from.

"This is Constable Sommer. Can you access the reservation file for Elín Árnadóttir?"

"Of course."

"Can you see the details, like when it was originally made?"

"I can. What are we looking for?"

"When and under what name was the original booking?" I asked.

"Hmm... looks like the reservation was made three months ago," the receptionist replied. "Miss Arna... dot..., the young lady... she made the reservation herself."

"For one?"

The lady took a few moments. "No, the original reservation was made for two."

"Name?"

"I'm sorry, I'm not very good with these foreign names," she said apologetically. "Viggo Krist... vee..."

"That's fine," I said, cutting her off. "We'll get the name from you on the way out. When was the reservation switched to one person?"

"Looks like that change was made ten days ago."

"*Takk,*" I said, and hung up the phone. "I'd say she broke up with her boyfriend a few weeks ago and decided to come anyway."

"Agreed," Whittaker responded. "Okay, any other observations?"

I shook my head, but asked myself what detail I was missing. Everything about Elín's room and possessions suggested a young woman on holiday. The hotel room didn't have a desperate or depressed feel about it. There was no mess, no condoms at the ready for a revenge-filled holiday fling, no alcohol stash.

"Seems pretty normal, doesn't it?" Whittaker commented.

"Too normal?" I asked, sure I was overlooking a vital clue.

Whittaker shook his head. "In our line of work, we see the worst of people. But don't lose sight of the fact that the majority of people's worlds turn without unlawful activity beyond occasion- ally speeding and including an extra receipt on their tax return. Sometimes it is what it is. A young woman on holiday caught in a circumstance not of her doing."

I hoped he was right, and with the shit I'd been through I tended to think everyone had a dark side, so I was probably looking for something about Elín to disappoint me.

"Bag the computer and let's get the boyfriend's name on the way out," Whittaker instructed me.

Using a large evidence bag I'd brought with me, I slipped the laptop and charger inside and sealed the edge. I then went to the chest of drawers and examined the young woman's clothing. Whit- taker was right; her outfits were stylish but simple. Jeans, leggings, T-shirts, and two bathing suits. The first was a one-piece and the second a bikini top and bottom, but not the kind that cut your arse in half.

"What did I miss?" Whittaker asked from the doorway.

"She'll need clothes," I replied, and picked a loose-fitting T- shirt, cotton baggy trousers, and a set of underwear to take with us.

"Good thinking," Whittaker said, patiently holding the door.

I knew from experience that body-hugging stylish was not what she'd want. Hiding beneath something loose and comfortable would be far more desirable. I paused by the open-front wardrobe and selected a pair of trainers over the flip-flops. She had two dresses hanging, both simple and elegant attire suitable for a bar or a nice dinner. I would wear any of the outfits she'd brought with her, but I wasn't sure what that meant exactly beyond us sharing uncomplicated taste.

We stopped by the front desk, collecting the name of the second person on the original reservation, then walked to the car park, where Jacob got out of the car when he saw us.

"I don't see any sign of da girl outside Foster's," he eagerly told us as we approached. "But one of da cars headin' south takes longer dan it should to appear on da udder CCTV at da fire station."

"Enough time to stop and let someone out of the car?" Whittaker asked.

"More time dan dat, I'd say, sir. Over a minute extra and dere's no stop sign or nuttin' between da two. Dat car musta stopped."

"No registration plate I assume?"

"No, sir," Jacob confirmed. "Pale coloured four-door is about da best I can say."

"I can take the relevant footage to the office and have the lab see what they can glean from it," Whittaker offered.

"I also got da footage from da hotel while you were inside," Jacob said, handing Whittaker three thumb drives. "I only had time for a quick look, but I see da girl leaving last night, and she was alone."

He gave Whittaker the notes he'd made with the timestamps.

"Good work, Tibbetts," the detective said, bringing a smile to Jacob's face.

Whittaker left for the office, so we drove across the street to Cafe del Sol in the plaza off Lawrence Boulevard. Twenty minutes later, we were halfway through our lunch sandwiches when my mobile rang. The caller ID said it was the hospital, so I answered through the patrol car's hands-free system.

"Hello?"

"Is dis Constable Sommer?" the voice I recognised as the reception nurse's asked.

"*Ja.*"

"Dat girl is awake and makin' more sense now. I believe you wanted to speak wit her?"

"*Ja.*" I glanced at my watch. It was nearly noon. "We'll be there in fifteen minutes."

Hearing my side of the conversation, Jacob was already rolling. I now had fifteen minutes in which to figure out what I was about to say to a traumatised young woman, a long way from home, who'd probably just endured the worst night of her life... and wouldn't remember any of it.

7

HOLDING HANDS

I walked more slowly than usual down the hallway. Elín's situation made my blood boil and I needed to put my own feelings aside to do my job. It was easy to project circumstances onto her situation without yet knowing what really happened, driven by my own anger and assumptions.

When I entered the room, she was sitting up with her eyes closed. A tray of food sat half eaten on a table swung away from the bed.

"Hey," I said from across the room, hoping not to startle her.

Her eyes opened and she blinked a few times; her brow creased as she took in my uniform and similar Nordic features to her own. Her eyes flicked around the room, as though she was re-establishing her bearings.

"I'm still in Grand Cayman, *já*?"

"*Ja*," I confirmed. "I'm Constable Sommer with the Royal Cayman Islands Police Service."

"You're not from here," Elín said sleepily, moving herself to a more comfortable position.

"Norway," I replied. "But they asked me to come by first thing this morning when they couldn't understand what you were saying."

I pulled a chair next to the bed and sat down.

"I don't remember seeing you," she said, "but I don't really remember anything since yesterday evening. Could you understand me?"

I grinned. "No, but I heard enough to guess you are Icelandic, and then I assumed you'd speak English when your head cleared."

"I have the worst headache," she moaned, and took a sip of water from a glass on the swinging table.

I nodded. "Did they explain the drug you had in your system?"

Elín rubbed her hands on her legs, scrunching the bed covers as she did so, then pulling the sheet up higher. "Yes. But I don't take drugs."

"If you did take recreational drugs, Rohypnol wouldn't be one you'd choose," I said. "Someone probably slipped it in your drink."

Elín clenched her teeth. "What happened? I don't remember anything."

Her voice was building to the edge of panic.

I held up a hand. "We don't know yet, but we'll try to find out. Let's start with what you do remember." I took my little spiral-bound notebook from my pocket and turned to a fresh page. "What's the last recollection you have from last night?"

She closed her eyes and shook her head. "It's all very... I don't know the word in English..."

"Hazy? Confused?" I offered.

"Já. I can see myself getting ready, but it's like I'm watching someone else."

"Where were you going?"

Elín thought for a moment. "I'd seen a club down the road. I was going to walk there."

"Onions?" I asked, trying to hide my disappointment.

"I think so. I don't know if I got there or not, though," she said, taking a breath and trying not to freak out. "I have small bits of memory that keep coming and going, but they make no sense."

"Do you remember at what time you left the hotel?"

She thought hard again, then shook her head. "Not really. It was dark. I remember drinking a martini and I don't usually drink martinis. These little clips and bits and pieces are driving me crazy. They feel like the parts of dreams that fall into your mind the next morning," she said, looking at me. I could see the fear in her eyes. "Do you ever have that?" she asked.

I nodded. But usually I knew exactly where those moments came from in the dark corners of my memory. Occasionally, they escaped their chains and jolted me awake.

"We have CCTV which shows you leaving the hotel at 8:35pm," I told her. "Now we know where you were heading, we'll see what other CCTV we can find between the hotel and Onions."

Elín swallowed hard and prepared herself to ask her next question. "What do you think happened to me?"

Her eyes filled with tears, and I thought about reaching out and taking her hand, but I didn't. As a policewoman I wasn't supposed to, although there was certain leeway when it came to comforting victims. But if I held her hand I would have to let go at some point and that moment always felt cripplingly awkward.

I needed to answer her question. She was looking at me expectantly, no doubt thinking the worst and hoping beyond all hope that it wasn't that bad.

"I think someone slipped a roofie in your drink. What happened between then and when you were found in West Bay is the question. We need your permission to perform an exam. That will answer one of the questions which I'm sure is on your mind."

Elín's head sank into the pillow and her whole body curled up into a ball. She mumbled to herself in Icelandic, and I let her take a minute to process what she'd probably been hiding from since she'd woken up.

"Maybe it's better I don't know," she whispered. "I have no memory of anything happening, so why find out?"

I started to answer, ready to explain how it would help us prosecute her attacker when the time came, but I held back. She had a point. What I would give to erase all memory of the repulsive things I'd endured? How would I feel if I had no recollection of the events, just someone telling me they happened?

"I don't know what to tell you, Elín. As the police, we want to know exactly what went on so we can catch the *drittsekk* and make him pay. But in your shoes, I'd want it all to go away too."

She looked at me. "Have there been others?"

I nodded. "One we know of for sure."

"Was she… you know?"

I shrugged my shoulders. "We don't know. She wouldn't be examined here and flew home."

Elín seemed to deflate and sink farther into the pillows propping her up. "And you have no idea who's doing this?"

I shook my head. "Not yet. The other girl had no idea where she'd been, and we weren't able to string anything together from CCTV to track her movements."

"So why do you think I'll be any different? I can't remember anything either."

"No, but we have a suspect vehicle from CCTV in West Bay," I said, stretching the truth a bit. "And you think you were in Onions, so that opens up more possibilities."

I paused, arguing with myself over whether to bring up another point or not. It felt like I was putting a sell job on her, but the truth was the truth.

"There is also the issue of STDs. An examination may provide us with DNA and let you know early on if there's a concern with an STD which can then be treated."

Elín gasped and broke into tears. I felt like a complete arse. I reached out and took her hand which she clenched with all her might.

"You'll get through this," I said, although I was glad she couldn't see my face through her tears.

"I don't know," she whispered between the sniffles as she tried to calm herself.

I could tell she was someone who hated to cry, like me.

Whoever said 'I had a good cry and felt better' was talking out their arse. All I get is pissed off and a headache.

"You don't have a choice," I said firmly. "You'll find a way."

Elín wiped her eyes so she could see me clearly. Her hand had relaxed in mine, and I felt the awkwardness I knew I would, but she didn't let go so I didn't take my hand away.

"You've been through this, haven't you?" she asked.

I wasn't sure if she was really perceptive, or if I was a lot more transparent than I thought, but her question threw me for a moment. I felt my brow tense into a frown.

"I'm sorry, it's not my business," she quickly added, and her hand slipped from mine.

"It's okay," I lied. "It's not something I talk about," I said, which was true. "I was recruited to a fancy private resort here on the island," I began, the words spilling out without a conscious choice to say a word. "It turned out to be a form of human trafficking. I was very young, and they taught us what we were doing was perfectly normal and okay. I was a runaway and they promised money and a new identity after one year, which were two things I badly needed. Our job was to escort the club members, and most of them were nice enough. They'd brainwashed us into believing this was all okay, so I could stand it most of the time.

"My year was almost up, and they gave me to a guy, a real sick fucker. He beat the shit out of me and forced himself on me. I wanted to curl up and die."

I took a deep breath and felt Elín's hand take mine once again. She was now comforting me which didn't feel right given her circumstance, but the words kept coming.

"But I didn't die, and it was part of the events which brought down the resort and the people running it. At the end of the one year in service, instead of giving the girls the money and passports, they were killing them and dumping the bodies in the sea. So, I guess I was lucky."

I'd never once thought I was lucky until that moment. I still wasn't sure I truly felt fortunate, but it was the most positive spin

I'd ever allowed myself to consider. I felt her grip tighten on my hand.

"I'm so sorry. That's awful."

I shrugged my shoulders. "The point is, I found a way to live again, and you will too." I forced a smile and slipped my hand free of hers. "Besides, we don't even know what happened last night, right? Perhaps you wandered around the island on your own all night."

"You don't believe that," Elín replied and rubbed her face with her hands. When she took them away, she looked at me again, but this time she had an intensity and determination burning in her eyes. "I'll have the exam."

I nodded, recognising the anger welling inside her which she'd need to make it through the shitty hand she'd been dealt.

"I'll be right back," I said, leaving to find the doctor.

Nothing ever happens as quickly as it should, especially in a hospital. If there's blood leaking in large amounts or someone has a heart attack in the lobby, people fly about and plug holes and do whatever thing they do for a heart attack. But for everything else, there always seems to be more waiting than the Department of Vehicle & Drivers' Licensing.

It was nearly two hours before everything was ready to perform the sexual assault forensic exam I'd told them to prepare for that morning. It would have been longer if she'd insisted on waiting for a female doctor. Doctor Emery was meticulous and surprisingly considerate and gentle. After the way he'd checked me out that morning, I'd guessed his bedside manner would be as bad as his ogling eyes, but he was very professional.

Elín insisted I remain in the room during the process, and we were back to holding hands. I think I was more uncomfortable with the procedure than she was. When the doctor was finished, he made sure he'd checked every box on the list of requirements before removing his gloves and rolling his chair next to the bed. Elín's grip practically crushed my hand.

"I don't get to say this often enough," he began, "but at this stage, I believe the news is good."

His patient excitedly propped herself up on the pillows, but I was waiting for what was coming next. I wasn't sure what the doctor classified as 'good news'.

"I can find no evidence of recent sexual intercourse, protected or unprotected. No signs of trauma, no traces of semen, nor the lubricant associated with condoms. The lab will need to confirm that from the swabs, but in my experience, I'd be able to tell from the exam."

Elín muttered to herself in Icelandic again, but the relief in her voice was unmistakable.

"We'll keep you here tonight, so the Rohypnol clears your system, and I hope to have at least initial lab results back before we release you late morning tomorrow." He stood and kept an eye on the nurse who was gathering up the paperwork and samples. "Just keep in mind the lab results will have the final word, but I believe my prognosis is correct."

He and the nurse left the room, and Elín slid down the pillows and truly relaxed for the first time since she'd come out of the drug-induced haze.

"I'll leave you to sleep," I said. "I'm glad it's good news."

She smiled at me. "Thank you. Especially for being with me through this."

Her eyes closed and I quietly left the room. I *was* glad Elín felt better, but I still had a bad feeling inside. For a second I worried it was disappointment I was feeling in some way, which made my stomach clench. Did I need someone to share in my own pain? Or a *drittsekker* to chase who fuelled my inner anger? Surely, I wasn't that selfish? And there was still someone out there slipping drugs into girls' drinks.

But the sense I couldn't shake was none of those things — or I convinced myself it wasn't. I still felt there was more to this.

8

FISH PIE VOODOO

While I'd been waiting for Elín's exam, Jacob had returned to West Bay Road and walked from The Locale Hotel to Onions, checking the businesses for exterior CCTV. When he picked me up from the hospital, he had footage from the petrol station on the corner and Craft, a self-proclaimed 'gastropub'. I had no idea what a gastropub was exactly, but they did have tasty food.

The Pizza Hut located between the two didn't have CCTV outside, and there was no one at Onions to ask. He'd tried calling but it went to a voicemail box that was full. Jacob drove towards West Bay while I began studying the footage on the laptop, starting with Craft. Using the timing we had for Elín leaving the hotel, I quickly found her walking along the pavement towards the nightclub. She was wearing a pale-coloured summer dress.

"What was she wearing when she left the hotel?" I blurted, startling Jacob.

"A dress I tink. Why?"

"*Dritt,*" I cursed myself for being sloppy, and called the mobile number I had for Rasha, our head scene of crime officer and forensics expert.

"Hello, Nora. You know I only received the bag of clothes an hour or so ago, right?" she said with a hint of humour in her English voice.

"I'm not calling about the results," I responded. "Well, I guess I sort of am," I corrected myself. "Do you have an inventory yet?"

I heard her muffled voice call out to someone else in the lab while she held the phone away from her mouth.

"We've done that much apparently. What do you need to know?"

"The inventory," I replied, as though it should be obvious.

There was a brief pause while Rasha presumably gathered the paperwork from her co-worker. "T-shirt and panties; that's it."

"She left for the evening in a dress, no T-shirt," I said, carefully studying the freeze-framed shot on the screen. I zoomed in a little, but the image was too blurry to make out much detail, so I returned to actual size. "And I can see a bra strap in the CCTV footage. We know she didn't return to the hotel, so she lost a dress and bra at some point and gained a T-shirt."

"I can't help you with the missing clothes," Rasha replied. "But I'll see what we can pull from the T-shirt."

"*Takk*," I said, and hung up.

"Maybe she just went to a party somewhere," Jacob suggested. "You know, like she had a good time but didn't go all da way… ended up in da guy's T-shirt."

That was always a possibility. A party where someone spiked all the drinks, or all the girls' drinks. Elín seemed cautious to me though, not the type to find herself at a wild party with a bunch of strangers. I returned to the CCTV as Jacob slowed past Onions. We both looked for signs of anyone there. At the last moment, Jacob turned sharply into the driveway between Craft and Onions.

"Hey," I complained, as I bashed against the door.

"Sorry, but dat car weren't dere earlier," he said, slowly rolling by a black SUV parked along the fence.

We parked and walked to the front entrance, which was locked. We banged loudly on the door a few times, but no one answered. Walking around the back, we found the rear entrance amongst an array of rubbish bins and empty crates. I knocked loudly and heard movement inside.

"Where do you want this box?" I called out. "It's a gift package of bottles from Cayman Spirits. I don't want to risk leaving it on the back step."

Jacob shook his head, but I heard the lock being turned and the door swung open. A large Caymanian stood before us wearing pleated trousers, a shiny black dress shirt and a large gold chain around his neck. His expression instantly turned from expectant to pissed off when he saw our uniforms.

"We have a few questions we'd like to ask you, sir. Are you the owner? I asked.

"Call my secretary and make an appointment," he said in a strong local accent.

He started to close the door, but I put my foot in the way. "We can talk at the station if that's what you'd prefer, sir."

"What da hell you want? I got work to do."

"Your name, sir?"

"Father fuckin' Christmas."

"Okay, Mr Christmas, do you have CCTV here in the North Pole?"

He rolled his eyes. "Not dis bullshit again."

Neither Jacob nor I had dealt with Onions before as it was outside our West Bay beat, but the place had a reputation for late night trouble, and we'd heard the owners were suspected of dealing drugs from the nightclub.

"We just need whatever footage you have from last night, sir," Jacob said, trying his luck with the *drittsekk*.

"Too bad, 'cos I ain't got nuttin' from da cameras — someone forget to hit record."

That was a laughable lie; everybody's systems were automated on timers.

"Mind if we come in and take a look at the cameras?" I asked.

"Damn right I mind, blondie," he replied, looking at me with a mixture of contempt and lechery. "Come back with a warrant, then I'll show you how I don't have any damn recordings."

He bashed the door against my foot, which hurt like crazy, but I refused to let it show on my face.

"I'd like to thank you for your co-operation today and we'll be sure to look out for your best interests anytime we're in the area," I said flatly, and moved my foot before he bashed it again. He gave me one last sneer and slammed the door closed.

We walked back to the driveway between the two buildings which led to a large — by Seven Mile Beach's standards — car park in the back. I looked up and saw a camera on the side of Craft, covering the driveway and hopefully the front door to Onions.

On the way back to the patrol car, I took a picture of the registration plate of the SUV so we could look up the owner. I also quickly ducked between the vehicle and the fence, hoping Craft's camera didn't extend this far back. I unscrewed the valve cap from the right front, dropped a small pebble inside the cap and screwed it back on until a slow, steady hiss emanated from the valve stem.

When I got back in the car, I had to listen to Jacob freaking out for five minutes about how we can't do that sort of thing and how much trouble we'd be in. It gave me time to bring up Craft's side camera footage from the thumb drive Jacob had got earlier and I watched Elín walk towards the entrance of the nightclub.

The camera didn't quite cover all the way to the door, which may have been deliberate with all the disturbances that happened outside the nightclub. The Craft management were probably too busy inventing words like 'gastropub' to get involved in next door's punch-ups.

"Nora, you're not listenin' to me, and dis is important," Jacob was saying as I swung the laptop around on its mount so he could see the screen.

"Look, here she is leaving the nightclub."

"Did you hear what I said?" he persisted.

"Of course I did. Don't do shit like that or we'll get in trouble. Now, look at Elín leaving."

Jacob shook his head in annoyance, but studied the screen as I played the footage.

"Who are dem two guys?" he asked.

"Keep watching," I told him.

The three of them walked down the driveway between the building before disappearing from the camera's view. A minute later, a white hire car drove out, and when I paused the footage, we could just make out the registration plate.

I quickly ran the plate to see which hire car company it was and then called their local number at the airport. The hire cars were all together in one small, chaotic area no bigger than the car park we were sitting in. I hoped we wouldn't have to go by there.

"Andy's Car Rental," came the local voice of a young woman.

"This is Constable Sommer. I need to know who rented one of your cars."

"Oh. I think you're supposed to come by 'ere so we can verify your identity before we give out dat information over da phone," she replied.

"Is dis Janice's girl?" Jacob asked before I could respond.

"It is, don't you know," the girl chuckled. "Who dis, den?"

"Jacob Tibbetts. I still tinkin' about dat pie your mama made da udder week. I ain't never tasted nuttin' dat good."

The girl laughed. "She mighty proud of dat recipe, don't you know. Bin known to throw people from da kitchen so dey don't learn her fish pie voodoo."

"You tell your mama I says hello, now."

"I will, Jacob. You gotta plate on dat car?"

I loved the way Jacob knew so many people on the island and the tight-knit community of the locals. It also pissed me off, as no matter how long I lived here I doubted I'd be accepted into that loop. Then again, I'd declined every invitation Jacob and his wife had extended to me over the time I'd known them, preferring to spend my free time alone or with the few friends I allowed into my life. I told myself that next time I'd say yes, but deep down I knew I probably wouldn't. I considered myself shitty company, so why inflict that on people I liked?

When Jacob hung up, we had a name and a hotel the guy had put on the paperwork when he'd rented the car. Tony Lunders from the UK, and he was staying at the Kimpton Seafire Resort. Jacob started the car and drove down the driveway to West Bay Road. I grinned as I noticed the black SUV was sitting low on the right front.

"She could have walked from Seafire to the cemetery," Jacob said as he waited for a break in the traffic.

"But she didn't, did she?"

"True," he replied, pulling out onto the main street. "She came from da north."

"But if this is the car we saw on the CCTV from the fire station and Foster's, we'll have our evidence. This guy, or him and his friend, drove her to West Bay and kicked her out."

"Could have been a party at da Seafire, right?" Jacob added.

"Let's go and see if they're at the hotel. I'll try and match up the car on the way. Guess I'd better call Whittaker and…" I never finished the sentence.

The radio had been relatively quiet, but now lit up with an urgent voice. "Multiple reports of a vehicle fire in the dirt lot behind the car park between the Dart building and CBAC sports club. Anyone in the vicinity please respond."

Jacob quickly U-turned on West Bay Road to take Lawrence over to Camana Bay. I flicked on the siren and lights, then responded to the call. We were less than a minute from the scene.

9

MORE COLD SWEATS

The car sat in brush land beyond the car parks, with thick, dark grey smoke billowing from the tops of the windows. It took a few moments for Jacob to spot a gap in the perimeter fence so we could reach the scene, and I called in the details as best I could. Jacob parked 20 metres from the burning four-door and pulled our boot release as he skidded to a stop. I leapt out and grabbed the fire extinguisher bottle we carried, while Jacob found a pair of work gloves.

He reached the car first as I struggled to pull the safety pin from the fire bottle. Jacob used a glove wadded up in his hand to try the driver's door, but it was locked. It hit me as strange that the fire was inside the car, rather than under the bonnet where most car fires originated. I could see orange flames licking the windows amid a violent swirl of smoke as the fire pulled air through the window gaps while simultaneously ditching the carbon dioxide-rich smoke out through the same vents.

My first thought was this was a prank. Probably kids getting carried away on a joy ride, but when Jacob staggered back, coughing from the smoke, I spotted movement inside the car.

"Someone is in there!" I yelled and shoved the nozzle in the two-inch gap at the top of the window.

Pulling the trigger, I sprayed the dry powder inside the car, aiming for the driver's seat area where I'd seen the motion, before sweeping it around to anywhere I spotted a hint of orange flame. The interior filled with a lighter grey smoke as the powder did its job and smothered the environment, stifling the flames. I stopped spraying and bashed the side window with the bottom of the steel bottle. The glass exploded with a sound like a gunshot and a thick cloud of smoke billowed from the new, larger opening, forcing me back a few steps.

The acrid smell of burnt rubber, paint and fabric was quickly overpowered by the stench of roasting flesh. I coughed from the smoke and fought back a wave of nausea, knowing it was the odour from a human filling my senses. Jacob broke the passenger side window with an emergency glass hammer he'd retrieved from the patrol car. Sirens wailed in the distance, but I knew they would be too late.

The interior cleared enough to make out the single figure in the driver's seat, head slumped forward, resting on their arms, which held the steering wheel. With a fresh air source, flames began building again in the footwell and back of the seat. I couldn't imagine the person was still alive, but I had to check.

Gulping in a lungful of fresh air, I stepped forward and reached in the window, picking their head up. If they had any life left in them, I was sure they'd want it extinguished like the fire. Their facial features were barely distinguishable, just a melted mass of red, brown and black. Hair was matted into hot, scorched flesh and I quickly let go, shaking my hand free of the human remains sticking to my fingers.

I gasped and pulled the trigger on the fire bottle, releasing a spray of dry powder, first at the person's head, and then at the flames trying to reignite in the wheel well. Jacob had now smashed the rear windows and I sprayed the back of the seat until the bottle ran dry, then dropped it to the floor and walked away.

"God in heaven, I've never seen anyting like dat before," Jacob spluttered between coughs. He sounded like he was almost sobbing.

I couldn't look back and I dared not look at my hand, where I knew the residue from someone's head still clung to my fingers.

"*Fy faen,*" I muttered, and felt Jacob's hand on my shoulder.

"Dere was nuttin' more we could do," he said, repeating the same words over and over again.

The female paramedic was just doing her job, but I was going to lose my shit with her if she didn't stop fussing over me and offering a blanket, a place to sit, and an oxygen mask. It was thirty-two degrees centigrade outside, and I'd just had my head in a fire… the last thing I wanted was a tin foil fucking blanket. Sucking on the oxygen for a minute had helped clear my lungs and my head, and she'd cleaned the human off my hands, which was the only thing I'd desperately needed. Now I was fine. Or as fine as I was going to get.

To my relief, Whittaker pulled up and I felt like I had somewhere to be instead of wandering around being chased by the paramedic lady until the fire guys told us it was safe. I'd tried to take a better look at the car, but Malky, the fire chief, had run me off until they were happy the fire wouldn't ignite again.

"There's someone in there?" Whittaker asked, in disbelief.

"*Ja.*"

"How on earth did they get stuck inside? The car doesn't look like it was in a crash."

"The car was perfect except for the fire," I responded.

Whittaker turned from the scene and looked me over. "Are you okay? You didn't get burnt, did you?" he asked, his face full of concern. "You've got black mess all over you, and I think your hair is singed."

I ran a hand through my hair, which felt dry and brittle. "I'm fine. So's Jacob."

"Good, good," he said, blowing out his cheeks in relief. "Do you think this was suicide?"

"Not unless the guy figured out how to strap both his hands to the steering wheel by himself."

"What?" Whittaker said, his hands on his hips. "The guy was tied to the car?"

"Jubilee Clips, my father called them, but I think you call them hose clamps." I'd noticed the discoloured stainless-steel bands before Malky had shooed me away.

"Good Lord," he muttered. "And the victim is male?"

I nodded. "According to the fire guys. They said his shorts were burnt away, so they could see his…"

"Okay, Nora, thank you. I get the point," he said, cutting me off and fiddling with his shirt collar. "'Yes, sir, he's confirmed as male' would have sufficed."

"Sorry," I muttered. I guess he didn't like the idea of a burnt dick. He should try getting a handful of gooey scalp. I knew I'd just added one more reason to wake in the middle of night with the cold sweats.

Malky walked over and said hello to the detective.

"Scene's secure now. We've got the temperature down so nothing should light back up."

"Thanks, Chief," Whittaker replied but didn't move.

I couldn't blame him. It wasn't a sight I was keen on viewing again, but I knew we needed to before the paramedics removed the body. Fire was an outstanding way of covering up evidence, which made it even more important to examine the scene carefully.

Another car pulled in and Rasha, our head SOCO, stepped out with two of her team. She looked at the burnt car then shook her head at Malky.

"Suppose you've doused everything with water and filled it with foam for me, haven't you?"

Malky laughed. "I had the lads leave the hoses on it a little while longer just for you, love."

Rasha playfully punched his arm as she walked by, directing her people as she went. Ten minutes later, she had the scene organised so that anyone close to the scene was required to wear a Tyvek forensics suit and sign in before passing under the taped perimeter they'd erected.

I suggested to Jacob that he track down the renter from the registration plate of the burned-out car. The plate surround had the hire company name on it, so it should be a quick phone call. He could also inform them not to expect their car back anytime soon. Not that it would be any use to them anymore. Jacob offered to organise the witness statements from the nearby car park as well, where onlookers had gathered at the fence. Both kept him away from the scene, which I knew he'd prefer.

I signed the clipboard and was about to duck under the tape in my stylish white Tyvek suit when a thought occurred to me. Jazzy would be expecting a pick-up about now.

"*Faen,*" I cursed under my breath, and took my gloves off to send my friend AJ a text.

By the time I'd made it to the once-white hire car, she'd texted back that she'd pick Jazzy up from school. How anyone thought it was okay for me to be responsible for a fourteen-year-old, even temporarily, was beyond me.

"Where was the fire concentrated when you arrived, Nora?" Rasha asked.

"Hard to see with the smoke inside," I replied, "but I don't recall seeing flames from the back seats."

"And you broke the windows?" she asked.

"I broke the driver's side with the fire bottle, and Jacob did the other three. They popped like they were about to shatter on their own."

Rasha nodded. "They would have."

"That gives us an idea of timing, doesn't it?" Whittaker asked.

"Vaguely," Rasha replied, carefully tilting the victim's head up with her gloved hands. "The glass explodes at a given temperature, but there's a lot of variables involved for it to reach that temperature."

"It looks like the fire was focused around the driver," Whittaker said, having moved around the car to the passenger side.

"He was executed," I replied, and they both looked at me, but didn't argue the point.

"It appears an accelerant may have been used around the driver's seat," Rasha said. "You got here just in time to preserve some of the key evidence, Nora," she continued absent-mindedly as she leaned over the body. "If the blaze had continued unabated, we wouldn't be able to see the varying levels of burn."

I knew Rasha was doing her job and being purely analytical, but I couldn't get the vision of the man's jerky movement from my mind, or the feel of his flesh sliding from his skull.

"I'd say I was a bit late," I responded with more agitation than she deserved. "He was alive when we first got here. I saw him moving."

"Right," Rasha replied, ducking out of the interior and looking at me through her lab glasses. "Sorry. That was callous of me."

I shrugged my shoulders. "This is a shitty way to die, no matter how we talk about it."

"Takes a lot of anger to do something like this," Whittaker commented, walking back around and taking a step away from the car. "I dread to think what the motive was."

"Maybe the killer doesn't like tourists," I said, joining him.

I heard the detective sigh behind his face mask, and his goggles steamed up for a moment. "Dear God, I hope this wasn't the work of a local," he whispered under his breath.

"Sir!" Jacob called out, and we both turned.

My partner was safely behind the taped boundary. In fact, he was at least five paces behind it.

"I have an ID on da renter, sir."

We walked to the yellow-taped perimeter so Jacob didn't have to yell. He moved one step closer.

"Ian Osgood," Jacob read from his notepad. "Thirty-four years old from da UK. Listed a friend's local address as where he was stayin'."

I turned back to look at the charred figure in the driver's seat. "I think it'll be a bit until we have a positive ID."

"True," Whittaker responded, slipping off his protective eyeglasses and face mask. "But we can check out this address and find out if his friends have seen him lately."

"Or if they smell of petrol," I muttered, ducking under the tape.

10

FISH TANK

Before Detective Whittaker would let me sit in his SUV, he made me revisit the paramedics for them to clean me up as best they could. We didn't have time to stop by the station as it was out of our way and the afternoon commuter traffic was already backing up. My dirty white RCIPS shirt would have to do.

We left Jacob with several other constables in search of more witnesses and CCTV from the area. We had no chance of finding any cameras with a view of the scrub land, but we hoped to capture the hire car as it approached.

The address we had was a modern house on Cook Quay, a cul-de-sac off a small slip road running parallel to the bypass at the south end of Governor's Creek. The property sat on a short canal leading into the main body of water. One of those Mercedes which couldn't decide if it was a car or an SUV was the only vehicle in the driveway, and a stone path led to an all-glass entranceway and front door.

Most Scandinavians love modern architecture which uses lots of glass in the design, but I can never understand it. I don't want people seeing inside my home; in fact, I want exactly the opposite. It's my business if I choose to run around the house with a pair of knickers on my head, riding a toy unicorn and singing along to Metallica. Some things are private.

Whittaker knocked, and we watched a woman in her mid-thirties walk towards us from the kitchen. There's another good argument against glass everywhere... she couldn't pretend she wasn't home.

"Hello, Mrs Loudermilk? Whittaker asked, using the name we'd looked up from the address.

"Yes. How may I help you?" the woman replied, looking me over disapprovingly.

She was a stern but pretty woman with a shapely figure accentuated by the tight-fitting V-neck lightweight jumper she was wearing with black leggings.

"I'm Detective Whittaker with the Royal Cayman Islands Police Service," he continued, showing her his badge, "and this is Constable Sommer. Do you currently have a Mister Ian Osgood staying with you, ma'am?"

"He's not here now, but yes, Ian is staying with us. What's this about?"

"May we come inside, Mrs Loudermilk?" Whittaker asked, and she somewhat reluctantly stepped aside for us to enter.

The house wasn't enormous, but the rear facing the canal was all tinted glass, making the living area feel larger than it was. The furnishings were simple, chic, and no doubt expensive. We paused where the entrance area opened into the kitchen on one side and lounge on the other. She closed the front door then joined us without offering to take us farther into her home.

"Is Mr Loudermilk home, ma'am?" Whittaker asked.

"Please, Rhea is fine, Detective, and no, Dalton isn't home yet, but he should be here in a few minutes." She put her hands on her hips and looked back and forth between us. "Can you tell me what's going on?"

"Of course, Rhea, I'll be happy to tell you the little we know if you'll indulge me another question or two first?"

She nodded, so he continued.

"When did you see Mr Osgood last?"

Rhea thought for a few moments, her eyes wandering around the room as she ran through the day's events in her mind. "Mid-morning, I suppose. He was here when I returned from my Pilates class, and that was a little before 9:30. After I showered, we had a cup of coffee and a chat together. It was some time after that he left, saying he was going to the beach and was meeting someone later for lunch."

"What time was that?" Whittaker asked, and glanced at me to make sure I was making notes.

"10:30, I'd say," she replied, and I added it to the notes I'd already been taking.

"Did he mention with whom he was having lunch?"

We both leaned in a few millimetres, hoping for a workable lead.

She shook her head. "He didn't say."

"No calls or texts since then?" the detective continued.

"Not with me, but we can check with Dalton when he gets here; he's more likely to have chatted with him."

"And what is Mr Osgood driving, ma'am?"

"He insisted on getting a rental so he wouldn't bother us during the day, which I told him was ridiculous, but he rented anyway. He could have used my car." She took a deep breath. "Can you please tell me what's going on, Detective? I'm beginning to worry myself to death."

If this was her worried-to-death look, I think she'd be a tough poker opponent. She appeared concerned at best to me.

"My apologies, Rhea," Whittaker said warmly. "I'm afraid there's been an incident involving the hire car Mr Osgood rented. It involves a fatality, but I cannot confirm that the deceased is in fact Mr Osgood."

Rhea Loudermilk's face tensed and her hand reached to the kitchen countertop as though she needed support, but I noticed her weight never shifted from her legs.

"An accident?" she asked, her voice a touch higher but steady.

"Our initial observations suggest we may be dealing with a murder," Whittaker explained, and I continued to watch her reaction closely.

Rhea's legs now gave way and she clutched at the countertop. Whittaker stepped forward and helped her to a dining chair. Her face had turned ashen.

"As I said, we cannot currently confirm the identity of the victim," the detective said softly.

"But it's Ian's car?" Rhea asked, her voice a hoarse whisper.

"That is confirmed, yes."

The front door opened, and I turned to see a man walk in dressed in a business suit with a large leather satchel slung over his shoulder. His expression switched to concern when he saw my uniform.

"What's happened?" he demanded.

"Dalton, I'm fine," Rhea responded, getting to her feet and moving to her husband. "It's Ian."

Loudermilk lowered his satchel to the tile floor and embraced his wife.

"Ian? What do you mean?"

"I'm Detective Whittaker, sir. There's been a fatal incident involving Mr Osgood's hire car, but we cannot yet confirm your friend is the victim."

Dalton Loudermilk was tall and broad shouldered. His suit hung perfectly from his chiselled frame, and he didn't have a hair out of place like he'd just stepped from the barbers. He clutched his wife with one arm but stared over her head at us.

"Victim? What the fuck happened?" he barked. "Why can't you identify him?"

I had no idea what Loudermilk did for a living, but based on the house and his demeanour, it was clear he had a high-paying position with plenty of subordinates.

"There was a fire, sir," Whittaker began, but the man quickly cut him off.

"I saw the smoke from the office earlier. Are you saying that was Ian's car? He's been burnt to fucking death?"

"Can we sit down, sir?" Whittaker asked pleasantly, trying to settle the man down with a change in positions.

"Fine," Loudermilk replied, and guided his wife back to a dining chair.

Whittaker and I sat opposite Rhea, but her husband paced back and forth.

"Mr Loudermilk. If you would please," Whittaker urged, pointing to the seat next to Rhea.

He finally sat down and pulled on his tie, shaking it loose around his neck and undoing the top button of his shirt.

"It was a car wreck?" he asked, his voice firm but less boisterous.

"No, sir, that doesn't appear to be the case," Whittaker replied. "I'm afraid we can't share too many details, mainly because we don't know very much at this stage, but also because the incident is being investigated as a murder."

Rhea grabbed her husband's arm but his focus was on the detective.

"You're saying Ian was murdered in his rental car which was then torched?" he asked, his tone switching from demanding to tense.

"Can you tell me what Mr Osgood was doing here on Grand Cayman?" Whittaker asked, ignoring Loudermilk's question.

"What do you mean, what was he doing?" the man responded defensively. "Having a fucking vacation, that's what he was doing."

"How long have you known Mr Osgood?" Whittaker continued, ignoring Loudermilk's tone.

The husband turned away, shaking his head.

"Years. We've been friends for years," Rhea responded. "We try and see each other once a year or so. Usually he comes here."

"And what does Mr Osgood do for a living?"

I noticed Whittaker used the present tense, which I didn't think was an accident.

"He's in real estate," Rhea replied. "What they call an estate agent in the UK," she added with a hint of a melancholy smile.

"I need to ask the obvious question, I'm afraid," Whittaker asked, looking at Dalton Loudermilk. "Can you think of anyone who might wish harm on your friend? Did he mention any issues, or perhaps you overheard an argument he may have had?"

The husband now looked directly at the detective. "So, you are saying it's Ian in the car."

"As I've told you, sir, we can't..."

"Cut the bullshit, Detective," Loudermilk snapped. "Why ask all these damn questions if it's not Ian?"

Whittaker sat back and took in a breath. I stared off into the distance towards the canal through the huge windows, or wall of glass, or whatever they called it when they build a house like a fish tank. I wanted to let this *drittsekk* have it, but instead I tried to convince myself that he was grief stricken and edgy, which accounted for his shitty manner. We sure as hell didn't set his mate on fire. I tried to save the poor bastard.

"It's Mr Osgood's hire car, and the deceased occupant is a male," Whittaker patiently explained. "Your friend hasn't shown up or contacted anyone that we're aware of. So yes, the victim is most likely your friend, but until we have medical verification, I can't confirm this as fact."

"When did you last hear from him?" I asked Loudermilk.

He scowled my way, then returned his attention to Whittaker. "He carries a wallet. Was there a wallet on the body?"

"The body had not been removed from the vehicle when we left, so I can't say as yet, Mr Loudermilk. Now, would you mind answering the constable's question?"

I resisted giving Loudermilk the middle finger as I figured Whittaker had just done that for me. I smiled on the inside.

"I don't know," Loudermilk replied, throwing his hands in the air. "I think he texted me this morning some time."

"Would you mind checking your mobile for the exact time, sir?" Whittaker asked firmly.

Loudermilk retrieved his oversized smartphone from his pocket. It looked like one of the latest, whizziest, ludicrously over-priced mini-TVs which also made phone calls.

"10:51," he replied, studying the screen.

"What did he say?" Whittaker asked.

"We'd talked about having lunch, but he was telling me he had to meet someone else."

"Did he say who, or where?" Whittaker continued.

"He didn't, and I was curious too, but I was in the middle of a series of meetings, so I figured I'd ask him later." His voice trailed off and his wife hugged his arm and rested her head on his shoulder.

"You were at your office all day?" I asked and Loudermilk glared at me again, but this time he answered.

"I stepped out for lunch with one of my managers; otherwise yes." His body tensed. "What the fuck does my day have to do with Ian's murder?"

"Sounds like nothing, but we have to ask," I responded, maintaining eye contact with the man. "I'm sure your manager can verify your story so we can move on."

The truth was we didn't have to ask anything, but TV crime shows had helped us with some of the more accusatory questions as they always used that line.

"How about you, Mrs Loudermilk?" I persisted. "Where was your Pilates class? Where else did you go today?"

Rhea looked stunned that she was now on the spot.

"The class was eight until nine, and I told you I was back here before 9:30."

"Did you go out again?" I asked.

"How about you go and find out if it's actually our friend who's been murdered?" Dalton Loudermilk shouted, jumping to his feet. "Enough of this bullshit. We were his best friends. Why the hell would we have anything to do with murdering the man? Now get on with your jobs and let us know the moment you have a positive ID."

Whittaker managed to get a contact number for Osgood's brother in the UK before Dalton herded us out the door. I climbed into Whittaker's Range Rover and lowered the window to let the steaming air escape until the AC kicked in. With my mobile, I clicked a photo of the silver Mercedes and an expensive-looking Audi I presumed belonged to Dalton Loudermilk. The detective reversed out of the driveway, then started down the cul-de-sac.

"What do you think?" Whittaker asked me.

"I don't think they strapped their friend to the steering wheel of his hire car and lit him on fire," I replied.

"I agree," Whittaker said, rubbing his chin.

"But she's hiding something," I added.

"Hmm," Whittaker muttered. "I got the same impression."

11

TUNA AND ANCHOVIES

As Whittaker pulled into West Bay station, Jacob was just coming out of the building. On seeing us, he walked over, and Whittaker lowered his window.

"Anything new, Jacob?"

"Nothing useful from da canvass, I'm afraid, sir. But we did get a hit from CCTV at the Camana Bay roundabout. I emailed you both a link to da file on da server."

"What does it show, Jacob?" the detective asked.

"Car comes from Lawrence Boulevard, then goes outta da camera view on da bypass south, just before Minerva Drive, where he probably turned in to cross the car park to where we found the car, sir."

"Time of day?"

"A few minutes after three, sir."

"Good work. We'll need to backtrack from there and see how far we can trace the car's movements. If what the Loudermilks tell us is true, he left their house around 10:30, so we have four and a half hours of unaccounted movement we need to fill in for Mr Osgood. I'll get someone working on that tonight at Central."

Jacob raised his hand. "One more ting, sir. In da footage dere's someone else in da car wit da driver."

"Why didn't you say that before, Jacob?" Whittaker asked. "Rather important, don't you think?"

"Yes, sir. Sorry, sir," Jacob babbled.

"That's probably my fault, sir," I volunteered, and Whittaker turned to me. "Jacob sometimes tends to blurt everything at once when he's excited."

"I've noticed," Whittaker interjected with a wry grin.

"Well, I've been urging him to organise his words a little better, sir. And use less of them."

Whittaker turned back to my partner. "Keep up the good work, Jacob. Sorting the priorities in delivering information will be the next step."

"Yes, sir, sorry again, sir."

"Well?" Whittaker urged.

"Oh, of course, sir. The other person in the car is in the back and wearing a hoodie or a dark hat. We couldn't make out any details."

———

I left the station with too much on my mind. It was hard to get the images of the fire out of my head and the smell from my nose. At least I'd had a change of clothes in my locker at the station, so now my uniform was balled up on the passenger side floor as I drove less than a kilometre to the dock where my friends AJ Bailey and Reg Moore kept their dive boats.

Reg and his wife Pearl were like island parents who looked after and kept an eye on a bunch of us, but mainly AJ. Reg had helped her start her own business, Mermaid Divers, and let her share the dock he ran his three boats from. AJ was a decade older than me and felt like my big sister.

Two years ago, she, along with Detective Whittaker, was responsible for bringing down the resort and saving my life. They also picked me up from the lowest point in my life when my boyfriend

Ridley was murdered. AJ kept me going, one breath at a time, and Whittaker persuaded me to join the Royal Cayman Islands Police Service, which gave me a purpose. They asked for nothing in return, and I suppose I haven't given them much, but I sucked with words, so that's the way it is.

AJ and her only full-time employee, Thomas, were getting her 36-foot Newton custom dive boat ready for a night dive trip, but the customers hadn't arrived yet. Jazzy was helping them pull rental gear out from the bow cabin and smiled at me as I walked up.

"Hey," I said, and AJ stuck her head out of the cabin.

"Hey, what are you up to? You should come out with us," she said, in her cheery English voice.

She was only five foot three, had a tanned and toned figure from working the boat every day, and shoulder-length blonde hair with purple streaks. Both arms were covered with beautiful underwater scene tattoos, and until anyone heard her speak, they might think she was the lead singer in a rock band. Her friendly persona and easy smile seemed in contradiction to her looks to some people, until they got to know her.

"I have to run into town," I said, making that decision on the spot.

Spending an hour underwater sounded tempting, and I loved diving at night when the reefs had a shift change of their inhabitants, but something else was tugging at me.

"What was all that smoke this afternoon," AJ asked, as she set up buoyancy control devices on tanks.

"A fire," I answered, my mind elsewhere.

AJ slumped her shoulders and shook her head at me.

"A car was set on fire out the back of Camana Bay in the scrub land."

"Hooligans?" she asked.

"No, I doubt it."

If Jazzy wasn't there, I would have told AJ more about it. She and Reg often worked for the police when they needed professional divers, which was enough of an excuse in my mind to share certain details with her the public couldn't know. But Jazzy had seen and heard enough trauma in her life already. I was supposed to be adding normality to her days... which, again, was a ridiculous notion.

"AJ pulled a wheelie on the way home," Jazzy blurted with a big grin.

AJ groaned from the other side of the boat. "What part of 'Don't say anything about that' was confusing to you?"

Jazzy grinned. "It was really cool."

"Grass," AJ muttered.

"You're supposed to be the responsible one," I said, giving AJ my attempt at a disappointed look, which probably didn't look any different from my perpetual blank stare.

"I'm not used to having someone on the back," AJ said in her defence. "We needed to get around a few slowpokes and I may have flown the front wheel for a few yards."

"A few yards?" Jazzy said, bursting out laughing. "A few hundred yards you mean."

AJ waved her off and pretended to be too busy to bother with it anymore.

"Come on, you'd better come with me as your auntie AJ can't be trusted," I said, and Jazzy hopped from the boat to the dock.

"You're welcome," AJ shouted after us and I knew she was hiding her smile as much as I was.

It felt good to have something to smile about, albeit briefly.

We walked past AJ's Ducati Multistrada motorcycle on the way to the Jeep.

"Did you think you were coming off the back?" I asked.

"Yeah," Jazzy replied, giggling. "At first, but then when I didn't, it was really cool."

I pulled myself into the lifted CJ-7 and started the engine.

"Where are we going?" Jazzy asked.

I backed out of the spot and drove up the short, steep slope to the road. "To see a friend."

"I'm starving," Jazzy added.

"You're always starving."

"Are we getting dinner?"

"Sure," I replied, and wondered if I could keep anything down after the day I'd had.

Elín was sitting up in bed reading a well-worn paperback when we walked in. She looked surprised to see me.

"I should have brought the book from your hotel room with your clothes. Sorry," I said, leading Jazzy to the guest chairs.

"That's okay," Elín replied and placed the book down.

"This is Jazzy," I said. "I hope you don't mind me bringing her with me."

Elín shook her head, and I could see she was studying us both, no doubt curious what my connection was with a dark-skinned teenage girl. "This is Elín," I continued, looking at my young charge.

"Are you two related?" Jazzy asked.

Elín laughed.

"No, Elín's from Iceland," I explained. "She's a friend."

"I know where that is," Jazzy exclaimed proudly. "It's north of Scotland and below Greenland."

Elín nodded. "I'm impressed. Not many people know exactly where it is."

"I had an atlas I used to study when I was bored," Jazzy said, her eyes wandering all around the hospital room.

With the basic introductions over with, I had no idea what to say or ask. Usually, I was perfectly content with what most people considered awkward silence, but we were visiting, so it seemed like I should be talking.

"You okay?" I asked.

It was pretty much a dumb question, but I figured she'd get the point. I deliberately didn't ask how she was doing, as I knew that had to be pretty shit considering how her holiday was going.

"The headache is starting to go away," she replied. "Were you able to figure anything out?"

"A little," I said and looked at Jazzy, who rolled her eyes.

"I know. Forget everything I'm about to hear," Jazzy groaned.

I returned my attention to the young woman who was looking at me in anticipation of discovering what may have happened during a night she couldn't remember.

"From CCTV, we know you went to Onions, and it appears you left with two guys in their car. At least one is a tourist who's staying at the Kimpton Seafire hotel. We were heading there to interview him when another thing came up that we had to deal with."

"The fire that was on the news? I saw something about it earlier," Elín asked, pointing to the small, muted TV mounted on the wall.

"*Ja*," I replied, reluctant to expand on the event that had pulled me from her case. "Do any of the small pieces you can remember include a hotel, or two men about our age?"

Elín thought for a moment. "I remember bright lights and loud music, but I assumed that was the nightclub. It's only short flashes I get, like in a movie when they do that flickering image for just a moment thing."

"Does it all feel like the same place? Same style of music? Same people?"

Elín sighed. "It's so hard to tell what's real and what's not; it all feels more like my imagination than something that really happened. I'm sorry."

"That's okay," I assured her.

She closed her eyes and concentrated for a few moments, and I held up my hand when I sensed Jazzy was about to say something. I was pretty sure what she wanted, and she could wait a few more minutes.

"I think there's dance music in some of these thoughts, or

memories, or whatever they are, and rock music in others." Elín said as she opened her eyes. "Some feel really crowded and some don't. Do you think that means anything?"

"Maybe, maybe not," I replied honestly. "It's nothing we could use in court, but it might help us tie in a location."

She appeared to relax, and I figured that was enough for tonight. I turned to Jazzy. "Go on then."

Jazzy didn't need telling twice. She shot out of her chair, heading for the door.

"We bought a pizza on the way over," I said. "We got enough for all of us. I figured the hospital food was probably shit, so you might be hungry."

Elín grinned. "I haven't been able to face food all day, but pizza sounds good. What kind?"

Jazzy raced back in with the large pizza box we'd left on a chair outside the room.

"Vegetables on half and plain cheese on the other half. Boring, but I don't eat meat, and the pizza place doesn't have the toppings we like in Norway."

"Anchovies?" Elín asked with a wry smile.

"Exactly," I agreed. "They freaked out when I first got here and asked if they had them."

"That's because little smelly fish on pizza is extra, super gross," Jazzy squealed, opening the box and offering Elín a slice.

"Tuna and anchovies are the best," Elín countered, and took a slice of veggie.

We ate in silence for a while, Jazzy occasionally coming up with a new topping she thought was disgusting and asking if we'd like it. Shortly after we finished the pizza, a nurse came by and informed us visiting time was over, so we cleared up our mess and prepared to leave.

"Nice to meet you, Jazzy," Elín told us. "And thank you both."

"Sure," I said, with a quick nod. "Tomorrow, we'll find those two guys."

Elín forced a smile. "I know you will."

12

FILTHY CARPET

2009

Allie finally began to relax. The crowds were endless, but they seemed harmlessly drunk and simply having a good time. There was also a heavy police presence, although they appeared to let most activities go unchecked, warning far more than arresting. She'd avoided lifting her top again, but Rachel hadn't been so shy, gathering an impressive collection of beads around her neck. She'd received two warnings from uniformed officers, but they'd both struggled to look her in the eyes as they'd ordered her to cover her breasts.

After inching along in traffic for another hour, Bruce finally found his place to park behind a tall hotel building. The car park was cordoned off with chain strung between stacks of concrete blocks and guarded by a dodgy-looking guy with jeans hanging halfway down his bum. Bruce showed the man a printed hotel confirmation and didn't bat an eyelid when the bloke charged forty dollars for the privilege of parking at the hotel he'd booked.

They walked to the beach and worked their way through the

crowd until they found a spot they could sit and watch the sunset. The sun was going down behind them, silhouetting the town, but the rich light on the wispy clouds over the ocean produced beautiful shades of orange, turning a deeper red just before the sun disappeared altogether. Allie had remembered her camera and kept taking pictures as the colours changed.

In the final few moments before the sun dipped behind the buildings, the crowd quietened, music was turned down, and the beach, packed with people as far as Allie could see, calmed for a few minutes. The second the top of the sun disappeared behind them, the whole place erupted in cheers and blasting music. They stood, and the mass of humanity jumping and moving made Allie feel slightly dizzy. It was like looking at a carpet of bugs where the individuals were lost, and the colony appeared to exist as one.

It struck her as the perfect metaphor for Spring Break. A colony of bugs. A large community, all acting in the same chaotic manner.

As the sky turned from deep blue to ink black, the crowds slowly thinned on the beach as people moved from the sand to the street, seeking out the lively hotels and bars which lined the waterfront. Bruce and Rachel led the way back to their hotel, and Allie wondered what the room arrangements would be. She hadn't been asked for any money, so she hoped Ozzy wasn't expecting a deviation from their strictly friends relationship.

The sheer number of people packed on the street was overwhelming. What should have been a five-minute stroll took them forty-five minutes. Drinks seemed to pass freely from hand to hand, regardless of whether people knew each other, and the beads for boobs spectacle continued relentlessly.

Checking into the hotel was another lengthy process, with a queue all the way out the front doors. Rachel berated Bruce for not taking care of it earlier but quickly forgot about it as a group of shirtless guys admired her with slurred complements.

"I have a credit card to pay for my part," Allie told Bruce, but he waved her off.

"Don't worry, you're a guest, and I'd be paying for the room regardless."

Allie thanked him and went back to people watching as hordes of young men and women bustled in and out of the hotel lobby.

The place was far from fancy and the decor didn't look like it had been updated since the place had been built, which Allie determined was not recently. Beyond the odour of sweaty bodies, an unpleasant, stale, mouldy smell filled the lobby, briefly relieved by fresh, humid air blowing in when the doors opened. When they finally made it up to the room, Allie found it to be no better than the lobby. The door even used a real key, like a motel or old guest house.

A scratched and beaten wooden dresser sat opposite two sagging double beds, and an ancient air conditioning unit hung loosely from a hole under the dirty window. Allie could see little gaps around the edges where the streetlights shone through. The rusty box rattled, whirred, and spewed out air which didn't feel much cooler than the steamy air outside.

"Have you texted Rafa?" Ozzy asked, plonking himself down on one of the beds and looking at Bruce.

"Yeah!" Rachel squealed from the bathroom where Allie could hear a steady stream hitting the water in the toilet bowl.

The door to the bathroom was wide open. So was the door to the room, and loud voices came and went from the hallway.

Bruce typed a message into his mobile and hit send as Rachel appeared from the loo, still adjusting her bikini bottoms.

"Rafa, Rafa," she chanted, then placed a big, sloppy kiss on Bruce's lips.

"Who's Rafa?" Allie quietly asked Ozzy, sitting next to him on the bed.

Ozzy grinned in the cheeky way he used to do when they were up to something naughty as kids, and for a moment, Allie recognised her old friend. He'd been gone less than a year, but since she'd arrived in Miami, she hardly recognised the lad who'd been one of her best friends for so many years. He'd been drinking a lot, and all he'd talked about was partying at Spring Break. She'd never heard the word 'party' used as a verb before.

His two friends were nice enough, but not the types she and Ozzy used to hang out with. She'd been to a few crazy parties before, but nothing even close to the madness surrounding her now. She felt like a voyeur. An alien in a completely foreign environment, dragged along in the wake of the festivities.

"Rafa's the Candy Man," Ozzy said, laughing. "He brings the party to us."

Allie could only guess that he was talking about drugs, but Ozzy was drunk, so she knew a sensible conversation was out of the question. Her friend slumped back, resting his head on the once-white pillow, which was now an oddly mottled creamy brown colour. Bruce's mobile phone dinged, and he checked the message, with Rachel excitedly bouncing next to him on the bed.

"He's in the hotel next door," Bruce announced with a broad smile. "He'll be over in twenty minutes."

Rachel pushed him over on the bed and climbed on top of him. "Then we have twenty minutes to fill," she said, releasing the well-worn clip on her bikini top, allowing the flimsy garment to tumble to the filthy carpeted floor.

Allie, who'd insisted on a dimly lit or darkened room whenever she and her boyfriend had made love, had no intentions of watching someone else have sex, and scurried to the door, pulling it to behind her. Without a key, she dare not close it and find herself locked out for the night. She was hoping that after this guy Rafa came by, they'd all go out for the evening, and she'd make an excuse to stay in the room. Her return ticket to London wasn't for another four days, but she was already wondering how much it would cost to leave early.

Wandering the hallway killing time, Allie found just about every room door open, and the same scenes playing out in each of them. She was invited to join many of them, and only ran across one person she suspected of being sober. It was a guy looking for his friend's room, who explained he'd just arrived. She figured he'd be inebriated within thirty minutes.

Allie had been surprised by America's twenty-one-year-old drinking age, which seemed ridiculous, but apparently it didn't apply, or wasn't enforced during Spring Break. Bruce was of legal age so he'd had no issue buying beer and liquor on the way down, and at first Allie had been annoyed she wouldn't be able to, but now it seemed irrelevant.

After twenty minutes of meandering the hotel, she returned to the room and found the door was now closed. She quietly knocked, but no one answered although she could hear voices inside. Allie knocked again, harder this time, and Ozzy opened the door.

"There you are!" he exclaimed, and ushered her in. "We were worried about you."

"The Joker's back!" Rachel yelled, devoid of any sign of worry.

There was a new guy in the room. He was Hispanic and looked a year or two older than the rest. He looked Allie over, and his mouth curled into a playful grin. His eyes were dark and mischievous but intriguing.

"She's with us," Bruce said. "She's cool."

The man who she assumed was Rafa nodded. "What can I get you?" he asked in a heavy accent.

"I'm good, thank you," Allie quickly replied, but Ozzy pushed her towards Rafa.

"She needs to loosen up," Ozzy said. "Our little Joker hasn't found her Spring Break spirit yet."

Allie's friend laughed as he spoke, and she noticed his pupils were even more dilated than they'd been earlier from the booze.

"Really, I'd rather not," Allie said, and shook herself free of Ozzy's arm around her.

Rafa held up both hands and laughed. "Hey chica, no sweat, baby."

"C'mon, Joker, sweetie," Rachel said with a fake pout, struggling to remain steady on her feet. "We just want you to have a good time."

Bruce laughed. "Let's hit the streets, Batmaniacs. It's time to light this sleepy little town up."

Rachel and Ozzy both cheered.

Rafa grinned. "Text me, bro. I gotta couple more homeys to hit up, then I'll join you."

They all performed what to Allie looked like a strange combination of handshakes, half-hugs, and hand slaps, before Rafa slipped out the door and the others gathered up the few things they wanted to take with them. Mainly money, ID, and beer.

Allie tried to melt into the corner of the room, hoping they'd leave without noticing she'd stayed behind, but no such luck. Ozzy and Rachel grabbed a hand each and dragged her out the door.

"No way, sister," Rachel enthused. "It's now my personal mission to get you wasted and laid before daybreak."

Ozzy laughed and gave his old friend a smile which made her feel incredibly uncomfortable.

13

SKIRMISHES

I drove West Bay Road north behind Seven Mile Beach on the way home, avoiding the bypass. I preferred driving amid the restaurants, hotels and condos instead of the dual carriageway, which felt so out of place on a Caribbean island. The traffic lights and tourist traffic made the trip longer, but my other incentive was to avoid driving by where I'd watched a man burn to death earlier that day.

Past the Watermark condos, we met Public Beach where West Bay Road was now forced 90 degrees right for a few hundred metres into a roundabout on the bypass. The road used to run along the waterfront all the way to West Bay, but the developer of Seafire had persuaded the government to redirect the road so his hotel could be slap-bang behind the beach. Much to the protests of the locals, whose voices fell on deaf ears.

I looked up at the tall hotel, its lighting a bright yellow-orange glow against the night sky, and turned left into the road leading to the side entrance.

"Where we going now?" Jazzy asked, her massive frizz of hair tied back in a ponytail to combat the wind rushing over the topless Jeep.

"This won't take long," I said, although I'd made the decision to stop on the fly, so I really didn't know what I was going to run into.

I pulled up to the entrance where a valet parking attendant magically appeared from somewhere, asking for my room number.

"Police," I said, and flashed my badge.

"Pull over there, miss, so you don't block the entrance," he replied, disappointed he'd left whatever game he was playing on his mobile for a non-tipping vehicle.

I moved up a few car lengths then parked, ignoring the attendant's suggestions that I drive farther away. I looked at my uniform under Jazzy's feet on the passenger side floor. As a constable I wasn't supposed to go running around, badge in hand, without my uniform, but I couldn't face the lingering smell of burnt... stuff.

Jumping out of the Jeep, Jazzy followed, and I paused, about to tell her to stay put, then changed my mind.

"Find somewhere to hang out in the lobby, okay?"

"Why can't I come with you?" she asked.

"Because I'm on official police business."

"You don't look very official," she pointed out.

"I'm undercover," I said, stretching the truth to its breaking point.

The parking guy gave us a frown as we entered the building through the automatic doors, arriving in the large and very extravagant lobby. I pointed at four plush and uncomfortable-looking chairs surrounding a table in the middle of the reception area.

"Don't steal anything," I whispered loudly enough for Jazzy to hear me, and she poked her tongue out in return, but went and sat down.

"Good evening, madam," the man at the front desk greeted me.

"Hey," I said, and showed him my badge. "You have a guy named Tony Lunders staying here. I need his room number."

"I'm sure you're aware that we require a warrant to issue a room number, madam."

I looked at his badge. Blake Johnson. Front Desk Manager. Great, I thought, I had to get the one guy who knew all the rules.

"No problem, I'll be back tomorrow with half the force in tow, warrant in hand," I said, taking a plunge I was sure I was about to regret. "I doubt this douchebag will be in his room at eleven in the morning, but if we send the firearms guys running around the place, I'm sure they'll find him before too long. We'll have to shut the hotel down for an hour or two, but we'll be as quick as possible. Blake."

He grinned and shook his head. "Nice try, Constable...?"

"Sommer," I reluctantly admitted. Apparently, he'd noticed my rank even if he hadn't caught my name.

"Constable Sommer. That's a nice strong-arm line but take a look at this from my side. It's illegal for me to give you the room number without a warrant. You're alone, out of uniform, and I have no way of knowing if you're after a real suspect or a one-night stand you're mad at for not calling you back. Please come back with a warrant."

Fy faen. My bluff had been well and truly called. Good sense dictated I should walk away. Jacob and I had planned on calling the room from the lobby earlier that day, but I had to go and push my luck.

"We have a young woman in George Town hospital recovering from being slipped a date rape drug," I said, ignoring the good sense in theory I possessed. "Through CCTV, we've traced her movements from a club in town. She left with Tony Lunders and his friend. Lunders listed your hotel on the hire car form. We have reason to believe Lunders is the man who slipped her the roofie, either at the club or here at the hotel. I'm not trying to shortcut the system, I'm simply following up on my own time as we're much more likely to find the guy in his room at this hour."

"Lunders?" Blake asked.

I nodded. I couldn't imagine he'd turn a 180 on his refusal, but I'd made some progress. The manager hit a few keys, then looked back up at me.

"We do have someone by that name staying with us," he said tentatively. "And last night, we received several complaints about noise from his room. We sent security up and apparently they were having quite a party. They were told to keep it down and we didn't hear any more complaints. I had security walk by again thirty minutes later, and he told me he could still hear music and voices, but it wasn't unreasonably loud."

I nodded. "Thanks." I drummed my fingers on the counter as I thought it through. He still couldn't give me a room number, but maybe we could go about this another way. "You can call his room and tell him there's someone in the lobby to see him, correct?"

"Of course," Blake replied. "But he's under no obligation to come down for the police without a warrant."

"I doubt he would come down," I agreed. "But he might for a blonde woman called Nora who says she was at the party last night."

Blake grimaced. "I can't lie for you, Constable."

"I wouldn't ask you to. I'll just move along the counter and ask one of your receptionists to do it."

Blake gritted his teeth. "This has to be tonight? You couldn't come back in the morning with the paperwork?"

"We'll be back with a warrant for Lunders, and for the CCTV I'm sure you have on each floor and in the car park. But I can't risk the bloke skipping out on us. He might not even answer the phone, in which case I'll see you tomorrow."

"Someone messed with the cameras on that floor last night," Blake admitted. "Smeared a gel or grease all over them. We had a hell of a job cleaning them."

"So that's not very suspicious, is it?" I scoffed. "Didn't whoever watches the cameras see it happening?"

"We don't have a dedicated person; the security guys rotate, taking turns, but no one saw it happening. You just see a hand smear something from behind. We looked to see if we could figure out who it was from other cameras, but they must have used the stairs. There aren't any cameras in the stairwell."

"Sounds like your CCTV needs some attention."

Blake grimaced. "Okay, look, let's do this. I'll call the room and tell him there's a woman here to see him. But I must insist you meet him by the elevators, and I'll have my security there with you. I'd rather have an organised presence knocking on his door tomorrow than a skirmish in the lobby tonight."

"Let's do it," I said, avoiding any promises about skirmishes. They were out of my hands. Mostly.

I walked over to Jazzy while I waited for Blake to organise one of the security men to join us.

"I'm hungry," Jazzy complained. "Can I order something here?"

"Hell no. Look at their prices."

"They don't put prices on this menu."

"That's because even they are embarrassed to put it in print. You had a pizza already. How can you be hungry again?"

"I'm a teenager mid growth spurt. I think I'm about to get really tall."

"You're mid nothing. You haven't grown a centimetre since you conned me into putting a roof over your head. You didn't tell me you have some kind of stomach worm that needs feeding every ten minutes."

"Okay, I'm on the cusp of a growth spurt."

Blake called me over to the front desk where he now stood on the customer side with a man in a pale blue security uniform.

"Stay here and don't order any food," I instructed Jazzy. "You can have something when we get home."

I heard her groan as I walked away.

"Leroy, this is Constable Sommer," Blake said, introducing us.

"You're Jacob's partner, aren't you, miss?" Leroy asked.

"*Ja.* Are you another cousin?" I asked, amazed at the extent of Jacob's family.

"Someting like dat, miss," he replied with a laugh. "I'm a Tibbetts, all right, so we're related somewhere along da line, but I couldn't tell you where."

"If you're both ready, we'll make the call," Blake said, now seemingly eager to get this over with.

We both nodded, and he had a receptionist hand him the receiver.

"Where are the lifts?" I asked Leroy, thinking through my plan for when the doors opened.

"Around dat corner," he said, and we both turned to Blake.

"*Faen*," I muttered to myself, and Blake handed the receiver back over the counter.

"No answer I'm afraid."

My adrenaline had begun to pump and now it all felt anticlimactic. I'd not only wasted part of my evening, but I'd risked getting in serious trouble for nothing. I thanked them both, and Blake said he'd leave a note for the day manager so he'd expect us. I promised Leroy I'd tell Jacob hi from him.

"C'mon," I told Jazzy, and she skipped to catch up.

"That wasn't very exciting," she said as the entrance doors slid open in front of us.

Walking in was the young man I recognised from the passport photograph Jacob had requested from immigration and emailed me earlier in the day.

"Tony Lunders?" I said and he looked me over with a grin.

"You've found him," he said, sounding like an American college kid from the movies I always turned off. His friend stopped alongside him and gave me the same lustful look.

I pulled out my badge. "Constable Sommer with the Royal Cayman Islands…"

I didn't get any further. They both turned and sprinted from the lobby, turning hard right around the building in the direction of the beach.

"Stay here!" I yelled to Jazzy and took off after them.

They'd surprised me coming through the door, then surprised me again by running. I was five paces behind them, they were young and fit, and they seemed to know where they were going. I saw brighter lights ahead and the pathway opened up before splitting either side of the lusciously landscaped pool.

I'd gained a step on them but was still way too far back to grab the friend who was trailing Lunders. They chose right and dodged around a couple dressed in tropical evening wear, just before a blur arrived from behind the shrubs at an alarming speed.

Leroy cleaned the friend off his feet and the two careened through more shrubs and crashed to the ground out of sight. Lunders made the mistake of checking over his shoulder at the chaos behind him and lost two paces to me. He grabbed at a deck chair, attempting to fling it in my path, but he swung wildly, and it missed, flying clear of me.

Every head turned from under the thatched cover of the pool bar as we sprinted past. Several people cheered but everyone on the pathway jumped out of the way, which wasn't helping me. Now I wished I had my uniform on, so they'd know I was a copper. Although that might've made them less likely to assist me.

The path continued curving behind the hotel building and would eventually run parallel to the beach. A row of low trees lined the path on the left, screening the little rentable beach view cabanas. Between the concrete path and the trees was a metre or so of grass and I decided that might be the softest landing I'd seen.

With a spring from my right foot, I lunged at full stretch, glancing his right shoulder, but catching a handful of his shirt. It was enough to drag him sideways until he tripped over himself and went sprawling to the ground, hitting first on the edge of the concrete, then rolling across the grass until the trees brought him to a stop.

I cleared the concrete but landed hard on a mixture of grass and Lunders's legs, his foot in my chest knocking all the wind from my lungs, followed by a smack to the head as I crashed into the trees. Wheezing and gasping, we both struggled to pick ourselves up and I knew the *drittsekk* was about to try running again. I punched him in the nearest soft tissue I could see, and he dropped to the ground. If I'd stopped him having kids someday, that was fine with me.

As I sat up, I saw Leroy dragging the friend towards us by the scruff of the neck. The kid had a nasty-looking graze across the side of his face. People fussed and followed, several with mobiles catching video of the scene. I'm sure they were all wondering what a young woman in leggings and a T-shirt was doing chasing men through the hotel, so I pulled out my badge.

"Police business, stay back," I wheezed.

The front desk manager bustled past the crowd and stood next to Leroy with his hands on his hips. "When I talked about skirmishes, this is exactly what I meant, Miss Sommer," Blake said, running his hands through his hair in desperation.

"That was way more exciting," Jazzy enthused, peeking around them both. "So this is what you do all day."

14

AVERAGE MAN

Detective Roy Whittaker, my superior and mentor, was not impressed. Once again. He'd been just about to leave his office at Central Station in George Town when I'd called him to say I had Tony Lunders and his buddy, Max Jones, at West Bay for questioning. Neither the hour nor the fact that I had them in custody bothered him, but the follow-up call from the irate manager of the Seafire had him wagging a finger at me as he paced back and forth, lecturing me on procedure. And something about it applying to me as well as everyone else. I'm not completely sure — I was thinking about my questions for Lunders.

As usual, once Whittaker had administered my bollocking, he returned to his calm demeanour and carried on as though nothing had happened. I dug out a spare uniform shirt and trousers from my locker and we entered the interview room where Tony Lunders sat, looking battered and forlorn.

"You can't assault me and hold me here like this," he complained. "There are laws against this shit."

Lunders was no taller than me and almost as skinny. He'd strutted into the Seafire like he'd owned the place, but despite his words, he didn't look so cocky now.

"Let's start with why you ran from Constable Sommer, Mr Lunders," Whittaker began.

Lunders shrugged his shoulders and shook his head as though it was no big deal. "I thought she was hotel security giving us a hard time again. Figured it would be a lark to give her the runaround."

Whittaker turned to me. "Did you show this gentleman your badge and introduce yourself, Constable?"

"*Ja*," I replied. "That's when he stopped looking at my chest and ran."

Lunders scoffed. "This is bullshit. One phone call and I'm out of here and you're in deep shit. You're getting sued for brutality," he added, pointing at me.

I smiled, but he wouldn't look directly at me.

"I assume you're unfamiliar with our laws here, Mr Lunders," Whittaker explained calmly. "We can hold you for quite some time without a call and without charging you if you're involved in a serious crime. Which you are."

That got the kid's attention. "What crime? Having a party in a hotel room isn't a crime for fuck's sake!"

"Depends what happens at the party, Mr Lunders," Whittaker responded.

"Jeez, man. A few drinks with friends, that's all. So we played the music a little loud and the neighbours bitched. No big deal; we turned it down, man."

Whittaker took a picture of Elín from his folder and slid it across the table. "Recognise this young woman?"

Lunders studied the picture, which I figured came from her social media page. She looked happy, smiling, knee deep in clear blue water. Probably taken here on the island just a few days ago.

"It looks like the chick we met at a club the other night, but I can't be sure," he said, pushing the picture away.

Whittaker nudged my leg. I didn't need prompting twice.

"You're on CCTV leaving the Onions nightclub with her last night," I pointed out. "Tomorrow morning, we'll have CCTV from your hotel which will show her arriving there with you. Is she looking more familiar yet?"

"So what?" Lunders exclaimed. "A chick came back to the room with us. Big deal. We had a party going — there were lots of people there."

"How many of the girls did you slip a roofie to?" I asked.

Lunders finally looked right at me. "What the fuck are you talking about?"

"Are we going to find Rohypnol in your room when our forensics team tears it apart in the morning?"

The kid's jaw dropped open and quivered a few times. The smartarse was lost for words now.

"I don't have any idea what Roe-hip-whatever is! Someone brought a little weed, we had drinks, that was it, man," he said, his voice shaking. "I don't even know what happened to that Swedish chick. She was weird."

I didn't bother correcting the fine geographical knowledge of the college student and focused on the timing.

"Walk us through what happened last night, from the nightclub to your hotel room," I told him, backing off the pressure enough for the kid to calm down.

His shoulders relaxed and he slumped in the chair. "We'd thrown a few lines out around the pool that day, and my WhatsApp starts lighting up when we were at the nightclub, chatting to that chick," he said, pointing to Elín's picture. "Pretty soon, I got a party brewing, so we bailed and invited her along. She was pretty wasted already and said she'd love to party." Lunders leaned over the table. "I didn't force her to come with us, man. She was game."

"Did you drive straight to the hotel?" Whittaker chimed in.

"Yeah," Lunders said, then thought for a second. "No, man, that's right. We stopped and picked up drinks at some place along the main drag."

"On the left or right?" Whittaker asked, and I knew he could narrow down the liquor store along West Bay Road by which side of the street it was on.

"Right. I think."

"Okay, what happened when you arrived at the hotel?"

Lunders shrugged his shoulders. "We went up to the room."

"Just the three of you?"

"Yeah, to start with. But Max drove and carried the booze, 'cos my phone was blowing up, man. We were back maybe five minutes is all, and people started rolling in."

"When did you take out the security cameras?" I asked.

I got the same befuddled look he'd given me about Rohypnol.

"I've no idea what you're talking about, man. What cameras? They have cameras in the fucking rooms? How is that legal?"

"Hallways, lobby, lifts, outside," I replied impatiently. "Not in the rooms."

"Oh, well I don't know anything about any cameras."

"We need names and numbers for the other guests at your party," Whittaker demanded.

Lunders laughed. "I've got no clue, man. People were coming and going, and I was having a good time, so I didn't pay much attention."

"You just told us your mobile was blowing up with messages. How about you start there?" I said.

Lunders looked sheepish, realising he was about to piss off a bunch of people who'd no doubt rather the police didn't have their numbers to come asking about a late night party. We had his mobile and other possessions in a bag up front, so we'd have to have him unlock it later.

"What happened to the girl in the photo?" I asked, tapping the picture.

Lunders threw his hands in the air. "I have no idea, man. She was fine when we started talking to her at the nightclub. We danced a few times, then like I said, she must have hit her limit or something, 'cos she got wasted real quick. She fell asleep in the car to the hotel, but made it to the room and people started showing up. Last I saw, some dude — her boyfriend I guess — showed up, and then I never saw her again. Didn't give it another thought until you brought her up."

"How many drinks did you buy her at the nightclub?" I asked.

"I don't think we bought her anything," Lunders replied. "She had one of them seltzer things the chicks dig. We offered, but she said she was fine. Don't know what she really had in that can, but it knocked her off her feet."

"Describe the boyfriend," I said, starting to piece together the possibility of another course of events.

Lunders rolled his eyes. "I don't know, man. I didn't pay much attention. He was... shit, I don't know what he was. Average I guess. Had a hat on I think, 'cos I don't remember his face at all. But she was leaning on him as he was trying to get her to leave; I remember that."

I sat back in my chair and looked at Whittaker.

"Here's what's going to happen, Mr Lunders," the detective explained. "You'll wait here and we'll either have more questions for you, or you'll be escorted to our jail for the night."

Lunders groaned and rubbed his forehead with the palm of his hand. "I didn't do anything, man. You guys can't lock me up like this."

"You'll be allowed a phone call later this evening, but we're keeping your mobile phone for now. You'll need to unlock it for us," Whittaker explained. "We won't be able to search your room until tomorrow morning, which is why we're providing you overnight accommodation. Your hotel room is sealed until our forensics team get there."

We both stood, and Lunders looked at us like a scolded dog.

"I don't know what happened to that girl, but I didn't have anything to do with it. I swear."

"We'll see if your friend, Mr Jones, has the same story about the evening as you do," Whittaker said, gathering up his file and the photograph of Elín. "That will be a start, Mr Lunders."

We left, and I sung the Counting Crows song in my head as I

walked down the hallway. I wasn't sure I could sit through an interview with 'Mr Jones' without cracking up.

I checked up front, where I was both pleased and annoyed to see AJ had already been to collect Jazzy. I was glad Jazzy didn't have to sit around any longer, and annoyed I'd once again been forced to lean on my friend to help me. I hated the idea that I wasn't self-sufficient. Since leaving Norway at age sixteen, I'd fended for myself and been free of tethers and obligations. Apart from the resort, I suppose. But that didn't count, as I'd thought I could leave if I'd needed to.

Now I was responsible for a teenage kid, had a regular job, and friends I owed for all the favours they did for me. When I thought about it like that, an urge to run grew like a balloon in my gut. But I hadn't run yet and wouldn't run now. I guess that's why they call them obligations.

Jones had close enough to the same story as Lunders, except he was damn near in tears. If I had to guess, Lunders's family had the money for fancy hotels and unlimited credit cards for the kid, while Jones was riding on his friend's coat tails. Interviewing him was simply a formality, and either the two of them were cover-up geniuses at telling the same story with enough varying details to be believable or they were telling the truth.

The two had arrived on the island after the incident with the woman from the UK, which wasn't to say they hadn't bought roofies from a local dealer, but my gut told me they were guilty of being idiots, not drugging tourists.

I found an available computer — which was all of them at this hour — and logged in, Whittaker standing behind me. I found the CCTV on the server from Craft restaurant and fast-forwarded to the timeframe we were interested in. Jacob and I had stopped looking after Lunders and Jones had driven away with Elín, but now I was interested in what happened afterwards.

Two women stepped around the corner from the nightclub and lit cigarettes, followed shortly afterwards by a man who kept walking out of the frame. Thirty seconds later, the same man drove out.

Whittaker leaned in closer. "We can't see his face," he muttered.

The driver's baseball cap and the camera position mounted above the driveway made it frustratingly impossible to see who he was.

"Caucasian," I said, looking at the skin tone of the hands on the wheel.

"What about the car?" Whittaker asked. "It doesn't have a front registration plate."

"No," I agreed. "But it looks remarkably like the pale coloured four-door we have in the West Bay footage."

15

INNOCENT DOGS

I would have preferred to be freediving the reef in front of my shack or having breakfast with Elín, but I wasn't doing either. I was sitting in a briefing room at Central Station with a bunch of fellow police officers and detectives, waiting for Whittaker to start the meeting.

As someone who didn't like a lot of talking, or being around too many people, meetings were not my favourite pastime. I understood the necessity, and the potential efficiency of delivering all the details to the whole group in one place, but inevitably I found myself sitting through tedious shit I already knew or didn't need to know.

I made sure I sat on the end of a row and put Jacob next to me. He liked people and enjoyed talking, so he could chat with his neighbour, leaving me alone with my thoughts.

Whittaker walked in the room and waved us back into our seats after everyone stood to attention.

"Let's get started and make this as short as possible," he began. "We have much to do."

I liked the sound of that. He gave everyone a moment to settle down before addressing the group.

"We have two major cases in play, for which we're pulling resources, meaning people, from other districts and departments to help out. On your email, and posted on the noticeboard once you leave, is a list of assignments, including manpower assigned to your task where applicable. Our priority focus is the car fire, as it's being investigated as a murder."

Detective Whittaker continued, but I noticed he covered peripheral nonsense, while everyone in the room looked at their mobile phones and studied the email. Jacob and I were assigned primarily to the arson case, but it was noted I would be the victim's point of contact with the Rohypnol inquiry. Once everyone's attention returned to the podium, Whittaker continued the briefing, but having been involved with both cases, there was nothing new for me and my mind drifted.

By the time we were finally dismissed, my coffee mug was empty, my feet wouldn't keep still, and I needed to pee. Our first assignment was tracking any likely suspects using immigration records from recent entries to the islands. I sent Jacob off to find an open computer while I used the loo, then met him in the shared office space where computers were available on a first come, first served basis.

"We have seven people wit felony records, entering during da last tree weeks," Jacob told me as I pulled a second chair next to him. "Looks like four have already left."

"Any of those four leave yesterday?" I asked.

"Nope. All before dat."

"Okay, who are the three?"

"We have a thirty-four-year-old woman, Louise Middleton, from da UK. She's staying in a condo at The Sovereign wit her husband. She was found guilty of embezzlement wit a suspended two-year sentence."

"Doesn't really fit the profile, does she?" I commented, and Jacob shook his head.

"Dis guy did eighteen years of a twenty-five-year sentence for murder. Dat's more likely, I'd say."

"Agreed. How old is he?"

"He was born in 1963, so dat makes him sixty."

"Bit old to be running around setting fire to people," I thought aloud. "When did he get out?"

"About a year ago," Jacob replied.

I couldn't decide if that made him prime to kill someone else, or unlikely to want to go back inside.

"He also from da UK," Jacob added. "Says he killed a man who was suspected of attacking his second wife. They never proved dat fella was involved."

It sounded to me like the bloke may have got a raw deal, but I didn't say anything.

"His name's Charles Winskell," Jacob continued. "He staying at a guest house in West Bay. Da third one is American. Jonas Richards. He served three of a four-year sentence for battery causing serious bodily injury. Looks like he beat da hell outta some fella outside a bar."

"That sounds more promising," I said. "When?"

"He got out eighteen months ago," Jacob read from the screen. "He was arrested about five years back. Twenty-nine years old. He's staying at da Grand Caymanian timeshare."

"Let's start with him," I said, and rose from my chair.

"Wait up," Jacob said, still looking at the screen. "Look at dis."

I leaned over his shoulder and scanned the report on the screen. "Does that say arson?"

"Yup," Jacob confirmed. "He was a person of interest in an insurance fraud arson case. Never brought charges."

"Anyone hurt in the fire?" I asked.

"Nope. No injuries reported, but da building burnt to da ground."

"Wait," I growled, pointing to the screen. "There was someone in there."

"Man…" Jacob muttered.

"That's fucked up," I snapped, motivated to interview our first person of interest. "He must have known there were two dogs in the place."

The Grand Caymanian hotel and timeshare resort consisted of two long, three-storey buildings built in a vee with the registration lobby where they met. At the open end of the vee was a waterfront and pier extending into the North Sound. Nestled between the buildings, a restaurant stood amongst tropical foliage, and beyond that a pool surrounded by deck chairs, umbrellas, and sunscreen-smothered bodies.

The front desk had called Jonas Richards's room, and no one had picked up. He hadn't booked any excursions for the day, but we had no way of knowing if he was on the property or not. He had a hire car for the three weeks he was on the island, so he could be driving himself around.

We left the reception and walked through the winding path-ways around the restaurant to the pool. Anyone who wasn't asleep or too focused on the book they were reading looked our way. Two coppers in uniform showing up at a resort usually attracted attention.

I noticed people were split into two groups as they stared at us. Most were curious and nosey; the others were tense and trying their best to melt into the surroundings. It amused me to watch the reactions. It was like drivers slowing to 10 mph below the speed limit as they passed another vehicle pulled over by the police. Were they expecting the copper to abandon the ticket they were writing to come blazing after them instead?

Looking at the picture of Richards on my mobile, we both surveyed the pool area, which had pretty much come to a standstill. A group of kids in the shallow end whispered and pointed at us. Three bronzed, bikini-clad women turned on their stools at the bar and watched us over their fruity cocktails. And a man who looked close enough to the picture on my mobile eyed us from behind a Clive Cussler novel.

I walked his way with Jacob a step behind me, and the man slapped the book down in his lap.

"I can't even take a fucking vacation without you guys bothering me. What is it now?"

"Mr Jonas Richards?" I asked.

The man laughed. "No, I'm Bruce Willis. You got the wrong guy."

"Can I see some form of identification, Mr Willis?" I asked as politely as I could considering he might have been responsible for torching two dogs and a man I had to wash off my fingers.

Jacob shook his head and nudged me.

"What?"

"Identification," Jacob repeated sternly to the man who continued to laugh sarcastically but reached into a rucksack and pulled out a wallet.

Jacob checked the Florida driver's licence the man held out. "Let's go somewhere more private. We have some questions for you, Mr Richards," Jacob insisted.

I was happy to let Jacob lead as I was still confused about the Willis bullshit. As someone who never watched TV, only sat through movies AJ subjected me to, and hated anything to do with politics, I didn't know many of the famous names like most people did. Sometimes it could make me look like an arse, and I figured one of those times just happened.

Richards stood up, swearing under his breath. "My room's right there," he said, pointing to a ground floor patio twenty metres away.

We followed as he stomped towards the room and away from the pool while everyone watched us leave. He pulled the sliding glass door open, and a wave of cool air rushed from the room. Inside was the standard bamboo island decor I hated, but the room was spacious and included a small kitchen, with a door to what I presumed was the bedroom.

"All right, what's all this about?" Richards asked after closing the slider.

"Can you tell us your movements yesterday, sir?" I asked.

"I was here most of the day," he replied.

"And what about when you weren't here?" I asked impatiently.

"I drove into town."

His minimal answers didn't help his cause in my eyes, and I took a deep breath to stay calm.

"What time was dat, sir?" Jacob asked, no doubt sensing my agitation. He'd become good at anticipating when to step in.

"Mid-afternoon," Richards replied.

"Three? Four?" Jacob asked.

"I'm on vacation. I didn't pay attention."

"Okay," Jacob continued. "Where did you go, sir?"

"I bought some booze and came back."

"Which liquor store was dat?" Jacob asked.

I was impressed how he kept pushing the man; he usually left that to me. I took the opportunity to let my eyes move around the room, which appeared tidier than I would have expected.

"The one by the grocery store in Camana Bay," Richards answered.

Two things caught my attention. The first was a screwdriver sitting on the kitchen counter next to a notepad and pen, and the second was the man's choice of liquor store.

"Why that shop?" I asked. "There's several much closer."

He stared at me with contempt which I hoped he saw reflected in my own eyes. Innocent until proven guilty is fine, and as it should be, but I had no doubt this *drittsekk* was guilty of something he was yet to be convicted for. That something might well be torching a pair of helpless dogs… and Ian Osgood.

"I needed a few groceries," Richards replied. "Are you gonna tell me what this shit is about or not? I've answered all your damn questions, so tell me what's going on, or get the hell out."

Jacob was about to speak, but I beat him to it. "Mind if we take a look around the rest of the room?"

I turned away from both men and faced the kitchen with my

mobile hidden from Richards's view in front of my chest. I clicked a picture of the counter.

"Get the fuck out," he growled in reply.

My mobile was back in my pocket by the time I turned and walked towards the sliding glass door.

16

LYING ABOUT SOMETHING

Jacob drove us away from the Grand Caymanian while I tried to decide which of the other two to interview first. It was mid-morning, so the likelihood of either being where they stayed was thin. I was about to pick the guest house in West Bay when Detective Whittaker phoned me. I put the call through the patrol car's hands-free system.

"Sir," I answered.

"Where are you two?" he asked.

"Just interviewed the first felon," I replied. "Leaving the Grand Caymanian now."

"What was your impression?"

"He's an arse, and he had a screwdriver which is odd for someone on holiday, but he didn't smell of burnt flesh."

Jacob groaned, and Whittaker took a beat before continuing.

"I don't think owning a screwdriver is grounds for a search warrant, Constable Sommer."

He was calling me Constable instead of Nora, which may have been for Jacob's benefit, or more likely it meant he had someone else with him.

"No, sir, but I'd say he's hiding something, it's just hard to say if it's related to this case or not."

"What's his name?"

"Jonas Richards, sir."

"I'll add his name to the board, and we'll see what else we can dig up on him," the detective said. "Where are you heading now?"

"West Bay. Sixty-year-old murderer, Charles Winskell, sir."

"That'll have to wait, I'm afraid. I need you to run by the airport and pick up an NCA officer from the UK. She's landing at 11:40am on the flight from Miami."

Jacob and I looked at each other. We hadn't been asked to be a taxi service before.

"We could get one more interview in before then, sir," I pointed out, not happy about the distraction.

"Negative, Constable," he replied firmly. "The officer will accompany you two on the interviews, so wait until she's with you."

I was about to say something, which I probably would have regretted, but Jacob fortunately spoke up.

"What's da NCA, sir? Who is dis lady?"

"National Crime Agency, Constable Tibbetts. Think of them like the UK's equivalent of the FBI. My brief is that Officer O'Neill may have information pertinent to our arson case, and I've been asked to allow her access to our investigation. I will meet with her this afternoon, but her boss asked me to throw her into the thick of things, and right now that's you two."

"You mean, you want her out of your hair until you figure out what to do with her?" I blurted.

Jacob went as stiff as a board behind the wheel.

"Nora, must you always say exactly what's on your mind?" Whittaker responded. "Even if it is accurate."

His voice was firm, but I detected a hint of amusement in there somewhere. Or perhaps that was wishful thinking on my part. I hadn't meant my question, which was more of a statement really, to be funny. I was simply pointing out what seemed obvious. Besides, I only ever verbalised a tiny amount of what was on my mind.

"Sorry, sir," I said, deciding the best way forward was to get off the call, but then I thought of another question. "Did you get the warrant for the Seafire, sir?"

Jacob smacked my arm, and I smacked his in return. Harder.

Whittaker made a disgruntled noise, then sighed. "Yes, I did."

"Then we could go by the hotel with the warrant," I suggested, keen to keep Elín's case moving along.

I knew Whittaker considered it important, but a high-profile and unusual case like murder threatened to leave Elín's assault undermanned.

"I have someone already there," he replied, sounding tired. Or more likely fed up with my questions.

"Who?"

"Whoever I decide is the best available person, Nora."

"Of course, sir," I replied, unsatisfied, but sensing I'd pushed my luck far enough with my boss.

Jacob's finger hovered over the end call button on the steering wheel, waiting for the first opportunity to end what was torture for him.

"Detective Weatherford," Whittaker said. "Is that satisfactory?"

"Yes, sir," I answered, surprised he was concerned how I felt about it. "I trust Weatherford."

Whittaker made a strange noise which sounded something between a laugh and a snort. "Pick up O'Neill at 11:40, continue with the interviews, and call me when you're done. Oh, and treat her with the appropriate respect afforded a superior officer. Which she is."

"Absolutely, sir," Jacob said quickly, and took the opportunity to hang up the call. "He da boss, Nora! You gotta show da man more respect."

"I respect Whittaker more than most people I know," I replied defensively. "You heard. He asked if I was good with Weatherford doing what I think we should be doing."

Jacob laughed. "He was bein' sarcastic!"

I was taken aback for a moment and replayed the conversation in my head. I knew I bothered the detective sometimes with my forthright manner, but I felt he understood and shared my belief that superfluous words and mindless chatter had no place in police work. Of course, I thought the same should apply to life in general, but Whittaker seemed to enjoy a social life, which usually meant conversing with other people. Something I tried to avoid when possible.

"Take us to Central — we need a computer," I replied, ready to move on.

"What's wrong wit dat computer right in front of you?" he asked, pointing to the patrol car's laptop.

"Too slow. We need to search more CCTV."

Jacob turned left onto the dual carriageway, heading south towards town. We had an hour and a half to kill before we picked up the NCA officer, and I didn't want to waste a minute of it.

The second chair was still sitting by the desk of the computer we'd used earlier, but this time I took over the keyboard and Jacob sat beside me. I pulled up a map from the server with all the government CCTV camera locations marked and angled the screen towards Jacob.

"Which one is closest to the Loudermilks' house?"

He studied the map for a moment. "Da house is on Mitchell's Creek, right?"

"I thought it was at the bottom of Governor's Creek?"

"Dat's called Mitchell's Creek," he confirmed.

Seemed odd to me that the same body of water had two names, but there again where one ocean or sea became another was a mystery to me too.

"Dere's a camera at da Lime Tree roundabout. If dey headin' south, dat'll see dem."

I took the reference number from the camera Jacob picked and found the files on the server. Whittaker already had someone looking for Osgood's movements, and I wasn't worried about that, so I started searching at 10:30am and set the playback on x4 fast-forward.

"What are we lookin' for?" Jacob asked.

"A silver Mercedes GLC 300."

"What da heck is one of dem?"

"A half-car, half-SUV, bloated bug-looking thing." I said, and showed Jacob the picture I'd taken with my mobile.

We both watched the screen and after two false sightings which turned out to be bloated silver beetles by other manufacturers, we spotted a silver Mercedes with a woman who looked like it could be Rhea Loudermilk behind the wheel. I looked again at the photo I'd taken in the Loudermilks' driveway, and checked the registration plate. It matched.

"I knew she was lying about something," I muttered.

Jacob looked at his watch. "We best be leavin'."

I ignored him and x8 fast-forwarded the footage. The cars flew through the roundabout like a Formula One race, and it became hard to decipher one from another, but I let it roll, stopping several times to check silvery blurs.

"Maybe she came home from da udder way," Jacob suggested.

She may well have done, but with the limited time we had, I could only check so much and finding another camera and the right timeline would take too long. I paused the replay at the next silver vehicle, and this time it was Rhea Loudermilk returning home, or at least heading north. She had to drive to the next roundabout then come back along a frontage road to reach her house. The timestamp was 12:52pm. Over two and a half hours before the unfortunate Osgood was set on fire.

"Okay. We gotta go now, Nora, else we'll be late."

I checked the time. It was still fifteen minutes before she was scheduled to land. "It'll take us ten minutes to get to the airport and she won't be through immigration, get her bag, and clear customs for ages. We have plenty of time."

Jacob shook his head and fidgeted nervously. In my opinion he worried about all the wrong things, and I was dying to know where Mrs Loudermilk spent a few hours she was reluctant to discuss. I was about to look for the next camera along the bypass when Jacob stopped me. I thought he was about to nag me to leave again, but instead he told me to switch to the camera facing south. I did, found the same timeline, and watched the silver Mercedes coming towards us on Esterly Tibbetts Highway.

"I'm going to get the camera from the next spot that way," I said, about to stop the playback.

Jacob made me wait again. "Rewind," he said.

We watched the Mercedes reverse along the bypass until it became a speck and disappeared into the distant roundabout.

"See, we need the next camera," I complained.

"See there!" he tapped the screen, and sure enough, the silver speck in the distance was now coming backwards towards us, until it veered left.

It was so far away I couldn't tell where, and I switched to the map on the screen.

"Ritz Carlton Drive," Jacob declared. "Has to be."

I looked from the map to the footage, then back again. Jacob was right. We could see Safehaven, the road we'd taken that morning to the Grand Caymanian, and she'd come out the only other road before the next roundabout. Ritz Carlton Drive. She'd been forced to turn left and go around the roundabout in order to head north.

"That's those fancy townhouse places and houses, right?" I asked. "The hotel itself is on Seven Mile Beach."

"Yup," he confirmed. "Dis is da homes on da Ritz golf course." He pushed his chair back and stood. "Please, can we go now before you get us both in big trouble?"

Seventeen minutes later, having caught every light and slow-arse tourist between the station and the airport, we drove slowly down the road outside Arrivals, looking for a woman we'd never seen or met.

"That gotta be her," Jacob said, pointing to a woman in her fifties wearing a slightly wrinkled sport coat and matching trousers.

The woman's dirty blonde hair didn't look like it had been brushed that morning, her skin tone was pale, and beads of sweat ran down her face.

"Heads or tails?" I asked.

"Huh?" Jacob responded, as he pulled over to the kerb.

"One of us has to go in the back. Heads or tails?"

"Oh. Tails."

I flicked the coin in the air, caught it and slapped it against the back of my other hand. I revealed the result to Jacob. He groaned.

I unwound the window. "Officer O'Neill?"

"Aye," she replied, looking me over with a frown. "Been waiting a while."

Jacob glared at me, but I jumped out before he could say anything. I offered to take the woman's suitcase, which I was pleased to see was carry-on sized. I guessed that meant she wasn't planning to stay long, but I was curious why she was here at all. I rolled the case to the back and put it in the boot.

"Which one of you is Tibbetts and which one is Sommer?" she asked, clutching an enormous tote bag/satchel/purse-like thing.

"I'm Constable Jacob Tibbetts, ma'am, and dis is Constable Nora Sommer," Jacob announced as he reluctantly climbed into the back seat, which, despite extended efforts and many chemicals, always smelled of body odour with a hint of vomit. O'Neill dropped her slender frame into the passenger seat, lugging her handbag with her.

"You're not what I expected, I must say," she said in a British dialect I couldn't place. It was one of the strong regional accents that seemed to change every few miles in England.

"I'm from Norway," I replied, being polite although I was sick of explaining why a Norwegian had come to be a policewoman in the Caribbean.

"You're more what I expected," she added, turning to look at Jacob behind the wire divider in the back.

He smiled. "Cayman Islands born and raised, ma'am."

She turned back to the front. "Bloody hot 'ere innit?"

"*Ja,*" I replied, wondering what she'd expected from a tropical island.

"No wonder things are catching on bloody fire," she added.

17

A CUPPA AND A BIT OF CAKE

As we drove out, Officer O'Neill didn't say a word but seemed to look around somewhat disapprovingly as we twisted and turned through the edge of the commercial park next to the airport.

"May I ask where you're from, ma'am?" Jacob asked, and I found myself curious about her answer.

"Well, England of course, pet," she replied as though it was the most juvenile question she'd ever been asked.

Jacob sat back in his seat, but I wasn't letting her off that easy. "Obviously, ma'am. But where in England is what my partner wanted to know."

"Oh. Liverpool," she replied, making the pool part twice as long as the liver part.

When I thought about it in that way, I pictured a pool of livers, and it made my skin crawl.

"Is this Whittaker fella ready to brief me?" she asked, and I knew she wasn't going to like my answer.

"We're on our way to interview two persons of interest, ma'am. We were told you wanted to attend the interviews."

"First of all, the message I got when I landed said there were three interviews, and if they're the names I was given, they all seem like clutching at straws to me."

"We already spoke to one," I told her without apology.

I was already eyeing the next bus stop to drop her off.

"Which one?"

"Jonas Richards, ma'am."

"Well, he was the only one worth a sniff. Why didn't you wait for me?"

"We didn't know you were coming," I retorted. "You want to come with us for the other two or not? Ma'am."

"Don't get all shirty with me, young lady."

"Are you hungry, ma'am?" Jacob asked from the back, before I had a chance to explain to Miss Stick-Up-Her-Arse how she'd fucked up our day and was about to be shoved out the door without stopping. He probably saved my job.

"I'd love a cuppa," she said, turning and smiling at Jacob. "A nice bit of cake wouldn't go amiss either."

The last thing I wanted to do was waste more time driving in the wrong direction and sitting around eating lunch, but I knew there was only one place we had a chance of getting her decent English tea.

"Nora, I was tinkin' the best place…" Jacob began.

"Water and the Elephant," I said before he could finish.

"Dat's da one," Jacob agreed.

Ten minutes of silent driving later, we were parked in front of a modern two-storey office building. Maybe O'Neill was expecting a quaint sixteenth-century cottage tea shop as her displeasure hung like a cloud over us as we walked towards the building. Or perhaps it was the hot, humid, blue sky Caribbean weather.

The ground floor housed several small eateries, including Water and the Elephant. The decor matched the modern feel of the building, but their menus included the largest variety of teas on the island. Fortunately for me, they also made wonderful coffee, as despite the island being a British Overseas Territory, most of the population preferred coffee.

O'Neill took her time perusing the cabinet of bakery treats, so I ordered my coffee and a superfood vegetable wrap, making sure to add 'to go' loudly enough for everyone to hear. The NCA officer finally chose her drink — the Royal Affair, a traditional English breakfast tea — after turning her nose up at the plethora of other flavoured teas and added what I had to admit looked like a delicious slice of chocolate brownie cake. When the server asked if it was for here or to go, I answered for her, which won me another scowl.

While Jacob ordered and we waited for our lunch, I stepped outside and called the guest house in West Bay I'd hoped to visit hours earlier. The woman, who said she was the owner, confirmed Charles Winskell was staying there, and in fact they'd just eaten lunch together. I thanked her, hung up, and quickly called The Sovereign.

The manager of the high-end beachfront condos didn't know Louise Middleton and knew no one under that name as an owner. I found the unit number she'd put on her immigration form, and he informed me the owner of that unit was Mr Nigel Bradley-Shaw. He connected me to the condo, and after five rings, a woman answered.

"Is this Louise Middleton?"

There was a brief pause before she responded. "This is Lulu, who's calling?"

Her voice was English and sounded posh, but with something else mixed in.

"Constable Sommer with the Royal Cayman Islands Police Service, ma'am. I was hoping to have a word with you about an incident you may have witnessed."

"Incident? What incident?" she responded as though the idea was ridiculous. "I think you have the wrong person."

"This will only take a few minutes, ma'am, and we can come to you."

"What bloody incident are you talking about? I think I'd know if I'd seen something the police should be involved in."

I heard a man's voice in the background and Lulu held the phone away from her mouth while she responded.

"It's nothing, dear, just a question about a dress I'm having altered. I'll bring you a drink to the balcony in just a mo."

Although her voice was faint, I could hear she now sounded perfectly English upper class.

"I don't know what the bloody hell this is about, but I'll meet you at three o'clock outside Book Nook, alright?"

Her voice had slipped again as she whispered into the phone. I agreed to the meeting, and she hung up before I'd even finished my words.

I kicked the door open to the cafe. "Let's go. Winskell's at the guest house now."

O'Neill frowned at me, and I wondered if that was her natural expression, glued to her face since she first decided the world was not to her approval. Jacob gathered up the food and drinks which the server had hurriedly packaged in a carry bag for us, handing the officer her tea.

"Drinking tea from a cardboard cup is a bloody sin," she mumbled, but exited through the door I held open for them both.

"What about da woman?" Jacob asked as we walked to the car.

"Three, by the bookshop on Seven Mile Beach," I replied, holding the back door open for him.

He was about to protest, presumably presenting the argument that another coin toss was due, but he saw the look on my face and slid into the back without a word. He retrieved his sandwich, and I took the bag as he wouldn't be able to pass anything through the wire divider.

"Why the bloody rush?" O'Neill asked as I pulled to the car park exit and waited for traffic to pass.

"Like you said, these are unlikely suspects, so let's get them done and move on," I replied.

I said it mainly to appease her ladyship, but I also agreed with her thought that Jonas Richards was the one of interest. Especially after meeting him.

"Detective Whittaker told us you have information which may be linked to this case," I said, deciding to risk her wrath on the chance of hearing something useful.

"Aye," she replied, between nibbles of chocolate cake. "And when he stops giving me the runaround, I daresay I'll share it with him."

So much for getting anything useful. We ate our lunch as I drove us north to West Bay and found the little guest house which rented a few rooms through VRBO or some other international system. The owner, a local lady with a warm manner and welcoming smile, looked concerned when she saw the uniforms, but I assured her it was a simple matter which wouldn't take long. She led us into a courtyard, where a burly man with grey hair and beard sat at a table under an umbrella with a paperback novel and a bottle of Corona.

"Sonny, dese police folk say dey have some questions for you."

"Mr Winskell?" I asked.

"Sonny," he replied, in a thick London accent which reminded me of my friends Reg and Pearl. In fact, the man could have been a relative of Reg's based on his appearance, and had a similar build, although scaled down. Reg was a bear of a man, and this bloke was a three-quarter-sized version. "Have a seat," he added. "How can I help you?"

I looked at the owner who was hovering close by, and she took the hint to leave. I couldn't be sure what she was up to with her tenant, but judging by the looks they exchanged, it was more than a simple bed and breakfast arrangement.

We sat at the other three chairs around the table, and I wondered who was supposed to conduct the interview now a senior ranked officer was with us. O'Neill didn't say anything, so I began.

"I'm Constable Sommer, this is Constable Tibbetts, and this is…"

"I'm Officer O'Neill, a training instructor accompanying these two today," she said, cutting me off.

It would have been easier if she'd told me her plan before we'd arrived, and I gave her a look which hopefully conveyed that message. She ignored me and waited for me to continue.

"Can you tell us your movements yesterday, sir?"

Sonny Winskell's tanned and wrinkled face set off a pair of sparkling blue eyes. He wore cargo shorts, cheap flip-flops, and a well-worn Boddingtons beer T-shirt which revealed faded dark green tattoos on his forearms. I recalled from his records he'd been in the Navy prior to spending eighteen years in prison.

"Sure, and then I presume you'll tell me why it is I'm being asked," he replied with an amused smile.

"Let's start in the morning, sir," I urged, making no promises.

Winskell looked at his beer for a few moments. "Alright then," he began. "I had breakfast here, then went to the beach for a swim, which I do most days. Back here by ten. Sat in the courtyard and read me book until lunchtime, then went inside. Gets a bit toasty out here when the sun's overhead. Like now, if you know what I mean."

"It's entirely too hot everywhere I've been so far, Mr Winskell," O'Neill said in a pleasant tone.

Apparently she could be nice when the need arose, and I guessed she was setting herself up as good cop.

"What did you do all afternoon?" I asked.

Winskell took another sip of beer, taking his time. "Knocked about. Read a bit, checked the sports online, watched telly. Nothing much really."

"You didn't go out anywhere?" I asked.

"Not till five-ish, I suppose. Found this pucker little pub up the road called The Fox and Hare. You know it?"

I nodded. "Was it busy?"

"A few dropping in after work," he replied and squinted at me. "Talk to Frank behind the bar; he'll tell you I was in. That's what you were gettin' at, right? Seeing if someone could verify I was there."

"What about all afternoon? Got anyone who can vouch for you then?" I asked, ignoring his question.

"I do as it happens," he said, drumming his fingers on his beer bottle.

"Should we ask your landlady to re-join us?"

Everybody stared at me, including Jacob and O'Neill.

Winskell's expression broke into a wry smile. "Don't miss much, do you?"

I nodded to Jacob, who took the hint and left the table in search of the owner.

"Do I get to know what this is all about?" Winskell asked.

I considered my response. His landlady was undoubtedly about to corroborate his alibi, so he couldn't have been in the scrub land yesterday at 3:30pm when Ian Osgood was burnt alive. Sonny also seemed like a pleasant man who I guessed had exacted his own justice on a man he believed to have attacked and assaulted his wife. I understood all the reasons why these things should be handled by law enforcement, but too often that's not what happens. Guilty people go free all the time. I couldn't help feeling a hint of respect for the man.

"We're questioning current visitors to the island who have felony records, sir. It's a standard line of inquiry when we have a major crime case," I said, deciding Winskell deserved my honesty. "Do you know a man named Ian Osgood?"

Sonny looked me in the eyes and smiled, then gave me a subtle nod. "Heard of Peter Osgood," he said. "I'm not a Chelsea fan, but he was bloody good in an England shirt. Can't say I know any Ian, love."

"How long are you staying, sir?" I asked, getting to my feet.

"Planned on three weeks," he replied, politely standing. "But I might stay longer seeing as things have been going rather nicely."

He gave me an amused wink.

"I'm sure you're becoming quite familiar with the island," I said, inventing ways to buy Jacob enough time. "Seeing as you're here awhile."

"Nice place, isn't it?" he replied amiably. "I'm not much for lying around on a beach, personally, but I do like the water. Being outside in general is a luxury too many people take for granted."

I nodded, finding it hard to imagine being locked up for almost as long as I'd been alive. "Have you been diving?"

He smiled. "I spent too many years making sure I stayed on the boat. I guess the Navy took away my desire to jump off one that was still floating. But I see you have plenty of operations offering to teach scuba."

"It's one of the main attractions here in the islands," I replied, figuring I'd given Jacob enough time by now.

"Can't say I'm too keen on relying on a little rubber hose to breathe," O'Neill chimed in. "Gives me the willies all those creepy things under the water."

Winskell laughed, a relaxed and natural chuckle. "I like sitting downtown by the harbour in George Town," he said. "When the cruise ships aren't docked, that is. Watch the locals come and go with their catch, and the dive boats heading out to look at all that creepy stuff." He grinned at O'Neill. "Place has just enough hustle and bustle but it's still small and feels like a Caribbean island. Catching the sunset from there is quite a sight, I must say."

"Daresay I'll have to try that out," O'Neill said. "The sunset part, that is."

"Thanks for your time, Mr Winskell," I said and rose from my chair. I knew what Jacob would have heard from the landlady, so it was time for us to move on.

18

MANICURES AND DIGGING FOR GOLD

O'Neill fanned herself with a file folder she pulled from her bag as I drove away from the guest house. Jacob told us about the very embarrassed landlady confirming Sonny Winskell's story, and by the time we reached West Bay Road and headed south, the car's air conditioning had turned the interior into an icebox. The NCA officer put her fan-file away and surprised me with a question.

"You were first to the burning car, weren't you?"

"*Ja*," I replied. "We arrived a few minutes too late."

O'Neill sat still, holding her bag in her lap and watching out the front window. I figured she was done talking. She wasn't.

"But you didn't see the arsonist?"

I thought about her question for a moment. I hadn't seen anyone, but the blazing car had consumed my focus. It felt like a loaded question, as obviously we would have reported seeing anyone suspicious or a potential witness. I wondered what she was digging for.

"No, ma'am," Jacob answered while I overthought O'Neill's objectives.

"The witnesses from the car park were interviewed," I added.

I wasn't sure what her angle was, but I decided to run through what we could have missed one more time. It couldn't hurt.

"Two people shot video with their mobiles, which we have, but it's after we'd arrived."

"So, where did he go?" O'Neill asked, sounding casual, but I knew the technique too well. Idle, seemingly harmless chatter, allowing the witness to back themselves into a corner or contradict their own words.

"I assume the point you're getting to is that the arsonist couldn't have been far away," I answered, annoyed at being treated like a witness instead of a policewoman.

Of course, I realised, we were witnesses. We just happened to be police constables as well. We were trained to observe and process situations in an organised manner, but a man being burned alive in a car tends to grab your focus.

"Your report states you saw him moving inside, so he was still alive when you arrived," O'Neill continued, her voice remaining impassive. "I didn't see anything about a remote method of igniting the fire, so we're talking a few minutes, wouldn't you say?"

"*Ja*," I agreed.

"So where was this fella?" she asked again.

"You're assuming the arsonist is male?" I questioned.

"Almost certainly," O'Neill rebutted.

"Women don't set fire to things?"

"Sure they do. But they don't *plan* on setting fire to people."

I thought about that for a moment. The National Crime Agency had to have access to overwhelming quantities of data regarding crimes.

"A crime of passion, and this was premeditated," I thought aloud.

"Precisely. So where did he go?"

"Da water ain't dat far away," Jacob said, leaning forward with his nose to the wire divider. "Could have staged a boat."

O'Neill's eyes never left the road ahead. "The canal behind is narrow, and aren't there condominiums to the south?"

"Yes, ma'am," Jacob replied. "Olea, dey called. Pretty snazzy places."

"Someone was assigned to canvass the units today and look for CCTV," I added, recalling Whittaker mentioning it in the morning briefing.

I turned into a small shopping plaza on the left and wound around to the far corner where Book Nook occupied the last space in the back row. I found a spot to park and looked around for Lulu Middleton. I didn't see anyone remotely matching the immigration photograph I had.

"Ask yourself this," O'Neill said, not showing any inclination of getting out of the car. "If you went to all this trouble of getting someone out in the middle of nowhere, strapped to a car and meticulously torched to inflict as much suffering as possible before they died, wouldn't you want to watch?"

Jacob groaned and sat back in the seat. I didn't like her phrasing either. The idea of being put in the shoes of the arsonist was creepy as hell, but her point was valid.

"He was one of the people at the fence, watching," I said, trying to recall the scene in my mind.

O'Neill pointed to the dashboard. "No dashcam I see."

I shook my head. "No bodycams either."

"I haven't seen the witness statements yet, but I'm guessing the questions they were asked weren't the ones we need the answers to," the officer said. "We know what happened with the car."

"There's no CCTV covering that car park," I commented, thinking along the line she was leading me. "We found the hire car arriving from the camera at the roundabout. The passenger was unidentifiable."

"That'll be your woman, I suspect," O'Neill said, gesticulating to a frazzled-looking lady in designer sunglasses, hurrying along the covered pavement towards Book Nook.

I stepped from the car. "Miss Middleton?"

The woman shook her head. "Why don't you announce it to the bloody world," she snapped, the polish missing from her posh accent once more.

I opened the back door for Jacob, and Officer O'Neill got out of the patrol car, walking around to join us. Middleton scurried under a wide, covered walkway between the rear and side buildings, plonking herself down in a seat at a wrought iron outdoor patio set.

"I see you brought half the station with you," she complained. "What is it you think I've witnessed, then?"

I introduced the three of us, sticking to O'Neill's training observer cover story, before beginning with, "Where were you yesterday, miss?"

"Wouldn't it be easier if you told me where whatever happened happened, and then I can tell you if I was there or not?"

Lulu Middleton was an imposing figure. She was tall for a woman, and broad shouldered, like a swimmer, with dark hair, cut in a bob. She was dressed in black yoga pants and a designer blouse cinched with a wide belt. Three buttons of her blouse were undone, displaying an un-swimmer-like cleavage, which filled the material before the custom cut tapered down to her slender waist. Toned arms jangled with gold bracelets as she lit a cigarette and exhaled a long plume of smoke.

"Run us through your day, please," I responded.

I couldn't see her eyes, or even half of her face, past the over-sized sunglasses, but I guessed she'd rolled her eyes at me. I noticed her features were sharp and she wore little make-up, at least in regard to powder and lipstick. Overall, she had a head-turning appearance, but I didn't think she was particularly pretty.

"Fine. Breakfast, gym, then I had a mani-pedi at ten."

"Gym at The Sovereign?" I interrupted.

"Yes. We lunched at Blue Cilantro, then Nigel had meetings, so I went home and read on the beach most of the afternoon. We had dinner at The Wharf, and home around nine," she rattled off. Then added, sarcastically, "Need to know what we did after that?"

"Alone at the beach?" I asked, ignoring her attitude.

"I saw numerous other people," she replied. "It's a public beach, seven miles long."

I wanted to correct her, as the beach was never actually seven miles long, and with the sand erosion, certainly didn't have nearly that length of uninterrupted beach anymore. But I stuck to the important questions.

"Was anyone specifically with you during this time?"

"No, I managed all by myself," she snipped.

"What timespan was this reading and managing by yourself?" I asked, unable to hold back completely.

Lulu let out a long sigh. "How about you tell me what you're getting at, then maybe I'll answer your asinine questions, or how about I just leave now?" She rose from her seat.

"Sit down, Miss Middleton," O'Neill ordered, and the woman complied.

"You're a visitor on foreign soil, and as such, I'd say it's best to answer any and all questions the local authorities may have for you."

"My residency paperwork is in progress," Lulu protested, but the vim had left her voice and her posh accent had almost evaporated.

"It'll be permanently stuck in progress, unless you start cooperating," O'Neill responded. If she wasn't careful, I was going to start liking her. I hid my smile and continued.

"Hours you were at the beach, please."

"About 2:30 until 4:30, maybe five," Lulu huffed.

"Alone, and never left the beach?" I persisted.

"I went inside to use the loo once or twice, but otherwise yes, I was on the beach the whole time."

"But no one was with you who could confirm that?"

Lulu threw her hands up, the expensive jewellery accompanying her movements like a percussion section. "I don't recall talking to anybody, but I'm sure someone noticed me there. The perv in 11 is always getting an eyeful whenever he can."

"Do you know an Ian Osgood, ma'am?" I asked, and wished I'd

asked her to take off the stupid glasses. Instead of her eyes, I watched her perfectly manicured hands and noticed something odd.

"No," she replied flatly. "Should I?"

Lulu took another drag on her cigarette, but I didn't notice her hands tense at the question. What I did notice was her surprisingly short, well-trimmed nails, void of nail varnish.

"What's the name of your nail salon?" I asked.

Her brow creased. "What?"

"Your nail salon," I repeated. "You mentioned a manicure yesterday morning. Where did you have that done?"

Lulu pointed to the building next to us. "Two doors down."

I'd never set foot in a nail salon in my life, but I figured today might be my first time, even if it wasn't to have any work done. I glanced at O'Neill to see if she had any further questions, but she was staring off into the distance and fanning herself again. I quickly looked at Jacob.

"How long are you 'ere for dis trip, ma'am?" he asked.

Lulu shrugged her shoulders. "Depends on whether Nigel insists I go back with him in a few weeks."

"He likes keeping his possessions close, does he?" O'Neill responded, obviously not as distant as she appeared.

Lulu bolted up from her seat, tipping the chair to the floor with a clatter. She leaned over the table, her face turning red, and a finger pointed at the NCA officer. "Nobody owns me, lady!"

Swearing under her breath, she threw her cigarette to the ground and stomped away. I rose to go after her, but O'Neill rested a hand on my arm.

"Let her go."

"But the fingernails," I whispered.

"I know," O'Neill assured me. "Not to mention she's got quite a temper, don't she?"

I sat back down and looked at the officer, wondering why we'd let Lulu walk away without questioning her further. Calling her out for being a gold-digger was brilliant, and obviously a deliberate move to bait the suspect, but I figured we had a great opportunity while she was riled to get her to slip.

"Don't worry, pet, we're not letting her off the hook." O'Neill looked past me to Jacob. "Be a love and go see if she had an appointment at the nail place. Ask them what she had done, alright?"

Jacob nodded and left the table. I felt like he was being sent away and I wondered why. When he was out of earshot, O'Neill turned her attention back to me.

"Seems like a nice lad," she said, the frown finally relaxing from her forehead.

"He's a good partner," I replied, ready to defend him.

"Aye, I daresay," O'Neill continued. "But a case like this is over his head."

I began to protest, but she held up a hand. "Don't get all uppity, pet, I didn't say he's a bad copper. I'm simply stating a fact. He don't think about his cases much when he goes home does he? But the likes of you and me can't get them out of our heads, can we?"

I felt I should be campaigning on behalf of Jacob, but it was tough to argue her point. He had a family who he adored and when he wasn't working, they were his total focus, which I admired. Regardless, she wasn't about to change her mind at the moment, so I let the point go, wondering what was coming next.

"Let's stop buggering about and go see your Detective Whittaker, shall we?"

I nodded, and we both stood. "You think she's a potential suspect though, right?"

"What would her motive be to barbecue some poor bugger?"

"Maybe she knew him," I suggested. "Perhaps he was going to screw up her honey trap she has going. I bet Nigel Bradley-Shaw doesn't know she did time for embezzlement."

She looked at me with a hint of the frown returning. "Okay, but that's all supposition, innit? Ask yourself what she has to lose by publicly torching a bloke."

NCA Officer Lisa O'Neill was an odd duck, but she was

processing evidence and information through an impressive set of filters and lenses. In one afternoon, I'd gone from wanting her out of our hair to hoping she'd stick around a while. I could learn a lot from the woman.

"She could lose her sugar daddy who she's obviously worked hard to secure," I admitted. "Lulu would be better off slitting Osgood's throat in the mangroves and letting the birds clean up her mess."

"A bit more graphic than I had in mind, love, but yeah, you get the point."

We walked towards the car, and O'Neill paused before getting in.

"There's already been a case like this one," she said, which brought me to an abrupt halt. "In Florida, six weeks ago. When your report went into the system, our computer flagged several similarities, and because this attack involved a UK citizen, we're taking an interest."

"An execution by fire?" I asked.

"Aye," she replied. "Jubilee Clips and all."

EFFICIENTLY INSENSITIVE

Detective Whittaker met us in the lobby of Central Station and apologised to Officer O'Neill for not being available sooner. Her stern expression let him know she wasn't buying any of it, and she asked to gather the key players in the investigation for a briefing. Fifteen minutes later, we sat in Whittaker's office, joined by Rasha and Station Sergeant Hadley. Jacob had not been invited, and I felt bad for him, but he smiled and pretended it didn't bother him.

Rasha gave us the grim details from the autopsy she'd attended, conducted at the hospital. Ian Osgood had suffered extensive and what would eventually have been fatal burns over his entire body — which was not news to anyone, especially me — but the cause of death was one of, or a combination of, two things: smoke inhalation and asphyxiation. The latter was exacerbated by the fire extinguisher powder, which was found in the man's throat and lungs.

Basically, he was going to die from the moment we'd arrived, but I probably sped up the process by stealing his last breaths with the fire extinguisher. Truth be told, I knew the powder would likely choke him if enough went in his mouth and had deliberately sprayed it at Ian's head. I couldn't imagine anyone wanting to hang on in excruciating pain for a day or two before succumbing to the burns. That part of the incident wouldn't keep me awake at night.

Very little else had been gleaned from the crime scene. The accelerant had been good old petrol, available from any of the twenty-two petrol stations in the Cayman Islands, or by syphoning from any one of the too many vehicles jamming up the roads. The only retrievable fingerprints belonged to Osgood and an employee at the hire car company, both found on the boot lid. Any clothing fibres of use had been lost to the fire or the extinguishing foam used by the fire department.

Sergeant Hadley had spent his day shepherding staff in conducting interviews and reviewing CCTV footage. Canvassing the vicinity had drawn a blank. Beyond the handful of witnesses at the fence, no one else saw the blazing car up close or any suspicious people near the car park.

"We tracked Osgood leaving the Loudermilks' around 10:30am in his hire car," Hadley explained, reading from his notes. "Lost him for an hour and a half, after which he drove south on West Bay Road. Lost him again until he's seen at the Camana Bay round-about when someone else is with him at 3:06pm."

He handed everyone a map with the victim's movements marked, along with the areas in which he eluded cameras. Potential exits from those areas via roads without CCTV were also noted. Either by design, or luck, it was clear he could have covered a much wider area during those times, making his whereabouts a needle in a haystack.

"What do we know about his habits or routines?" O'Neill asked.

When no one else answered, Whittaker spoke up. "That's a good question, and one we should ask the Loudermilks. Beyond him mentioning going to the beach and his lunch meeting, we have little insight into his day."

"So, 10:30am until noon is likely to be at the beach, and then he drives to his lunch meeting which lasts until three," O'Neill surmised.

"I'd say that's likely," Whittaker agreed.

"His mobile is missing, correct? How about the phone records?" she asked.

"Correct, and we've requested the records," Whittaker replied. "But it's a UK service and they're notoriously slow at getting back to us."

O'Neill made a note on a pad she held. "Let me see if I can expedite that for you."

The detective nodded his thanks.

"The Loudermilks may also know if he's hung out with anyone else while he's been here," I said.

Whittaker nodded again, making notes of his own.

"And Rhea Loudermilk didn't stay home all morning — we know she left after Osgood," I added.

"Where did she go?" Whittaker asked, looking up.

"I don't know; we ran out of time and had to go to the airport," I replied.

I was stating a fact, but Whittaker fidgeted in his seat, and Hadley couldn't hide a grin.

"She comes back shortly before 1:00pm, but I don't know where she went, or if she left again," I said. "We should take a more detailed look."

"I'll add it to the list," Hadley said in a grumpy tone, losing his grin and raising an eyebrow at me.

"What about the felon interviews?" Whittaker asked.

"Jonas Richards is a *drittsekk* with an arson charge on his record. He had a screwdriver in his room and admitted to being away from the hotel mid-afternoon, shopping at the liquor and grocery shops by Camana Bay."

"I did a little digging on him after your visit," Whittaker added. "I've emailed the detective from the arson case to see what his impressions were, and I'm waiting to hear back. I daresay that'll be tomorrow at the earliest. I pulled the details on his hire car, so that's another one for you, I'm afraid, Sergeant."

Hadley grumbled something under his breath as he added the chore to his list.

"If we can place him in the vicinity at the right time, I can get a search warrant for his car and hotel room," Whittaker said.

"He's from Florida, correct?" O'Neill asked.

"His licence was Pompano Beach," I confirmed.

"The first incident, six weeks ago, was in South Florida, about 30 miles from Miami in the Everglades," O'Neill said. "Do we see any connection between Richards and the victim?"

"Currently, the only connection we have between Osgood and anyone on the island is the Loudermilks," Whittaker replied.

"Seems a stretch to imagine them inviting their long-time friend over for another stay, only to torch the bloke," Hadley commented.

"We have Rhea leaving the house after Osgood; maybe they're up to something and the husband found out?" I offered. "Dalton's pretty much a dick and a hothead."

Hadley stifled a laugh.

"Despite Constable Sommer's poorly worded assessment, she's correct," Whittaker said. "Dalton Loudermilk was more angry than upset."

"And Rhea was faking being upset," I added. "She was scared when we told her what had happened. Maybe Osgood ditched her, and she got mad enough to kill him."

"Possibilities, I agree," O'Neill countered. "But unless you can place either of the Loudermilks in Florida six weeks ago, I'd say they're not our killers."

Whittaker looked at Hadley.

"On it," Hadley grunted. "I'll check with immigration."

"Okay, Richards is top of our list so far," Whittaker declared. "Who's next, Constable?"

"Charles Winskell. Goes by Sonny. He did eighteen on a twenty-five-year sentence for murdering a bloke he believed assaulted his wife. He was screwing his landlady while Osgood was being torched."

Whittaker's shoulders slumped a little. "Nora…"

"Sorry, sir," I said, trying to figure out what I'd said wrong this time. "At the time Mr Osgood was murdered," I said, correcting myself. Apparently, I come across as being insensitive sometimes, but English is my second language, and I deliberately choose the shortest number of words to get my point across. I call it efficient, but unfortunately, not everyone appreciates my brevity.

"And moving on to the third interview," O'Neill said, and for some reason she had a grin on her face. I would've sworn she wasn't capable of smiling until that moment.

"Louise Middleton, who goes by Lulu, did time for embezzlement, and is currently ripping off some rich bloke called Nigel Bradley-Shaw," I explained. "She has a thin alibi. Claims she was alone on the beach all afternoon. She's applying for residency, so I'm not sure how she's pulling that off with a felony record, but unless we can find a tie to Osgood, and place her in Florida at the time of the first murder, she's an unlikely suspect."

"Thank you," Whittaker said, letting out a sigh. "Sounds like we have more CCTV to review, immigration records to check, and the Loudermilks to revisit. I'll call them shortly, now we have confirmation on the victim, right after I contact next of kin. Officer O'Neill, can you share anything more from the Florida case which might help us here?"

The NCA officer thought for a moment. "Not much, I'm afraid. I'll leave my copy of the police file they sent me with you for the evening, Detective. Feel free to make a copy, but you'll see they're stumped. No CCTV anywhere near where it happened, very little traffic, and no homes nearby. They have zero suspects and not even a single witness. We should verify with US immigration that Richards was indeed in the US when the first attack occurred, and see if any of our other suspects were there at the time." She turned to Hadley. "I'd like Constable Sommer and I to interview the eyewitnesses again. Can you arrange that for the morning?"

Hadley looked as surprised as I felt, for different reasons, I'm sure.

"Certainly," he replied, and was about to say something more, but decided against it. If he intended on questioning the value of revisiting witnesses he was sure had seen nothing of use, he was smart to keep quiet.

I liked the way O'Neill had used 'our' when talking about the suspects, it gave me confidence she was invested in helping catch the killer, but my shock came from her asking me to accompany her on the interviews. Things had improved between us as the day had worn on, but I still figured she'd be glad to be rid of me and would expect Whittaker to accompany her.

My mobile buzzed in my pocket, and I sneaked a look. I had two text messages, one I'd missed earlier, and the one I'd noticed now. The first was Jacob telling me he was heading home. It was 5:30 and he'd sent it half an hour ago. I had my Jeep with me as we'd met here in the morning, so that was fine. I sent him a thumbs-up. The recent message was from Elín, asking if I could pick her up and take her to the hotel.

I looked up, wondering how much longer the briefing would take. Everyone was staring at me. "What?"

"Officer O'Neill was asking what time you'd like to meet in the morning, Nora," Whittaker said, obviously repeating what I'd missed.

"Seven," I replied, without much thought.

"Okay. Pick me up at seven then," O'Neill said. "I'm staying at the Marriott."

I quickly realised I'd just screwed myself, and Sergeant Hadley. He'd now be expected to line up the interviews for first thing in the morning, and I had to get Jacob up early to meet me at West Bay station before picking up the NCA officer. I could feel Hadley's eyes glaring at me.

"We could drop by the Loudermilks first," I said, and Hadley's laser vision cooled a notch.

"Fine with me, pet," O'Neill said. "Now how's about you run me to my hotel?"

"Yes, ma'am," I replied, and wondered if she'd still want to use me as her taxi after a ride in the Jeep.

20

RASSGAT

I made sure I asked Officer O'Neill if it was okay to pop by the hospital and pick up a friend before we went to her hotel. I explained the hospital was only half a kilometre away and she agreed, providing she was able to sit up front. I guess she'd smelled the back seat of the patrol car, but I didn't bother telling her she didn't have to worry about that.

We walked across the car park, her wheeled carry-on bag clattering over the asphalt until I heard it come to a stop. My Jeep was the only vehicle left before us.

"That's your bloody car, isn't it?"

I climbed inside and started the engine so it could warm up for a minute or two. I hopped back out and offered to take her bag, which she reluctantly handed over.

"How are we getting to the hotel, taking the mountain pass?" she grumbled. "Where's the roof? And the doors? It doesn't have any bloody doors."

"It was my boyfriend's," I said, knowing that didn't explain much, but I didn't know what else to say.

"Where's he gone then?" she asked, looking at the passenger side, trying to figure out how to climb in.

"He's dead," I replied, and pointed to the grab handle and the tubular running board. "Hold there and use the step."

O'Neill swung herself up and into the Jeep more nimbly than her hesitation had suggested.

"Don't suppose the air conditioning works, does it?" she said as I returned to the driver's seat.

I looked at her, puzzled by the question. A grin crept over her face, and I laughed. She'd now logged two smiles and a joke. She was turning into a regular comedian.

"Please don't kill me in this contraption," she said, as I pulled to the car park exit, the 4.2-litre engine rumbling under the bonnet.

Two turns later and we pulled up in front of the hospital. I'd texted Elín and told her I'd be there in fifteen minutes, and as we came to a stop, I saw her waiting just inside the sliding doors. Though I hadn't expected to see who was standing next to her.

"You miss the bus?" I asked Jazzy as I jumped out to help Elín.

I wasn't sure what I was supposed to think or feel when the teenage girl I was responsible for showed up somewhere I didn't expect, but I was irritated at first.

"No," Jazzy replied. "I just wanted to visit."

"How were you planning on getting home?" I asked, more sternly than I intended.

"You, or the bus."

I was about to tip the driver's seat forward so Elín and Jazzy could get in the back, but Officer O'Neill had already jumped out and was struggling to get the passenger seat tipped forward.

"It's okay…" I began to say, but she managed to figure out the seat lever, and climbed into the back.

"Best she rides up front if she just came outta there," O'Neill said, nodding towards the hospital building.

She looked funnier in the back than she had done in the front, sitting all prim and proper with her enormous satchel/purse thing on her lap.

"Elín and Jazzy, this is Officer O'Neill. She's here from the UK, helping us with a case."

"Call me Lisa. We're off duty now," she said.

Jazzy clambered over the back and plonked herself into the back seat next to the NCA officer, and I helped Elín into the passenger seat.

"Are you two related, then?" O'Neill asked, looking at Elín and then me.

"She's from Iceland," I said, wondering how much more explanation was needed.

"Oh," she said, but looked confused.

"I'm here on holiday," Elín added.

"And you ended up in hospital? That buggers up your trip. Sorry about that, love. Are you alright now?"

"Já, I'll be okay."

"Right, so you two look like sisters, but you're not related and not even from the same country," O'Neill said, then turned to Jazzy. "And who are you then?"

"She's my boss," Jazzy replied with a straight face, pointing to me as I climbed back in.

"It don't sound like you always do what the boss tells you," O'Neill replied, and I laughed.

"She's got you figured out," I said, looking in the rear-view mirror as I pulled away.

"Are you a detective?" Jazzy asked.

"Sort of," O'Neill replied. "I work for a branch of law enforcement called the National Crime Agency. They call us officers, but we do the same job as a detective. Most of the time."

Jazzy turned her attention back to me. "What are we doing for dinner? I'm hungry, and Elín has had shitty hospital food for two days."

"I'm fine," Elín said. "I appreciate everything you've already done. I don't want to be any more trouble."

"You're no trouble," I told her. "That one in the back makes all the trouble."

"Bloody hell, love," O'Neill said, barely audible over the wind noise as I drove north on West Bay Road. "I only asked for a ride to the hotel."

My eyes flicked to the rear-view mirror and my heart stopped. Being a bit lippy was one thing, but a very senior officer thinking I was insulting her was going to be big trouble if she... I saw the grin on her face and my heart started beating again. Two smiles and now two jokes.

"I'm hungry, pet," she shouted to be heard. "Any place around here to get a good English supper? Not much for fish meself."

I looked over at Elín. "Want to eat with us?"

She nodded and smiled. "I'd like that." She leaned over closer and spoke quietly. "I don't know why, because nothing bad happened there that I know of, but I'm not so keen to go back to the hotel room."

I nodded, not sure what I could say, and noticed we'd reached the Marriott on the left-hand side. "That's your hotel, ma'am. I'll bring you back after we eat. There's a pub in West Bay with English food."

"The Fox and Hare!" Jazzy announced. "My favourite."

It had been the first place I'd taken Jazzy to eat when I was trying to lure her off the streets and into proper care. As it turned out, 'proper care' wound up being me, which I don't think fit the criteria, but the pub became her favourite spot, which I guess meant something.

On the right, we passed by Onions nightclub, and I noticed Elín was looking and her fingers dug into her knee. She gasped.

"Are you okay?" I asked, reaching a hand over and gripping her arm.

"I was there, wasn't I?"

"*Ja*, but you're safe now," I said, trying to reassure her.

The right-turn light was red at the junction ahead, backing up traffic enough to bring everyone to a stop.

"*Fy faen*," I muttered to myself. It was shit timing. This location, between The Locale Hotel ahead on the left and the club just behind us on the right, was where Elín's life had been changed forever. Her hand shot out and she emitted a guttural sound, like a desperate, wounded animal. She was pointing to a pale-coloured car pulling out of the driveway between Onions and the restaurant, Craft.

"It's him!" I spat, and tried turning right to U-turn and give chase.

Cars were now forming a line in the central turn lane, blocking me in. I leaned out of the Jeep so the driver could see my uniform.

"Let me cross!" I yelled, but the guy behind the wheel was pretending he didn't see me and inched forward, thinking I was trying to jam in front of him... which he was busy doing to the rest of the people trying to make the turn light.

"Police! Let me cross!" I shouted, and the man finally looked over.

But he didn't look at me — his eyes were on the back of the Jeep. Over my shoulder I saw O'Neill hanging out the side with her badge held almost against the man's side window. The car in front moved forward and I lurched the Jeep into the gap, then whipped hard right, cutting off traffic in the other lane. With angry horn honks sounding behind me, I accelerated hard, trying to pick out the pale car in the line of vehicles ahead.

Jazzy leaned forward between the front seats. "Who are we chasing?" she asked excitedly.

My left hand shot back against her chest as though I could stop her body weight flying forward if something happened. "Put your belt on!" I ordered, and she sank back into the bench seat and fought with the crappy rear belt.

"I'd like to know the same thing, Nora," O'Neill shouted. "And I have my belt on, thank you."

"The suspect in Elín's..." I began, and stopped myself before I said attack. "Case," I finished, and swerved into the shared centre turn lane, passing several cars, wishing I had a police light and siren to turn on.

I spotted the pale car four cars up ahead, but with vehicles using the turn lane, I couldn't leapfrog around the traffic to reach him. I fumbled in my pocket and pulled out my mobile phone, using my thumbprint to unlock the screen.

"Here," I said, passing it to Elín. "Open the camera and get ready to shoot video."

I took a brief opportunity to swerve around two more cars, cutting off the second one to duck back in line, avoiding an oncoming van. The chaos was enough to alert the driver in the car we were chasing, and he now zipped into the turn lane and sped around several cars, barging in line before doing the same again. I took the same opportunities, but he'd already pissed off the cars ahead, and they closed the gaps to not let the second crazy driver cut in.

I was stuck in the middle lane with an SUV coming towards me, and a tight line of cars in my lane refusing to let me merge. I swerved right into the oncoming lane, dodged around the SUV, whose driver closed his eyes, then gouged back into my lane before the next vehicle blocking the centre.

"Mary mother of Jesus," O'Neill yelled from the back. "You're gonna bloody kill us!"

Behind us, a cloud of dust billowed in the air where someone had dropped wheels off onto the dirt and marl hard shoulder. Elín had gamely held my mobile above her head, arms waving side to side as I'd steered around the traffic, and I hoped somewhere on the footage would be the registration plate of the car I had seen was beige. We couldn't be certain this was our guy, but he was running, which usually meant they were guilty of something.

I pulled to the centre again and looked down the road for the car, but it was gone. He should have been no more than two or three cars ahead, but he'd vanished.

"*Faen,*" I swore, and braked hard, indicated right, and U-turned again, using a driveway to complete the manoeuvre, much to the displeasure of a few more tourists in white hire cars.

I sped back a hundred metres to where the dust had almost settled. Sure enough, there was a turning on what had been our left but was now to our right. I indicated, moved to the centre lane, and someone politely waved me across in front of them. Marbel Drive was a narrow lane with residences scattered along both sides. With the sun low in the sky behind us, the power poles and palm trees cast long shadows down the street. The houses, mostly tucked back from the road behind gravel driveways and front lawns, were shrouded in shade from the surrounding trees. Two small cul-de-sacs led away on opposite sides, and at the end of the lane, the houses stopped and the road turned to a single lane marl trail leading through a dense wood.

The driver could have pulled into any home with a garage and pulled the door closed before we'd arrived, but a hint of a chalky, dry taste rested on my tongue as I drove slowly down the gravel trail. The dust had visually settled, but someone had recently kicked it up.

"Go," O'Neill said from behind me. "He went this way."

I accelerated and felt like saying 'this is why I have a Jeep', but kept it to myself. The trail kinked left, went another hundred metres, then met the Esterly Tibbets bypass south of Camana Bay and opposite Mount Trashmore, the island's dump. He had to have turned left as the highway was divided by a wall, but I knew we were too far behind to catch him. Two kilometres down the road, his options for roads to take became endless.

"Look at the video," I told Elín, and she held my mobile so we could both see the screen.

O'Neill undid her seatbelt and leaned forward to watch with us. The footage was jerky, as Elín was bounced around by my erratic driving, but the beige car was visible a couple of times. With the dying light, movement, and distance between us, added to the fact I had the cheapest smartphone I could buy, we couldn't make out the plate.

"It's a Kia," Jazzy said, standing on the back seat and looking over Elín's shoulder. "That's their old badge on the boot. They have a new one now."

Elín handed me back my mobile and I noticed her hand was shaking.

"First thing tomorrow, I'll get CCTV from the Camana Bay roundabout. We'll get a reg plate and find this *drittsekk*."

She nodded, but still looked pale and scared.

"You can stay with me tonight, if you want," I offered.

Her eyes lit up. "Are you sure?"

"*Ja*. I have a tiny house, and only one bed, but we'll figure it out."

I watched the colour instantly reappear in her cheeks and she heaved a sigh of relief. "I don't mind sleeping on the floor."

"You can have the bed, I'll take the sofa," Jazzy said, squeezing Elín's shoulder."

We all sat back and took a few deep breaths.

"*Rassgat*," Elín said, looking at me. "You called him a *drittsekk*. I think that's *rassgat* in Icelandic."

"Cool," Jazzy said from the back. "That's another one I can use at school."

"Okay, now we have that sorted, and by some stroke of luck we're all alive, how about we get some supper?" O'Neill asked, settling back into her seated pose. "The British government can treat us if you get me there in one piece without scaring me to death again."

21

GLASTONBURY FESTIVAL ON STEROIDS

2009

Allie took an occasional sip from the beer they'd thrust upon her and wondered whether she was simply being too uptight about the whole event. This wasn't a gathering of dropouts and fringe members of society; most of the young people she saw were clean-cut uni student types. She'd seen the hilarious American teen and college movies from the eighties, but never believed the wild parties and prolific drug use was based on truth. From her new perspective, the movies seemed to be a tame version of Spring Break in Fort Lauderdale.

From the room, they'd moved to the swimming pool in front of the hotel next door where people were jam packed from street to building. Music played, the crowd swayed, and from a small stage at one end, a DJ coordinated a variety of games. The current activity was a belly flop competition from the springboard at the other end of the pool. Allie winced as men of varying sizes and commitment attempted to make the most far-reaching splash with their bodies. Current leader was a US Marine from Champaign, Illinois, who was about to go head-to-head for the crown with a very overweight student from Minnesota.

"These people come from thousands of miles across the country just for Spring Break?" Allie asked Ozzy, who stood next to her.

"You did," he pointed out.

"I came to see you and have a few days at the beach," she countered. "When you said come for Spring Break, I thought it was because you wouldn't have classes. Not this."

Ozzy shook his head. "Can you imagine anything like this happening back home?"

Allie laughed. "It's like a Glasto Festival at the beach without the rain and mud, but on steroids. Times a hundred."

"And this is the tamed-down version. According to Bruce, it was even bigger back before they clamped down and barred cars from the beach."

"The cars drove on the sand?" Allie asked.

Ozzy grinned in the boyish way she remembered. "That procession of cars we were in today going up and down used to do the same thing, but on the beach itself."

"They didn't sink into the sand, and all get stuck?"

He shrugged his shoulders. "You stood on the beach there. It's solid as rock, yeah? Must have been fine for the cars or they wouldn't have done it."

Allie stared at her friend. There were moments when she felt it was just like old times. He was in there somewhere, hiding behind this new facade of drinking and desperation to get to the next party. The same distractions were readily available in the universities back home, but neither of them had been consumed by booze, drugs, or the crowd who never made their morning classes. But it all seemed shinier here. Bigger, brighter, more open and accessible.

So many in the crowd looked like the perfect-bodied stars of reality TV shows. The men were bronzed, chiselled, and square jawed with perfect hair, while the women were stunning in skimpy bathing suits Allie had only seen on the beaches of France and

Spain. She'd thought the one she'd brought was daring, but now it seemed run of the mill.

England wasn't renowned for its gorgeous beaches and reliable summers and these perfect bodies would be one in a hundred on the sands of Blackpool.

While she could understand how the newness and novelty of it all could be appealing, for Allie the whole scene was too bizarre. She felt like they'd been dropped into a barely believable movie. It was also clear to see that Ozzy had been swept up in the rapids instead of staying on the bank and watching the torrid waters rage by.

"How are your classes going?" she asked.

Ozzy looked at her with a dazed expression. "Classes? Why would you ask about uni when we're in the middle of the biggest party on the planet? Huh, Joker?" He grinned, but the boyish expression was gone again.

"Don't call me that," she said, unable to hide her annoyance.

"Bugger me, Allie, can't you lighten up for once in your life?"

She turned and glared at the young man who was once her closest friend. "Why are you doing this? Why would you throw your education and future away over booze and parties? What's come over you?"

"What's come over me?" he yelled over the noise around them. "Can't you enjoy yourself for five fucking minutes, Allie? You're turning into your damn mother." His face had turned red, and he waved his arms as much as he could within the crush of people. "Is that how you plan to spend the rest of your life? Sitting by and watching the world happen to everybody else?"

Allie's first reaction was to slap her friend who'd now become a complete stranger to her. The young man she'd known for years would never be that spiteful or mean. But she held back, and instead, pushed through the crowd, pinballing off bathing suit-clad people who spilt their drinks on her as she shoved and barged her way out. But the sea of bodies never seemed to end, and hands kept touching her body, and voices invited her to stop and join them.

Finally, she came to a halt and looked up. She'd been sure she'd been heading towards the tall hotel building but it was nowhere in sight. Instead, the streetlights lining the frontage road shone brightly down, and Allie aimed their way. Meeting a low wall topped with a metal railing, she edged along, dodging bodies, and trying not to inhale the smoke from cigarettes, cigars, and joints. Finding the driveway entrance, she fought across the bustling pavement and stepped between the slow-moving cars to reach the beach. It was still packed with people, but nothing like the sardine-can crush of the hotel pool.

Allie walked towards the ocean and sat down on the hard-packed sand just above the waterline. Lights twinkled from unseen boats and the gently lapping waves helped to dampen the raucous noise from the town. Resting her elbows on her knees, she held her head in her hands and couldn't hold back the tears from running down her cheeks.

Allie cried out of frustration. For the loss of someone she'd held so dearly as a friend. For the ease in which the cruel words fell effortlessly from his lips. For the truth behind some of the words he never would have said a year ago.

All she could think about now was escaping. Leaving this madhouse and doing whatever it took to catch an earlier flight home. If it wasn't for the hurt she felt and her need to be back in her own world where life was boring to many, she might have considered hiring a car and driving to the Keys, or Disney World in Orlando. A trip that was full of possibilities and excitement just a few days ago was now a horrible dream Allie couldn't wake up from.

"Are you okay, ma'am?" came a man's voice and Allie wiped the tears from her face.

She turned to see a policeman standing a few yards away, his partner continuing down the beach. Allie stood and dusted herself off.

"I'm fine, thank you."

The officer lingered a moment. "Australian?"

Allie laughed. "English."

The man smiled. "My apologies, I always get it wrong."

"You're not alone. Since I landed, I've had about fifty percent guesses on English, and the rest has been a mixed bag of Australian, Kiwi, and one lady even asked if I was South African."

"Well, I'm sorry we're not better at distinguishing between the accents."

"That's okay," she replied. "I can tell New York from Southern, and after that I'm lost."

The radio on the officer's belt called out a disturbance, and Allie noticed his partner, now 50 feet away, replied, saying they were close by and would respond.

"Be careful and have a nice evening, miss," the friendly cop said, and turned to join his partner.

"Thank you," she responded, wishing they could have talked longer.

For a few moments, she hadn't felt alone, and longed for more of that security. It was too late to ask the policeman how she could safely get back to Miami, and Allie kicked herself for not thinking of that sooner. She considered following the two and asking once they'd dealt with whatever disturbance they'd been called to, but that felt like she'd be stalking the poor man.

Looking towards the road, she took a deep breath and contemplated her next move. It meant braving the crowds once more, but the hotel staff would know if there was public transport to Miami airport. She also needed to retrieve her bag from the hotel they'd checked into, so angling along the beach, Allie aimed for their hotel entrance, and hoped the queue wasn't still out the door.

22

BROKEN

If it had been Friday night, my friend, Pearl Moore, would have been setting up ready to play her regular gig, but we were a day early, and the little stage in the corner was empty. The Fox and Hare was owned by English expats who tried their best to give the pub a genuine feel. From the outside it was a plain, two-storey building on a street corner in West Bay, but inside, the dark wood, decor, and spectacular oak bar made it feel like you'd been transported to a countryside pub. Not that I'd ever been inside a pub in England, but that's what people told me.

It was around 6:30pm, and the after-work crowd had left and the dinner crowd were only just starting to show up, so we were able to get a booth. I wished I'd had time to change, as I felt self-conscious in my uniform, which drew a few looks. If AJ had been with us, she'd have known half the regulars in the pub, because she's nice to people and socialises, but the only person I knew was the bartender, Frank. He gave me a wave as we sat down, and I noticed the staring eyes on me shifted back to their own tables, as though I'd been validated by Frank's approval.

Jazzy handed out menus and started chattering about which

items she liked. I looked around our group. A prim and proper looking lady in her fifties, with two Nordic-looking young women, one in a police uniform, and a wild, frizzy-haired, dark-skinned local girl. Maybe I wasn't the singular focus of the stares after all.

The waitress came by and asked for our drink order. I hesitated a moment, and O'Neill must have guessed what I was thinking.

"I won't tell," she said, so I ordered a glass of wine, despite being in uniform.

She ordered a Scotch on the rocks, Elín, a glass of white wine, and Jazzy complained because I wouldn't let her order the same. She settled on a soda but not before explaining to everyone how I let her have a small glass of wine at home sometimes. I hoped someone from social services wasn't within earshot.

"So, seeing as I've found myself mixed up in this already," O'Neill said, looking at Elín, "can you tell me what happened to you, if you don't mind talking about it?"

Elín glanced at Jazzy, and then me.

"It's okay. She needs to know what's out there," I said, trusting Elín would be more delicate in telling her story than I might be. The booth had high, wood panel dividers between them which made the spaces feel private. I could hear the voices of people behind me, but couldn't make out exactly what they were saying, although I hadn't tried to listen carefully.

"I was drugged by a guy in a bar, the club we were passing by when we saw the car," Elín explained, "and the night is a blur from there. They found me miles away by the side of the road."

"GHB?" O'Neill asked, and Elín looked confused.

"Rohypnol," I said. "Second case we've had in the past few weeks."

"I'm sorry, love," O'Neill said, returning her attention to Elín. "I've dealt with a few cases involving these drugs back in the UK, but we were focused on the suppliers. Nasty stuff."

"What's GHB, or row-hip-na…" Jazzy asked, keeping her voice respectfully low.

"Row-hip-noll," I pronounced for her. "They're called date rape drugs. *Drittsekker* slip them into someone's drink and it makes the person drowsy and easy to be taken advantage of. The victim usually can't remember what happened."

"Oh shit," Jazzy whispered, turning to Elín. "I didn't know you were…"

I was glad she stopped, and I'm sure Elín was too.

"We don't know what he did," Elín replied. "But we don't think I was raped."

Jazzy rested her head against Elín's shoulder. "Good."

"Where are you on the case?" O'Neill asked me.

"Running across the car might be a lucky break. We didn't have anything on the suspect. Two American college idiots took Elín from the club to their hotel, but we don't think they were involved. She just happened to be chatting with them at the club. They organised a party in their hotel room and the suspect followed them. He took her from the party and that's where we lose them."

"And you can't remember anything?" O'Neill asked Elín.

She shook her head. "Little bits and pieces that don't make sense. Flashing lights at the club, then some other flashing lights, and voices, but they're not clear. I remember getting ready in my hotel room, then waking up in the hospital. Everything between is a blur."

"Do you want to check the CCTV in the morning before we go see the Loudermilks?" O'Neill asked me. "We could still be at their house by eight or so."

"She goes to an exercise class which starts at eight," I replied. "I don't know if she goes every day, but I was thinking it best to catch her before, or after, in case she's not home."

"Be better if we have Sergeant Hadley's report on the CCTV of where she went, right?" O'Neill suggested. "Doubt he'll have that until later in the morning. We can go to the station first, then once we have the info on her and appointments to interview the witnesses from the fence, we'll head out."

"Okay," I agreed. "I'll see if we can get a more comfortable SUV as well. That way one of us doesn't have to sit in the cage."

O'Neill grinned. "Aye, 'cos I'll pull rank if you try and stick me back there."

We ordered food and chatted for an hour or so, avoiding further talk about the cases. I was interested in hearing about the National Crime Agency, and O'Neill didn't seem to mind discussing their role and the kind of cases they handled. She picked up the bill, as promised, and we wandered outside, freeing up the booth for the crowd who'd been steadily filling the pub.

In the car park, walking towards the Jeep, I noticed someone I recognised. It was the landlady from the guest house, and getting into the passenger seat of her car was Sonny Winskell. Apparently, their relationship had moved on to public appearances. She gave me an awkward wave and he nodded, his rugged face creasing into a pleasant smile.

"That's Winskell, isn't it?" O'Neill asked as we climbed into my Jeep.

"Yeah," I confirmed. "I didn't see them inside, did you?"

"No, me neither."

I ran back through our conversations in my mind, as I was sure O'Neill was doing. As best I could remember, his name hadn't come up, and we didn't discuss anything I would consider compromising.

I dropped Jazzy and Elín by the side of the road near my shack. There was no official driveway or path, as the lot was trapped between the old Spanish Bay Reef Resort land, which was surrounded by a tall wire fence, and the sea. Access was supposed to be down a public path, 300 metres up the road, then along the beach. But I'd created a hole in the fence and cleared a narrow trail through the trees to save time and hassle. The resort buildings had been torn down years ago and nobody ever came there, so my secret easement hadn't been discovered yet.

O'Neill was struggling to stay awake as I drove her to Seven Mile Beach and the Marriott Resort. If she'd been in the back of a comfortable car, she'd have been out like a light, but the rough ride of the Jeep kept jolting her awake. She mumbled thanks as she clambered out and I handed over her carry-on roller bag.

As I watched her walk inside, I realised I hadn't asked the woman if she was married, divorced, had kids... none of the things people consider normal conversation. In most cases, I was fine with that as I didn't really care one way or the other — which wasn't to say I didn't care if the person was happy or not, but I would never meet O'Neill's husband, if she had one, so why do I need to know anything about him? I had enough shit I was trying to keep straight in my head, so dumping superfluous details in there simply clogged up space I needed for more important stuff. But I found myself curious about O'Neill.

Driving home on West Bay Road, I checked every passing car, looking for the beige Kia. I knew I couldn't get that lucky, running into the guy twice in one night, but now alone in the Jeep, with no one else to be concerned with, I wouldn't let him get away again. I felt the adrenaline feeding through my veins as an anger grew inside, and it was he who was lucky I arrived home without running across him.

My shack was tiny, but I loved it. A man named Archie Winters gave it to me so the *drittsekk* who owned the old Spanish Bay Reef Resort land couldn't steal it. I hoped to give it back to Archie one day, because that would mean he'd returned to the Cayman Islands, but I doubted that would happen. The police had a few things to talk to Archie about, and as I was a constable, it would be awkward, but an easy decision for me. I'd do anything to help Archie.

Nestled in the trees, the shack was raised off the ground to allow hurricane surge to rush underneath, and the front windows and deck overlooked Spanish Bay. The view was huge but the living quarters were only a little over seven metres deep by three metres wide, the bathroom and closet the only divided rooms. The front door was in the middle of the deck, between two windows, and inside the sofa faced the left window, and on the right was the kitchen. Farther back, down the left side, a dining table separated the living area from my bed, with the bathroom and closet on the right.

Elín and Jazzy sat at the dining table, and they both looked up and said hi when I walked in. It looked like Elín was showing Jazzy where she was from on a map on her mobile phone. Elín had a glass of wine in front of her, and Jazzy had a fruit juice.

"Did you meet Edvard?" I asked.

"He must be in the woods," Jazzy replied. "I looked."

"She told me about him but we didn't see him," Elín said, and smiled. "I love your home."

I nodded. "*Takk*. He'll be by in the morning for breakfast. You two will have to feed him as I'll be leaving early."

"Want a glass of wine?" Jazzy asked, getting up from her chair and eagerly gliding over to the fridge.

I plodded to the back of the house in search of a T-shirt and tracksuit bottoms, ready to ditch my uniform. "Sure," I replied. "And yes, you can have a small glass too." Her tactics weren't very subtle.

"I didn't know if it was okay, so I said she should wait until you're home," Elín said.

I laughed. "Don't trust a word she says," I replied, ruffling Jazzy's crazy mop of hair as she handed me a wine glass. "She's a treacherous elf."

Jazzy grinned and sat back down, taking a sip of her own wine.

My shack had been my refuge and sanctuary after my boyfriend, Ridley, had been murdered in front of me. My private space where I could be alone to grieve in my own way. For nearly two years, AJ had been the only person I'd let into that world, until Jazzy came into my life.

As I changed clothes and listened to the teenager firing curious questions at our guest while fidgeting excitedly in her chair, I realised I wasn't uncomfortable around Elín. Her presence in my private space felt okay, in the same way bringing Jazzy home had been. It was a good feeling, but I couldn't help but wonder why.

Was there something about her being Nordic that reminded me of home? It didn't feel like that was the reason. When the answer hit me, it bowled my contentment aside and replaced it with a familiar anguish, not only for myself, but for my new friend.

We were all broken.

23

YOU'LL LIVE, PET

Sergeant Hadley was not happy with us first thing in the morning. He softened a little when Jacob and I offered to help with the mountain of CCTV review which needed to be done. I focused on the beige Kia, and Jacob started on tracking down Rhea Loudermilk's movements on the day of the murder. Hadley had two other constables working on the CCTV and immigration records, while he tried to contact the eyewitnesses from the fire. Officer O'Neill joined Whittaker in his office, where they pieced together a timeline for the victim and each suspect as more information came their way.

Having an accurate time of day to search, it didn't take me long to find the Kia on the roundabout CCTV. With plenty of streetlamps at the intersection, I was able to read the registration plate and tracked down the owner. Ruby Fraser, aged forty-nine. Her address was on Parkway Drive, a small neighbourhood not far from Marbel Drive, where we chased her car the night before. Ruby was listed as divorced with a son, Jason, who lived at the house. She worked for a lawyers' office in George Town. I wondered if the firm handled criminal cases.

I gathered up the paperwork I'd printed, shoved them inside a file folder, and ran upstairs two steps at a time, rushing to Whittaker's office.

"I have an address for the guy who drugged Elín," I announced, and then corrected myself. "The man we suspect of drugging Elín, sir."

"Officer O'Neill was just telling me about your off-duty chase through Seven Mile Beach," Detective Whittaker said sternly. "I also saw a number of complaints from motorists in last night's report log. A souped-up blue Jeep was mentioned several times."

"We almost had him, sir," I replied, not willing to consider the chase was reckless. "I'm sure a beige Kia was also reported. It belongs to a lady who lives not far from where we chased the guy, and she has a twenty-four-year-old son who lives with her. Can you get a warrant?"

Whittaker stood and took the print out from me, studying the details.

"Elín IDed the car?" he asked.

I looked at O'Neill.

"The girl certainly had a reaction when she spotted the vehicle, Roy," O'Neill said.

I handed him another piece of paper from my file. "And here's a comparison of the car from Foster's CCTV, and last night's, plus a Kia Optima from the internet."

Whittaker looked at the three images. They weren't all at exactly the same angle, but the profile of the car looked the same to me. I waited for his reaction.

"Okay," he said. "I'll send someone by the house."

"I can go, sir," I blurted.

"You need to focus on the arson case, Nora," he replied firmly. "Don't you have witnesses to revisit, and Rhea Loudermilk to interview?"

"That's all being set up now, sir. I have time."

"We need results from the CCTV before we talk to Loudermilk, Roy," O'Neill added, much to my surprise. "Your sergeant is working on lining up the witness interviews, so I think there's time if you can drum up a warrant right quick."

Whittaker looked at his watch, then picked up his phone. Twenty minutes later, O'Neill was sitting next to me in the SUV patrol vehicle I'd managed to commandeer for the day, following Whittaker's Range Rover. Jacob had stayed at central to help Hadley, and the plan was for Whittaker to return to the station with Jason Fraser, leaving the two of us to visit Rhea Loudermilk.

The neighbourhood was a warren of narrow lanes, lined with older homes on large lots, nestled amongst established trees and replanted palms. It was behind West Bay Road and a stone's throw from Seven Mile Beach, but had the less extravagant appearance of full-time residents who had probably owned these homes for years. The Frasers' house was a green bungalow with a nicely paved semicircular driveway wrapping around a palm in the centre of a flower bed. The place was small, immaculate, and someone either spent a lot of time on the landscaping or paid good money for it.

The house didn't have a garage or a driveway alongside, but a bright blue 3 Series BMW compact sat alone in front. No sign of the Kia. We parked our two vehicles so they blocked the entry and exit, and walked to the front door. Whittaker knocked, and a dog barked from inside. After a few moments, we heard a woman's voice telling the dog to be quiet, and the door opened.

"Mrs Fraser?" Whittaker asked, showing the woman his badge.

"How can I help you?" she replied, keeping the dog at bay with one foot.

She wore a dark blazer over a cream blouse with a grey skirt. Her auburn hair was trimmed at her shoulders, with deep red highlights, and her subtle make-up immaculately applied. "I'm just leaving for the office," she added.

"I'm sorry for troubling you, Mrs Fraser," Whittaker continued. "But I was wondering if your son was home?"

"What do you want with Jason?" she replied.

"Is he home, ma'am?" Whittaker repeated in a firmer tone.

"No, he's not. He didn't come home last night. He must have stayed at a friend's."

"May we come inside, ma'am?" Whittaker asked.

"You'll have to come back," she responded testily. "You're making me late for work."

Whittaker unfolded the search warrant and handed it to the woman. She finally released the door, letting it slowly swing open as she took the pieces of paper.

"I need to call my office," she snapped, stepping back.

The dog, a furry white yappy thing, took its opportunity to dodge past her legs and ran out, circling me and Officer O'Neill.

"Get back inside, Snowball," she shouted at the dog, who ignored her. "Damn it. Get inside!" she ordered, and the dog scurried through the front door.

Mrs Fraser stepped back, and allowed Whittaker room to come inside, followed by O'Neill. I stood still, deciding to wait outside for a reason I didn't know. I was about to reconsider, but the door closed before I could say anything. Shit, I thought, that was stupid. I really wanted to see this guy's room to get a read on why a twenty-four-year-old was still living at home with his mum. I walked to the side of the house, where a gate accessed the back through a neat, waist-high wooden fence. I was about to walk to the other side when I heard movement and turned back.

A young man dropped to the stone pathway alongside the building, and I quickly stepped out of view. He had two options, based on what I'd briefly seen. Head to the back of the house, where I presumed he'd risk being seen out the rear windows, or try and leave through the side gate. The house was divided from the neighbour's property by a tall wood panel fence, which looked like it would break under the weight of a person trying to climb over. I listened carefully.

After a few moments of hearing nothing, I guessed he'd quietly stepped to the backyard, so I peeked around the building. Jason Fraser was crouched where he'd landed on the path, staring right at me.

"We just want to talk," I said, but I knew he'd run.

Fraser leapt from a crouch to a sprint like an athlete out of the blocks. I vaulted the gate and took off behind him, but he had a healthy head start. The backyard was a concrete patio with a pool, then grass to the wood panel fence which appeared to wrap around three sides of the house. Fraser was making for the far corner which at first appeared to be a dead end where I'd easily trap him, but with the agility of a cat, he used the sloped roof of a doghouse as a launch to jump over the high fence in one fluid motion.

I had no idea what was on the other side, but I guessed he wouldn't have gone there if it was a pit full of spiked sticks. With somewhat less grace and a lot less confidence, I copied his moves and vaulted from the doghouse, using a hand on the top of the fence to guide me up and over the fence. I spotted my landing on what turned out to be the neighbour's garden six feet below me.

To soften the landing, I tucked and rolled, feeling the hard ground pummelling my shoulder through my thin, white shirt. Coming to my feet, I had no idea where he'd gone. The garden stretched 20 metres to the house and was shaded by five or six large, old trees. I looked around for movement, and seeing nothing, I figured he'd already made it down the side of the building and run ahead.

I saw the swing coming, but was already going too fast to avoid the blow. Fraser stepped from behind a tree and threw a punch, aimed at my face. I managed to get a swinging hand up high enough that he hit my arm, which consequently smacked me in my own face. I was lifted off my feet and crashed into the ground with a thud which knocked the wind out of me.

My face hurt like hell and I gasped for breath, but I instinctively covered up with my arms in case a second punch was coming. It didn't, and by the time I sat up and could see straight, he was gone.

"*Fy faen*," I muttered, and heard a commotion behind me.

Struggling to my feet, I turned as Whittaker's head appeared over the fence.

"Are you okay?" he asked.

"*Ja*," I said, not that I particularly felt all right.

I'd been thrown down and smacked in the face, which wasn't great, but worse was the fact the *drittsekk* had got away from me twice now.

"You're bleeding," Whittaker pointed out.

"Okay," I said, wiping a hand across my face. It smeared with blood from my nose, but at least it wasn't broken. At least, it felt like the same shape it had always been.

"Do you need an ambulance?" he asked, and I heard his feet slipping on the doghouse roof.

I pictured his polished dress shoes slipping and sliding and couldn't help but grin. Which hurt my face.

"Get down before you fall down, sir."

"Yes, okay," he said, and disappeared. "Can you get back over?" I heard him ask.

I looked at the fence. It was lattice panels of thin wood between four-by-four posts sunk into the ground. I stepped to the next panel along from where I knew the doghouse was located on the other side, and kicked the shit out of the thin wood. Three kicks and a shoulder barge later, I was in the Frasers' backyard.

"Did you get the bugger?" O'Neill asked, standing next to Whittaker, who was bending down, wiping marks from his shoes.

"*Nei.* He blindsided me."

She put her hand under my chin and inspected my face. "You'll live, pet. Nothing broken."

We walked back to the house where Ruby Fraser stood by the back door, hands on hips. "You'll pay for that fence."

"You'd best lodge a complaint at the station," I told her.

"I shall," she snapped back.

I grabbed her arm and spun her around, slipping a cuff on her wrist. "Just so happens you're going there right now," I took great pleasure in saying. "Ruby Fraser, I'm arresting you for wasting police time, and perverting the course of justice."

24

THE ADULTERY EFFECT

My nosebleed finally stopped after walking around with tissue paper up each nostril for fifteen minutes. If I gave a shit what people thought, I'd have sat in the SUV and avoided the stupid jokes the other constables made. But I didn't, so I didn't, and the half a dozen guys who showed up all had their fun while I was more interested in what I could find in Jason Fraser's room.

His laptop was password protected, so we bagged it and sent it back to the station for our Technical Support Unit to figure out how to access the files, and I couldn't find any external hard drives or thumb drives. He had a nice digital camera, but no memory card inside or anywhere else in the room. His mobile was gone and we tried calling it but went immediately to voicemail. Whittaker put in a request to track the phone but undoubtedly Fraser had already pulled the battery.

The rest of the room yielded nothing of interest. I couldn't rule out the possibility that it was all a coincidence, and he happened to have the same car as the real suspect. Maybe he ran because he had pot in the vehicle with him... but it seemed like a stretch. Why did he run this morning? And what had he done with the Kia? His mother had immediately demanded her lawyer and wouldn't say another word, which didn't score her son any 'innocent' points in my view.

Whittaker issued a warrant for the arrest of Jason Fraser, along with an alert to all police stations to be on the lookout for the suspect and his beige Kia. A picture was also emailed to the local news station, and while we were still at the house, a likeness of Jason Fraser was being aired to the population of Grand Cayman. The TV exposure would generate a lot of false sightings, but unless the *drittsekk* had somewhere close by to hide, it would also flush out our man. The problem was sorting the calls and determining which leads to chase.

I finally received a text from Jacob, telling me to check my email. I took a look then tracked down O'Neill, who was talking with Whittaker outside.

"We have CCTV from Rhea Loudermilk's movements on the day of the murder," I said, holding up the screen for them both to read.

"Unless she has verifiable proof of her whereabouts, bring her into the station for questioning," Whittaker was quick to say. "Arrest her on suspicion if she refuses."

"Scroll down," I told him, and he used a finger to move farther down the text.

"So, Osgood returned to the Loudermilks' house before leaving again," O'Neill commented as she read.

"*Ja*, but I don't think they were at the house at the same time."

"It's close," Whittaker noted. "But it appears you're right. We'll wrap up here. You two go and see Mrs Loudermilk and see what she has to say for herself."

"She didn't lie to us," I said, reminding myself more than making the point to my boss. "Her husband interrupted before she could answer when we asked if she'd gone anywhere else yesterday."

Whittaker nodded. "That's true, but she had plenty of opportunity to tell us while we were there, or any time afterwards. She's hardly been forthright."

Forthright wasn't a word I knew in English, so I made a mental note to look it up later and walked to the SUV. He was right, there was nothing more we could do here, and I was ready to find out why Rhea Loudermilk had chosen to hide her movements from us. I had a feeling what that might be, but I needed to keep an open mind.

"How do you want to approach this?" O'Neill asked me as I sped north, using Jason Fraser's short cut to the bypass to save time.

I thought about her question for a moment or two. "I would start by asking about Osgood and his habits, friends, and general patterns, just to put her at ease. Then ask her to run through her day and give her the chance to come clean."

"Okay," O'Neill responded, which made me wonder.

Was that *okay*, as in great plan, or *okay*, as in that's a dumb idea but go for it if that's the best you've got? I looked over. O'Neill sat bolt upright with her satchel/bag thing in her lap, staring straight out the front window. The woman baffled me. She was this rigid, tea-drinking, stick-up-her-arse Brit all day, then last night she'd seemed relaxed, personable, and deeply concerned for Elín. I thought we'd broken down a wall between us, and although she wasn't being as prickly as she was on day one, her professional distance was back in play.

My main reason for caring about any of this was the fact that she significantly outranked me, and I couldn't get a good read on whether she'd object if I used methods outside the standard hand-book. I didn't have a current plan to go off the reservation, but these situations tended to sneak up on me and I often reacted rather than made a decision to use unorthodox tactics.

The Mercedes beetle-shaped car was in the driveway, so I parked behind it, and we walked to the door. I couldn't see Rhea through the huge glass panels, but that didn't mean she hadn't noticed us arriving. I was surprised when she opened the door before we reached it.

"Have you found whoever did this to poor Ian?" she greeted us.

"Investigation is still ongoing," I said, knowing that was a really annoying phrase to hear. "May we come inside?"

She didn't verbally invite us inside, but stood back and allowed us room to enter.

"This is Officer O'Neill," I said once the door closed behind us.

"I'm from the National Crime Agency in the UK," O'Neill said, taking over. Apparently, her ruse was up now.

Rhea gave her a nod and offered seats at the dining table. I noticed the huge windows overlooking the back garden and canal were more tinted than when we'd been here before. I guessed they adjusted with the sunlight's intensity or a control panel.

"We were hoping you could give us a few more details about Ian's movements since he'd arrived," I began. "He's been on the island quite a few times, so I'm sure he knew his way around."

"Yes, he visited us most years."

"Did he have a routine or particular place he liked to go?"

Rhea thought for a moment. "He preferred Public Beach. He's a swimmer... he was a swimmer," she corrected herself. "He didn't go every day, but quite often. He'd always come back with a coffee from Coccoloba's. I think he often ate breakfast there."

"It's a beachfront cafe," I explained to O'Neill, who'd looked over at me. "Part of the Kimpton Seafire Resort next to Public Beach."

O'Neill nodded and let me continue.

"Did Mr Osgood have any friends on the island, other than you and your husband?"

Rhea frowned as she thought it over. "He met a woman a few years back, but I think that fizzled after he went home. He hasn't mentioned her since. I can't say I know about anyone else."

"And you've no idea who he was having lunch with?" I asked.

Rhea shook her head. "Sorry, I don't."

I forced a smile, designed to further put her at ease, but my forced smiles always felt transparent from this side of my face. Rhea was staring at the table, so it didn't matter anyway.

"Can you run me through your movements on Wednesday, so

we can lock down the times we know Mr Osgood was here at the house," I asked, maintaining a relaxed tone.

Rhea's head picked up and she looked at me, a crease forming on her brow. "I told you the other day, I had my Pilates class from eight until nine."

"And Mr Osgood was here when you left, and also when you returned, correct?"

"That's right. Then he left the house around 10:30," Rhea confirmed, and I could tell she was hoping it would end there.

"Okay, and that's the last time you saw him?"

Rhea nodded.

"He didn't return to the house later in the day?"

Every muscle in Rhea Loudermilk's body tightened a small amount, but the overall effect caused her to flinch. Jacob's notes had Osgood's car leaving the Loudermilks' house at 10:34am as Rhea had confirmed, but he returned again at 11:05am for 44 minutes. We knew she'd already left her house, narrowly missing him by a few minutes.

"I didn't see him," Rhea finally said, which wasn't a lie.

"You couldn't have," O'Neill interjected. "You weren't here when Osgood came back to the house half an hour after he first left."

The colour drained from Rhea's face as she scrambled to come up with a plausible response.

"I think I did run out for a bit," she said, tapping the table with her hand. "I ran by a friend's place for a few minutes."

"A few minutes, pet?" O'Neill scoffed. "You were gone for two hours."

Rhea stood up. "I didn't offer you coffee. Would you like some?"

"Sit back down," O'Neill snapped. "Next time you stand, it'll be for us to put cuffs on you."

Rhea sat down and was about to start arguing, but O'Neill didn't give her the chance.

"I don't want to hear it, love. Obstruction of justice in a murder inquiry is a serious offence, not to mention the fact that you don't have an alibi for the time of the murder. Quit mucking us about and start telling the truth, starting with where you were in the morning, and then in the afternoon when your mate Ian was being torched."

Rhea Loudermilk was now paralysed with fear. Her hands were shaking and tears ran down her cheeks.

"Enough theatrics. Out with it," O'Neill demanded.

"I didn't lie about being at a friend's," Rhea blubbered. "I went to see a friend."

"Same friend, morning and afternoon?" I asked, taking over from O'Neill as I had another nugget of information.

Rhea nodded.

"So, you're having an affair," I said, rolling on a hunch.

She nodded again, and the tears flowed unabated, accompanied by groans and sniffles.

"Where did you meet? At his house?"

Rhea wiped her nose with the back of her wrist. "The Ritz-Carlton Deckhouses."

I nodded to O'Neill. It was where Jacob and I had seen Rhea's Mercedes turn when we'd first looked at the CCTV yesterday, and Jacob had confirmed the same for the afternoon.

"His name?" I asked. "We'll need to confirm your story."

"Dalton can't know about this; it'll ruin our marriage," Rhea begged.

"Funny how screwing other people has that effect," O'Neill said without a hint of sympathy.

"You don't understand," Rhea moaned, her head in her hands.

"Tell us who, so we can confirm your story, or you're coming down the station with us," I told her. "Be a lot harder to keep this quiet if you're arrested."

Rhea wiped her face and gathered herself together, finally looking up at me.

"His name?" I repeated.

"Jamie Willow," she replied, "and she's not a he."

25

MICKEY MOUSE EARS

It was nearly 1:00pm when we reached Central Station. We'd sat through more tears as Jamie Willow confirmed her affair with Rhea Loudermilk, and verified they'd met twice on Wednesday. We'd then grabbed lunch from Water and the Elephant again, as their tea was 'acceptable' according to O'Neill. We'd agreed that while it was still possible Rhea had slipped away from her girlfriend's house and Jamie was covering for her, it seemed incredibly unlikely. We certainly couldn't see a motive, but as yet we hadn't come up with a motive why anyone would set Ian Osgood ablaze.

Sergeant Hadley had lined up interviews with two of the three witnesses who'd been by the fence when Jacob and I had arrived at the fire. The third, a lady on business from Montreal, had returned home and Detective Whittaker had spoken to her over the phone. She'd said she was too traumatised by the whole affair to remember any details.

We walked into the interview room where a young Caymanian businessman, Clement Ebanks, waited for us. He worked for the Dart Corporation who owned and operated a large office building next to the car park which backed up to the scrub land. We introduced ourselves, then sat down.

"Walk us through what you saw, Mr Ebanks," I urged.

The distress was clear on his face as he began. "I was leaving work a little early as I had an electrician coming by my house, and I saw the smoke. I always park at the back of the lot so I don't get door dings. I figured they were burning brush, but then I noticed someone walking over to the fence, so I became curious. I walked around a van and that's when I saw the smoke coming from the windows and the flames inside a car. I had no idea there was someone still in there. Right after that, you and your partner came flying through."

"You didn't call 9-1-1?"

"No. I asked the other guy at the fence and he said he'd already called when he saw the smoke. Said he didn't know it was a car on fire until he'd got closer."

"Would you recognise the other man again if you saw him?"

"Sure. I did. He was in the reception when I arrived here."

"Did you see anyone else there from when you were walking to your car until the fire truck arrived?" I asked, giving him a broad time period to consider.

"More people came over after you arrived, but before that, I didn't see anyone else except the guy I mentioned at the fence," Clement replied.

"You were the only two in the car park?" I asked. "Think back to walking from the building to your car."

Clement took his time responding. "I'm not saying there wasn't anyone else in the car park, but I don't recall seeing anyone. As I said, I was leaving early. At five, the place would have been flooded with people leaving work. You should ask the other guy, though. Maybe he or his friend can remember more."

"His friend?" I blurted, as both O'Neill and I leaned over the table.

"Yeah, the guy I talked to was going over to the fence when I saw him. I think he'd just made the call. He joined someone else by the fence, but he must of taken off by the time I got there."

"You didn't see him go?"

Clement shook his head and looked confused. "I barely recall seeing him at all, but for some reason I had it my mind he was with the other dude."

We left Clement and hurriedly found the other witness, Ron Powery, and another available interview room. His arse had barely hit the seat when I threw all courtesy out the window and got to the point.

"You saw the fire, correct?"

The man nodded, appearing startled.

"Who else did you see?"

"I saw you," he replied, and smiled.

"Before we arrived, sir," I snapped, trying to hang on to some thread of patience.

"The fella I met again today in the reception," he began, "I remember him. Nice guy. He works at…"

"Obviously we know about him, he's here at the station. What we're interested in is who else may have been there. Were you with anyone else?"

"Oh, sorry," he bumbled. "No, I was alone. I had just arrived for a meeting at Dart and saw the smoke." He looked at me, apparently unsure what else I wanted to know.

"*Fy faen!* Did you see anyone else near the fence or the burning car?"

"Only the guy who ran to get help. He was calling you. I told him I'd already called 9-1-1, but I heard him telling someone what was going on, and he was going to find a fire extinguisher."

I took a breath and looked at O'Neill. From the expression on her face, I was sure she agreed with my thought. The man Powery described was the killer. The details our witness could drag from his memory would be crucial. I couldn't screw this up.

"Mr Powery, I'd like you to take a few moments, relax, and take yourself back to the moment you stepped from your car in the car park."

He looked at me, thrown by the sudden change in pace and energy in the room.

I smiled. "Take your time, sir."

Powery closed his eyes and I watched his body slowly begin to relax.

"What's the first thing you noticed?" I asked softly.

"I'd seen the smoke when I'd driven up," he replied, keeping his eyes closed. "I think that's why I parked so far away from the building. I was curious. When I got out of the car, I could see there was a vehicle beyond the fence, and the smoke was coming from the window tops."

"Could you see inside the car?"

He shook his head. "It was full of smoke and then I saw some flames. Honestly, my first thought was the fire department were doing training, but there weren't any fire trucks there."

"So, you left your car and walked towards the fence, right?"

He nodded.

"Tell me what you saw as you walked."

"I saw someone at the fence. I remember they had their hand to their ear like they were on a cell phone."

"Perfect. Tell me about their appearance."

Powery frowned and went to say something, but stopped.

"Tall, short, fat, thin. Focus on your first impression," I said, hoping to pry an image from his mind.

The man had run over to see a burning car, so it was unlikely the other person he noticed for a moment would have been particularly memorable. I was hoping for any morsel he could recall.

"I don't think I ever saw a face," Powery said. "I'm sure there was someone there, because I spoke to them, but I can't picture them at all."

"You referred to them as a guy earlier, Mr Powery. What told you the person was male?"

He opened his eyes. "I really don't know. I can't picture their face, or even their hair."

"But they spoke to you," I prompted.

"Yes!" he blurted. "The voice sounded male. It must have been that." He looked at me with distress in his eyes. "All I see in my mind is that burning car. I remember thinking how bizarre it looked with the swirling dark grey smoke funnelling out of the window tops and the flames flickering inside. I looked for a way through the fence, but couldn't see anything nearby." His head dropped into his hands. "That's when I saw something moving inside and realised there could be a person in there."

"Let's focus on the man you saw, Mr Powery," I said, trying to realign his attention.

Powery looked up at me with moist eyes. "I was paralysed. I just stood there and watched." He dropped his head again. "I didn't do a thing to help, and there was someone inside, wasn't there?"

"There was nothing you could do for the victim, Mr Powery. But you're helping us catch the killer now. Any details you can share about this stranger could be the difference between us catching him or him getting away with murder."

He nodded and wiped his cheeks. "Right, I'm sorry." Closing his eyes once again, he took a few deep breaths.

"You spoke to the stranger. Did he turn around when he replied?" I asked.

"He turned, I think," Powery replied, without sounding confident. "He must have, as he left, but I think he turned away from me."

"Okay. This is important, Mr Powery. He spoke to you and the voice was male. Did he have an accent of some sort?"

The man sat before me rubbing his temples and I allowed him the time he needed. After a while, he opened his eyes. "I have no idea. I'm so sorry. Somehow, I recall the words, but I can't hear him say them."

"But you're sure the voice was male?"

Powery shook his head. "That's what comes to mind so I guess that's the impression I took away."

"Okay. What comes to mind when you try and picture the

stranger? Was his clothing light or dark? Could you see his skin colour?"

Once again, he shook his head. "I really can't see him clearly in my head. I don't want to mislead you, and I'm just not sure."

I sat back and looked over at O'Neill, who'd remained silent until now. She reached into her bag and retrieved a computer tablet.

"I'm going to show you a series of pictures, Mr Powery. All you have to do is tell me if any of the images trigger any recollection at all of the person you saw."

She turned on the tablet and waited for it to boot up, then signed in.

"Don't overthink this, okay?" she continued as she opened a software program and began selecting a variety of inputs. "To begin with all I want to know is if the image makes you think of the person or not, it doesn't matter about details. If you see a kid wearing Mickey Mouse ears and the person you saw was an old man, but you remember now he had Mickey Mouse ears, then just say yes. Okay?"

Powery nodded, but as with most people facing a spontaneous test of any kind, he appeared nervous. O'Neill showed me the image on her screen before spinning it around to face our witness. It was the silhouette of a figure standing with his hands at his sides. I guessed it was a male, but I couldn't be certain. They were generally average in all proportions, and I couldn't even tell whether they were facing me, or away from me.

"Hmm, I'd say yes, I suppose," Powery said, and O'Neill spun the screen back around.

With a few clicks, the figure had the hand on the left to their ear, as though they were making a call on a mobile phone. She swung the tablet around.

"Other hand," Powery said immediately. "Oh, I'm sorry, you didn't want details, did you?"

O'Neill smiled, and made more changes to the options. "That's okay. If anything stands out, you can tell me."

When she showed him the image again, he slowly nodded. "Something's not right, I'm not sure what, though."

Before he could study the image for too long, O'Neill made another change, this time removing the figure's hair.

Powery shook his head. "No that's worse, something's still not right."

O'Neill spun the tablet around to face us, and pondered a moment, before playing around in a few drop-down menus until finding something she wanted. When she showed our witness, his reaction was instant.

"That's it!" he said, pointing at the screen. "I remember now! My first thought was why would anyone wear a hooded sweatshirt in this heat? That's why I couldn't see the phone. It was inside the hood."

"Is it also why you assumed the person was a young male?" I asked, and hoped I hadn't just stepped on O'Neill's toes.

Powery thought for a moment. "Maybe," he admitted, but once again seemed unsure. "It must have been a combination of the build, voice, and the way they were dressed," he added. "I came away with the impression it was a young man standing there, but truthfully, I can't be sure."

I sat back and let O'Neill continue with her software, showing Powery more additions and changes to the image. None of it sparked anything new except a maybe on a baseball cap under the hood. Everything else she tried either confused him or was further away from being what he remembered. Powery's vague description did match the equally hazy image we had of the figure in the back of Ian Osgood's car from the roundabout CCTV. Or more accurately, it didn't contradict what we could barely make out.

But none of it would stand up for a second in court, or more importantly, lead us closer to finding a suspect. The killer was probably male. Well, based on the crime they committed, we were already pretty certain that was the case. The one thing I kept returning to in my mind was the voice Powery heard, and his impression of them being young.

Ron Powery was a local man born and raised, who was used to dealing with both English and Americans in the workplace and socially. It was completely believable that neither accent would have stood out to him, but a person's age is usually detectable in their speech, at least to the degree of not confusing a sixty-year-old man with a twenty-nine-year-old.

When we finally released Ron Powery, with the instruction to call us if anything more came to mind, I walked with O'Neill up to Whittaker's office.

"What do you think?" I asked as we scaled the stairs.

"I think we need to take a much deeper look at Jonas Richards, pet, and see if there's any way he was in Florida three weeks ago."

"*Ja,*" I replied, pleased to hear we were on the same page.

26

ONE SIMPLE PHONE CALL

We waited outside as Detective Whittaker was on a phone call when we arrived at his office. Seeing us, he waved us in, and politely but quickly ended his call. He looked stressed. Or perhaps harassed, as he had the rare knack of usually appearing completely unflustered in most situations.

"According to witnesses calling our hotline, Mr Fraser is running around every corner of the island," he said, shaking his head. "I had to add a second constable answering the phone earlier, as one couldn't keep up. We're following up on the reports which seem more promising, but we're stretched thin."

"Any seem plausible?" O'Neill asked, and I was pleased to hear she was still invested in a case which had nothing to do with her.

"Two sightings near West Bay dock within fifteen minutes of each other around lunchtime," Whittaker replied. "But sweeps of the area produced nothing. Anything new from your interviews in the arson case?"

O'Neill nodded to me, so I gave my boss a concise briefing, trying to phrase the details in language he approved of.

I then took a moment before concluding, "Jonas Richards fits the limited description the best, sir." And then I added something else as the idea struck me. "Although our date rape drug suspect also fits as well or better."

"You think the two cases might be connected?" Whittaker asked in surprise, looking at O'Neill for confirmation.

She shrugged her shoulders. "I hadn't thought of that until now," she responded.

"Neither had I," I admitted. "And man in a hoodie describes half the male population of the western world under thirty years old, but it's not as popular here where it's so hot."

"Bloody right it is," O'Neill agreed about the hot part.

Whittaker tapped his pen on a stack of papers. "Okay, let's keep an open mind to that possibility, and turn up the heat on Richards."

I looked at him. Half of me wanted to chuckle and the other half was stunned Whittaker of all people would make a joke like that. He stared right back. I guess he didn't make the connection and I reminded myself how my train of thought rarely aligned with normal people's.

"Immigration records, sir?" I asked, moving on. "It would really help us if we could place one of these people in Florida six weeks ago."

"Still waiting on US authorities to get back to us," he replied.

"Where did they fly here from?" O'Neill asked. "Might be a place to start that we could check right away."

Whittaker shook his head. "They all came in from Miami. But that's because most flights from the US or Europe connect through Miami."

"Can we see the first leg of their flights?" O'Neill asked.

"Yes, that we should have access to. I'll get those details for you."

"We already know Richards was in Florida as he lives there," I pointed out. "We're still short on enough for a warrant though, right sir?"

Whittaker nodded. "The judge will give me a fair amount of leeway as this is a murder case, but everything we have is theory without a lick of evidence. You're sure the Loudermilks are in the clear?" he continued. "I suppose an affair is a strong motivator for the wife to lie to us, but what about her husband?"

"Jacob followed up with him at his work, and a co-worker corroborated his lunch story," I replied. "He has his own private office so in theory he could have slipped away in the afternoon, but the receptionist told Jacob that Loudermilk was there all afternoon. She put calls through to him and said she saw him several times."

"We shouldn't rule out Louise Middleton either," I said, the idea coming to me as I pictured her broad-shouldered athletic build. "I know the voice doesn't match, but maybe she disguised her tone and the witnesses already presumed the figure in the hoodie was male."

"If she was in Florida at the time of the first murder, I agree, she should stay on the list," O'Neill responded. "From our eyewitness account, the killer took care to conceal themselves, so putting on a voice wouldn't be a stretch to imagine."

Whittaker yawned and rolled his shoulders. "Forgive me," he apologised. "I'm sure we're all in need of a little more sleep this week. I need to follow up on a few of these items, but why don't you head home."

I stood and paused a moment. "Do you need a ride?" I asked O'Neill.

"I'm good, pet. I'll stay a while longer with Roy. He's kindly babysitting me tonight."

"Okay," I said, pleased to have a simpler evening, although I was beginning to enjoy the officer's company. "Perhaps you can tell the detective about your cool software. We need something like that."

Curious, Whittaker looked up from his paperwork. "What software is this?"

O'Neill winked at me. "I'll see where he takes me for dinner before I decide if he has clearance to see it or not."

. . .

I felt a little guilty driving home at 5:00pm. We'd started at 7:00am, so it wasn't like I'd put in a short day, but when a murderer and date rape drug *drittsekk* were still running around the island, it seemed like we should only stop when we couldn't go on anymore. Of course, that didn't make much sense as we'd all be useless with no sleep, but I still felt like I wasn't doing everything possible and it didn't sit well. The dull ache in my bruised face also contributed to my inability to put the job aside.

I'd texted during the day with Jazzy, who'd sworn she'd taken the bus to and from school. If she missed classes, the school would report her absences to the Department of Children & Family Services, who'd then be on my arse, and if I couldn't keep up her attendance, she'd be back with a 'regular' foster home. So I believed her. I could also track her mobile, so unless she'd given it to a friend, I could see where she'd been.

Parking the Jeep by the side of Conch Point Road, I traipsed through the woods and quietly approached the voices I could hear on the deck. The first one to turn and look at me was Edvard the blue iguana, who prepared himself for a rapid retreat until he saw it was me and decided a slow shuffle away from the steps was good enough.

"I hope it's okay, Nora, but I'm still here," Elín said, sitting in one of the chairs. "Oh shit! What happened to your face?"

"I ran into someone," I replied, noticing she'd changed clothes.

"She does dat a lot," Jazzy commented from the other chair with a mischievous grin on her face.

I hoped her glee had more to do with their day than my beaten-up face. "I'm guessing you checked out of the hotel," I said, choosing to wait until later to explain how I'd let the man who'd attacked her get away.

"I told her to," Jazzy claimed, putting her hand in the air.

"I bet you did," I said, raising an eyebrow at her.

"I'm sure I can get a room there again, or maybe somewhere else," Elín was quick to say, and started to get up.

"It's fine," I said, waving her back to her seat. Edvard tilted his head and stared at me. "You're in on this too, I suppose." He blinked once. That could have meant yes, but if I waited a bit longer, he'd eventually blink again, confirming lizards don't understand humans and just happen to occasionally blink.

"I can cook us dinner if you wouldn't mind running me to the store to buy some food," Elín offered.

I looked at the sky, and then at my watch. We had an hour or so of good daylight left. "Ever been spearfishing?"

Elín shook her head. "I've been snorkelling, and was thinking of trying scuba diving before I went home... but then... you know..."

"Put a swimsuit on. We'll go and catch dinner," I told her. "Miss Full-of-Great-Ideas can cook the fish we bring back."

"I didn't think you could spearfish here? Isn't it a marine park?"

"You can hunt lionfish wit a license 'cos dey're invasive and cullin' is da only way to control da population," Jazzy enthusiastically explained. "And she's makin' me cook 'cos dey're a pain in da arse to fillet with all da venomous spines."

I opened the door to the shack. "Only fair you cook if we catch."

"What about what I catch?" Jazzy complained, scrambling to follow me inside.

"Have you done your homework?" I asked, holding the door for Elín to come with us.

"I don't have any."

"Bullshit."

"I only have a little bit, and mind da language 'round my sensitive ears."

"Then you'll have time to cook the rice while we're gone."

I heard her let out a teenage groan. The kind I remembered making myself a few times, which now seemed so long ago. Before everything went wrong and my life was turned upside down.

"Start the rice on boil and you can come too," I said, caving like a total pushover. "But you're doing homework after dinner."

"What! And no TV?" Jazzy said, laughing in the free-spirited way only a youngster can.

I smiled. Despite all she'd been through herself, there was

still a child inside who was appearing more and more. Having Elín around was good for Jazzy. She struggled to relate to the other kids her age at school, and leaned towards older students, who she didn't share any classes with. I was shit at being her friend and twice as shit at being a guardian, but I kept trying to remind myself she was better off now than living on the streets.

I noticed Elín was looking around the room.

"We don't have a TV," I said, and she grinned at Jazzy's sarcastic humour.

With fins, masks, snorkels, and weight belts in hand, we walked out the door, which I closed behind me. Before I could reach the steps, I heard my mobile ringing inside.

"*Faen*," I muttered to myself, and wrangled with whether to ignore it or not.

Usually, the decision would be easy, but with two big cases on the go, I set my gear on a chair and went back inside. The caller ID wasn't the police station, but a number I did have stored.

"*Hallo*, Raylene," I answered.

"Hi Nora," the woman from the Department of Children & Family Services greeted me.

She was the one who'd gone out on a limb to place Jazzy in my care, bending several foster family rules in the process. She sometimes checked in to see how things were going, but something in her voice told me this call was different. My mind raced through all the things Jazzy could possibly have done to warrant the phone call as I waited to hear what the woman had to say.

"I have good news," she said, forcing a cheery tone. "We have a family who would love to meet Jasmine."

The rest of the details Raylene carefully gave me fell from the phone and clattered to the floor all around me. I'm sure my subconscious caught the key information of where and when a meeting was to take place, but as I closed the door once again and gathered my gear from the chair, the two pounds of lead on the belt felt like an anchor in my hands.

Elín and Jazzy were chattering away by the steps into the tiny old marina which used to be part of the Spanish Reef Resort.

"Anything important?" Elín asked, and I knew she was hoping for news regarding her case. I had news for her, but it wasn't what she wanted to hear and I'd already delayed telling her. She'd still have to wait. My mouth felt dry and I didn't think I could form the words to explain the call to Jazzy just yet, and I honestly had no clue how she'd take it. Either way, I knew I was going to feel like shit. It was amazing how one simple phone call or conversation could impact someone's life. If I hadn't gone back inside the shack to answer the phone, I'd be blissfully unaware, instead of filled with dread.

"Let's catch dinner," I said, unable to look either of them in the eyes.

27

COOL, REFRESHING WATER

2009

The lobby of the hotel was more like a London tube station than a reception area. There was no real queue, but a small crowd gathered around the glass-screened counter, some asking questions and the rest contributing drunken encouragement and insults in equal measure. A steady stream of bodies paraded through the lobby, smelling of sweat and sunscreen, with the front doors constantly swinging open and closed.

Allie hovered close by the counter, waiting for an opportunity to speak to one of the two receptionists who were attempting to pacify the crowd. Every other guy waltzing by invited her to join them at the 'most awesome party', and the other half bumped into her as they tacked their way across the room. Finally, one of the exhausted-looking Asian men was free, and Allie put both hands on the counter to protect her position.

"How can I help you?" the man asked, his eyes tired and defeated.

"I need to get to Miami airport, please. Is there a bus or shuttle?"

He looked her over for a moment and shook his head. "Tonight?"

"Yes. As soon as possible, please."

His face briefly cracked a smile. "No one is mad enough to come near here after dark. The next shuttle won't be until 9:00am. They leave from one of the hotels inland from the beach. A two-mile walk, I'd guess."

Allie's shoulders sagged. She didn't even know if her ticket was changeable. It had been a discounted seat through a third-party website. It cost a fortune to make a call from her UK mobile, which wasn't a fancy smartphone, and she didn't bring a computer to get online.

"Can I get a key to the room I'm in please?" she asked.

"Is your name on the room?"

"No, I'm staying with friends, I just need to get my bag."

The man paused a moment and they both tried to ignore the loud guys behind her shouting about getting help with the air conditioner which had apparently fallen out of the wall in their room.

"What's the number?" the receptionist asked, either feeling sympathetic to her cause or happy to delay helping the next idiots he had to deal with.

Allie gave him the room number and the man knelt behind the counter where she guessed they kept the rack of key hooks. He reappeared a moment later.

"Both keys are gone, I'm afraid."

One of the guys behind banged into Allie, shoving her against the counter.

"Shit. Sorry, hon," the brawny shirtless man slurred. "Hey, are you any good at fixing air conditioners?"

His friend erupted into laughter and Allie pushed the first guy away with her elbow.

"Could somebody let me in the room for a quick sec? I'll grab my bag and be out of your hair."

The receptionist scoffed. "I'm sorry, miss. There's only the two of us here, and as you can see, we can't leave the desk."

Allie groaned. "Is there a master key I could borrow for a minute? Please, I need to get out of this madhouse."

The man shook his head and looked past her. "I'm sorry, I can't help you. Next."

Allie relinquished her spot at the counter and drifted to a quiet corner of the lobby, until the overwhelming stench of vomit sent her in the opposite direction. She felt like curling up into a ball and crying again, but there was nowhere quiet to hide. She wasn't scared of the people — most were simply having a good time, albeit drunk and obnoxious — but the situation itself was overwhelming. Her only safe havens felt like the room or the airport, and she had no way to access either one.

After wandering for a while, and thinking, Allie decided her best course of action was to wait near the room. At some point, whether it was soon or the next morning, the Batman Brigade would return to the room, and she would take her bag and leave. That was step one. She'd work on the airport portion once she had her possessions, which included her passport.

Finding the room, she checked the door, which was of course locked, then banged a few times in case someone had returned. Nothing. She slumped to the grubby carpet and tucked in her feet so the occasional straggler weaving down the hallway didn't kick her.

Maybe she should find the group and apologise? Get a key and tell them she'd leave it at the front desk for them. She felt bad for stomping off, and the more she looked back, the more Allie wondered if it had all been an overreaction. Nothing had been quite the same with her friend since the moment she'd landed in Miami. Allie had never knowingly spent time around anyone using drugs, so she had no idea if that was his problem, but he'd been distracted and inconsistent, as well as obsessed with the new crowd he was hanging out with.

"What's happening?" someone said casually.

Allie looked from the white trainers, up the tanned legs to a silhouetted figure standing over her.

"Are you okay?" he said, his accented voice sounding familiar.

He stepped to one side, away from the ceiling light, so Allie could see his face, and she realised it was Rafa, the man she'd met earlier. He smiled and she caught that mischievous look in his eyes. He was a good-looking guy, and under different circumstances, and if he wasn't what appeared to be a drug dealer, she'd find him attractive.

"I'm fine," she replied. "My stuff is in the room and I don't have a key."

He nodded. "I doubt they'll be back for a while. It's early."

It didn't feel early to Allie. She was ready to call it a night, but that wasn't going to be an option the way things were going.

"Do you know where they are?" he asked.

"They were at the pool next door, but that was a while back. Who knows now."

Rafa took out his mobile and typed a text. "Let's see."

He slipped his rucksack off his shoulder and slid down the wall beside her. Allie wondered exactly what was in the bag, then decided she'd rather not know.

"You don't seem impressed with Spring Break in South Florida," he said, with humour in his voice.

"It's not quite what I expected," Allie admitted. "I'm not really the throw caution to the wind kinda girl."

Rafa shrugged his shoulders. "That's probably better in the long run."

Allie looked over at the man in the poorly lit hallway where they both sat on the filthy carpet. She had expected more of the same peer pressure the others had given her.

"I'm surprised to hear you say that."

"Why?" he asked.

Looking into his eyes she realised he appeared to be as sober as she was. "According to your friends you're the life of the party."

Rafa laughed quietly. "I bring what they want to the party. It makes me popular, but most of these privileged assholes wouldn't give me the time of day if I wasn't their Candy Man."

Allie wanted to ask Rafa why he did what he did, as he seemed like a nice and intelligent guy, but she didn't want to offend him. Apart from her brief conversation with the policeman, this was the safest and least agitated she'd felt all evening. Another oddity, since she'd been nervous of him earlier.

"They seem like arseholes to me too," she said.

He laughed again. "I like the way you say that. Americans probably have no idea you're insulting them when you call them an *arsehole*," he said, making a failed attempt at sounding English.

Allie grinned. "I don't know, but I want to try it now."

Two girls in cut-off shorts and bikini tops walked down the hallway hanging on each other, giggling and talking in the loud whispers drunk people do when they think they're being quiet.

"Hello there, arseholes," Allie said, accentuating her accent. "Could you tell me where the loo is?"

They both stared at her, burst out laughing, then kept walking. "What the fuck did she say?" one asked and they both fell into fits of drunken laughter once more.

"See," Rafa said with a big grin. "And like I said earlier, you're better off being you than another one of them."

"Thank you," Allie said.

For the first time since they'd driven into Fort Lauderdale, she didn't feel like an outcast. An alien in a foreign land, a minority that no one could relate to. She wondered if that was how people of different skin colour or race felt in certain situations.

Rafa's mobile had buzzed several times but he'd dismissed each text. This time, he read the message and eased to his feet, offering Allie a hand. She accepted and stood next to him.

"Where are they?"

"A deck party a few hotels down. I know where it is," Rafa said.

"How do I get there?" Allie asked, not relishing the battle through the crowds. The task felt like finding a needle in a human haystack.

"I gotcha," he said, and began walking down the hallway.

Allie quickly caught up. "Are you sure? You probably have… you know… things to do?"

Rafa smiled. "At Spring Break, I have the luxury of an unlimited supply of customers. Most will come to me wherever I am, so shortly that'll be at the deck party."

He knew every short cut, stairwell, walkway, and road to avoid the worst of the crowds, and fifteen minutes later, they joined a throng of people outside another run-down hotel. The deck was one floor above the street, contained by a railing which looked like it would burst at any moment. Rafa took her hand and led her through the crowd until he somehow found the group. She was convinced that without him she would have spent the night looking for them even if she'd found the right party.

A sound system thumped with the heavy beat of electronic dance music, and a horde of bodies near the stage moved with the rhythm. Farther away from the stage, people gathered in groups, talking loudly to be heard over the music.

"Where did you go?" Ozzy shouted, and Allie was surprised to see a look of concern on his face.

"I'm sorry, but I need to leave," she said, cupping her hand to his ear.

"To the room?" he asked. "I'll get a key and take you."

"Yes," she shouted. "I need to get my bag, but then I mean I'm *leaving* leaving. This isn't for me. I need to go home."

Ozzy stepped back with a hand on her arm, looking into her eyes. He nodded and moved closer. "I'm so sorry, Allie, I know this is crazy, and I haven't been the best…" he trailed off, or she lost the words to the ambient noise.

He shouted something in Bruce's ear, who nodded, and dug a key from his pocket, handing it to Ozzy.

"Okay, come on then," he said, holding the key for her to see.

"You don't have to come," she shouted back. "I'll leave the key at the front desk."

Ozzy waved her off. "No, I want to make sure you're okay. I'll come with you."

Yelling back and forth in the midst of the party, there was no way to contest the point of him coming along, and she wasn't even sure she could find her way, so she relented. Ozzy held up a plastic bottle of water and offered it to her. Allie realised she was parched and gladly took a swig.

"Keep it," he said, showing her he had another.

Allie looked past Ozzy to where Rafa stood by the railing in what appeared to be a heated exchange with a shady-looking guy wearing a bandana wrapped around his head. She wanted to thank Rafa for his help, but Ozzy was gently herding her away.

"What's up with Rafa?" she yelled to Ozzy, who glanced back.

"Guess he doesn't like the competition stepping in when he's not around," Ozzy replied and pushed on through the crowd.

Allie realised she was wishing it was Rafa taking her away instead of her childhood friend, and felt a pang of guilt. Ozzy seemed genuinely sorry, and back at the room they'd have a chance to mend the fence before she left. It was better this way. She took a long swig of the cool, refreshing water and followed along.

28

MORNING OF ALL MORNINGS

I felt like I'd seen every hour of the night on the bedside clock. Sleep had come in fits and starts, and each time I woke it seemed like I'd barely nodded off before my eyes were open again. I promised myself I wouldn't get up until sunrise, but at 5:45 I couldn't stand it any longer. Moving about the room quietly, I turned on the coffee maker, washed my face, and dressed without Elín or Jazzy stirring. It was Saturday, so any disturbance before eight would be met by a very disgruntled teenager.

I'd hoped a good night's sleep would bring clarity and perspective to the challenges clogging my mind, and it may well have done. But instead, barely feeling rested at all, I was functioning on autopilot, and the problems engulfed me like the thick fog that would roll off Oslofjord and consume my native home city. Just to top things off, my face ached and I looked like I'd come out the loser in a boxing match. Which I had.

Staring at the mirror, I reflected on the conversations I'd finally faced last night. Elín had been admirably philosophical about Fraser getting away and was more concerned about my well-being once she knew the bluish-green colouring on my nose and upper cheeks had come from her attacker. Jazzy took her news in silence.

For someone who usually machine-gunned questions about everything, her stoic response left me scrambling to understand what was going on inside her mind. Was she upset at the idea of a proper foster family, or was she hiding her excitement for my sake?

This was the shit that happened when I let myself get close to people, and an anger welled inside. I'd sworn I wouldn't let this happen again, and yet here I was with my guts churning and my head hurting, about to lose someone who meant everything to me. I tiptoed to the kitchen, filled my travel mug with coffee, and crept quietly outside as the thin glow of dawn chased the stars away.

Once clear of waking the others, I stomped through the woods, swearing under my breath, as the guilt of my self-centred thoughts made me feel even worse. All that mattered was whatever gave Jazzy the best chance in life. She shouldn't have to worry about my feelings. I stopped and stood still in the near darkness, surrounded by casuarina and sea grape trees, trying to decide whether to go back and wake Jazzy or let the kid sleep.

"*Fy faen,*" I groaned, and pressed on towards my Jeep.

Waking her at six in the morning to tell her it was okay to leave wouldn't resolve anything, but would guarantee her day started as badly as mine was going. Letting the CJ-7 warm-up for a few minutes, I contemplated where to go first. It was still too early to pick up O'Neill, so I decided to drop by West Bay station and use the computer there for a while. I could see if anything new had been added to either case file and do my own research into Jonas Richards.

Driving through West Bay, I came to Reverend Blackman Road and indicated left to go the last few hundred metres to the station. When I came to a stop at the intersection, I changed my mind and turned right, then left on Town Hall Road. I needed something positive to lift this funk off my shoulders, and seeing AJ usually helped cheer me up. She would be preparing her dive boat for the morning trip, so I turned right onto North West Point Road then immediately into the little car park by the water.

Reg was leaning against the door jamb to the tiny hut which doubled as their office, storeroom, and loo.

"You're up early," he said, as I hopped from the Jeep and walked towards the dock.

"We're all working overtime," I replied, which was true, but not the reason I was up this early.

"Getting anywhere on that arson case?" he asked.

"Maybe," I said, and again I wasn't lying. "We have a suspect but no real evidence."

Reg nodded and grunted. He was one person who understood my preference for economy with words. He usually chose what he said carefully and was worth listening to if he had an opinion to share.

"She's on her boat, grumpy as ever," Reg said with a grin.

I continued down the wood planks of the pier towards AJ's dive boat, *Hazel's Odyssey*, moored opposite two of Reg's boats. The crews, busy setting up gear for customers, all said hi or waved to me.

"Hey," I said, stepping onto the deck.

"What's up, Miss Nora?" Thomas greeted me with a big smile.

He was contagiously happy under almost any circumstances, and polar opposite of AJ Bailey until the sun was well above the horizon. She detested early mornings although my friend was still the cheeriest grump I'd ever met. AJ was a naturally warm and joyous person, so even her grouchy start to most days had an underlying humour.

"Are you working today?" AJ asked, appearing from the bow cabin with arms full of dive gear.

"*Ja*. All weekend I expect."

"Do you think this arsonist bloke is still on the island?" she asked, placing pieces of gear in front of dive tanks held in racks mounted behind the benches lining the aft deck.

"If it's the suspect we're looking into, then *ja*, he's still here."

AJ stopped what she was doing and looked at me. "Blimey. I

assumed someone doing something as awful as that wasn't from the island. You think it was a resident?"

"*Nei*, but we think they're still here."

"Why would a murderer stick around?" she asked. "I'd have thought they'd be on the first plane out. I think I'd be in Timbuktu by now, as far away from the scene of the crime, right?"

She made a good point, and one I didn't have an answer to. Maybe the murderer *had* left already. My dull, sleep-deprived mind wandered as I considered whether we should check the departures for the past few days, until Thomas called us over from the stern.

"I thought dat were a buoy half underwater over dere," he said, pointing in the direction of the overnight moorings. "But someting ain't right."

AJ and I both stared in the early morning light across the water, scanning the empty mooring buoys. He was right. One of them looked more like a big coconut peeking above the surface instead of a colourful plastic ball.

"What the heck is that?" AJ muttered.

The more I looked, the more a creepy feeling gripped my chest. "Thomas, can you see if there's a kayak I can borrow?" I asked, and sat down on one of the benches, removing my shoes and socks.

"We can take the boat out there, Nora," AJ offered.

"That's okay," I replied. "It's probably nothing."

But I had a bad feeling it wasn't nothing. Thomas carried one of the kayaks they used to paddle out to their boats in the morning down the pier and lowered it over the side behind the swim step of *Hazel's Odyssey*. I carefully eased myself into the moulded seat and felt the warm Caribbean water soak my trousers and underwear. He handed me the paddle and I shoved away from the boat.

"Shout if you need help," AJ said as I paddled away.

It only took a few minutes to cover the hundred metres to where the boats spent each night in six to eight feet of water. Tying them to the moorings saved the vessels from thumping against the pier if the waves picked up, which was hard on both the boats and the dock.

Each mooring had to be approved by the Department of Environment. The older ones tended to be something heavy like an engine block or concrete-filled barrel buried as deep as they could get it in the sand. Newer ones were more likely to be hefty stainless-steel eyelets screwed into the bedrock. A length of rope, longer than the depth of the highest tide, ran from the anchor in the seabed to the surface, floated by a buoy. A second length of line with a loop in the end connected just below the buoy, allowed the crews to tie in.

As I approached, my fears were quickly realised. Poking a few centimetres above the water was not a buoy, nor a coconut, but the top of a human being's head. Careful not to run into the body, I stopped a metre short and could see the body through the crystal-clear water. A male, but I couldn't tell much more.

I'd left my mobile on the boat so I didn't get it wet, but now I needed to make a call — 9-1-1 was the obvious, but as a police constable was already at the scene, I considered skipping that step. Whittaker would be the one to assign the case to another detective or take the lead himself. Unless this guy had managed to wrap himself in the mooring line, fully clothed, this was going to be another murder, which Whittaker always handled. Of course, we usually only had three or four murders a year on the island, which with a population of 75,000 plus tens of thousands more in visitors at any given time, was incredibly low. Two in a week was unheard of.

I waved to AJ and watched her scramble up the ladder to the fly-bridge. Thomas cast the lines clear, and within a minute, the 36-foot Newton was idling my way.

"Don't come too close," I shouted as *Hazel's Odyssey* neared. "If you can, drop anchor and drift back so the swim step is about six feet away."

"Bugger me!" AJ yelled down. "Is that a body?"

"*Ja*, now get the boat set up. I need to call Whittaker."

I watched her expertly manoeuvre the boat using the twin engines to steer into position. She looked at the other boats lightly tugging on their lines to judge which way she needed to orientate the Newton and waved to Thomas at the bow when she wanted the anchor released. It took a long minute for the boat to take up the slack and Thomas played out line until AJ signalled once more, then he tied the line to a cleat. The swim step bobbed nearby and I paddled over, scooting my arse out of the kayak which Thomas then pulled around the starboard side and secured.

"Here," AJ said, handing me her mobile. She knew Detective Whittaker well so it didn't surprise me she had his number handy.

"Sir?" I asked, putting the phone to my ear.

"What's going on, Nora? AJ said you have a body?"

"*Ja.* You'd better get down here. This wasn't an accident."

"I was just leaving the house," he replied. "It'll take me fifteen minutes. Have you called for back-up?"

"*Nei.* But I can call Sergeant Redburn and have him send a car. We don't need half the station showing up, sir."

"I'll make the calls while I'm driving," Whittaker said, and I heard his car door closing. "Any idea who the victim is?"

I hesitated and looked into the water where the top of the man's head was gently swaying with the ebb current.

"*Ja,* but I need to get in the water to be certain."

"I'll be there as quickly as I can," he responded and hung up.

Thomas was staring at the body with a horrified look on his face and AJ nudged my arm.

"Here, I'm guessing you need to get wet?" she said, handing me a Mermaid Divers rash guard she'd pulled from the cabin.

I unbuttoned my white police uniform shirt and Thomas almost fell off the swim step. He muttered a few apologies and looked the other way.

"You could change in the cabin, Nora!" AJ said.

I undid my bra, tossed it to the bench, and slipped into the rash guard.

"They're breasts," I said impatiently. "All women have them and most have much better ones than mine."

I dropped my uniform trousers.

"I can find you a bathing suit if you give me a minute," AJ sputtered, and Thomas crossed himself, although he couldn't see me at all.

I grabbed the nearest dive mask and dropped into the water. Surfacing, I slid the mask on, making sure my long hair was held by the strap. If I'd thought the morning had got off to a shitty start, it had hit high gear now. So much for nipping by and having AJ improve my mood.

After taking a few deep breaths, I ducked under the water and confirmed my suspicion from what I'd seen from above. I was looking straight into the lifeless eyes of Jason Fraser.

29

PLAYING GRAB-ARSE WITH A CORPSE

Within fifteen minutes, the shoreline became a lot busier, and to make matters worse, the tide was going out. Millimetre by millimetre, more of Fraser's head was slowly being revealed, floated by the mooring buoy tied around his chest. Crew from several of the dive ops who used West Bay Public Dock to load their customers swam or paddled out to bring their boats to shore. They were all curious and everyone knew AJ so they shouted questions and wanted to know what the fuss was about. Once they neared, there was no hiding the fact it was a body in the water, but I waved them clear.

I'd decided to leave the corpse in the water, not wanting to disturb the scene before Whittaker arrived, and subsequently Rasha, who he'd undoubtedly called. Besides, moving him now wouldn't make him less dead, but I did have AJ splash the water with her feet to try and keep the nibbling fish away.

"So, this is the bloke who was on the news?" AJ asked, when I returned from putting on a pair of colourful Mermaid Divers Lycra shorts she'd given me.

I figured I shouldn't be in my knickers when the boss arrived.

"Yeah. We're pretty certain he's been giving date rape drugs to tourists. One of his victims has been staying at my place. She was too scared to go back to her hotel."

AJ was happy to relinquish the role of water splasher and move away from the body. I sat down and took over.

"Karma took care of him pretty sharpish, yeah?" she commented.

I nodded. "*Ja.* Wouldn't it be great if karma would do that every time? I'd be happy to be put out of business."

"Do you think one of his victims drowned him?" AJ asked, sitting back down next to me, crossing her legs like a school kid.

"It wasn't Elín," I assured her. "She was with me all night. The only other victim we know about is back in the UK."

"Maybe there was another one who didn't come forward," AJ suggested, then I felt her lean in closer. "You didn't… you know… did you?" she whispered.

My best and only true friend knew more about me, what I'd been through, and what I was capable of doing, than anyone else. I'd taken the law into my own hands at times and crossed more than a few lines. If Detective Whittaker knew these truths, he'd be forced to not only kick me off the force, but arrest me. I was fortunate he chose to believe the best in me.

"*Nei.* But I'd probably shake the hand of the person who did."

AJ nudged me with her elbow. "Don't say that. Not out loud anyway."

I glanced over my shoulder across the bright blue water and saw one of the smaller Joint Marine Unit rigid-inflatable boats approaching.

"Are you sure this idiot didn't just fall overboard and get tangled in the mooring line?" AJ asked optimistically.

"I'm sure," I replied. "Tide's going out, right?"

"Yup, high tide was four or five I think, so low tide will be late morning."

"Making low tide last night about ten or eleven?"

"That should be about right," AJ agreed.

"So, my guess is he was tied to the mooring sometime between eight and midnight," I explained. "More likely the later time when no one was around."

AJ fidgeted and grabbed my arm. "Are you saying someone tied this bloke to the mooring pin with his head above water, then let him slowly drown as the tide came in?"

"*Ja*, that's exactly what I think happened."

"Bloody hell, there's some messed up people in this world," she muttered.

"You're right, and you're looking at one of them," I said, pointing to the top of Fraser's head.

"Yeah, but two wrongs and all that, Nora," AJ said.

I stood as the police boat neared. I was more than happy with the outcome for Jason Fraser, but I had a dark and troubled soul, and AJ had a beautiful one. Debating the justice of his execution was pointless, but what troubled me now was who killed him.

Whittaker stepped from the wheelhouse of the RIB and looked at the body in the water. I recognised Ben Crooks at the helm, keeping the Joint Marine Unit boat steady a few metres from us.

"If you want to pull anchor, AJ, we'll take your position," Whittaker called over. "I'm sure you have customers waiting."

"Thanks, Roy," AJ shouted back and she and Thomas went to work, weighing anchor.

"It's Jason Fraser, sir," I said, keeping my voice just loud enough for Whittaker to hear me, knowing the sound would carry across the open water.

"Really?" he said, shaking his head.

I hopped boats, then once AJ was clear, it didn't take long for Ben and his crew to follow the same process she had and anchor with their stern near the scene. I ran through the details with Whittaker, letting him know my theory about the killer's method.

"Nobody heard him scream for help?" he responded. "If what you're saying is true, his mouth would have been above water for some time."

"Unless the killer set the depth to cover his mouth and leave his nose exposed," I offered. "It could still take thirty minutes to an hour for the water to rise over his nose if the ocean was really calm."

Whittaker rubbed the back of his neck. "Putting ourselves in the mind of a killer is a very disturbing part of this job."

Most of the time I found it fascinating and challenging, but I didn't share that thought.

"AJ brought up a good point, sir. Perhaps there's a victim we don't know about who took matters into their own hands."

The detective looked at me sceptically. "I'm not saying there aren't any other victims, but as with the arson murder, this doesn't seem like the work of a female."

"I agree," I replied. "But it might be the work of a victim's lover or father."

Whittaker's expression shifted to a frown and he nodded. "That I could believe."

We both heard a motor getting louder and looked towards the public dock. A small skiff was on its way out with Rasha onboard.

"Does this answer your theory about the two cases being connected?" Whittaker asked, turning back to me. "You suggested Fraser could also be the arsonist, right?"

"*Nei, og ja,*" I replied. "If Fraser committed both crimes he could have twice as many enemies, so we're no closer to knowing that part. And yes, I brought up the possibility, but if that's the case, instead of one murderer, we now have two. Although this one is finished, so I guess we're back to looking for one."

Whittaker thought for a moment as the skiff slowed to tie alongside. "*If* Fraser was indeed the date rape drug attacker," he pointed out. "We're yet to find any damning evidence to support our thin vehicle match. We can't be sure this is our man."

"Someone thought he was," I said, looking down at the body in the water.

The fish were now gathering again since I'd stopped running interference.

"We didn't give the press any information about the crime, only that Fraser was wanted in connection with an incident," Whittaker replied. "I don't think we tipped off a vigilante."

"What in the world is going on this week?" Rasha said as she carefully stepped from the skiff to the RIB with a helping hand from Whittaker.

"I'm not sure, but I'm ready for it to stop," the detective replied.

Rasha peered over the stern around the side of the four powerful outboards. AJ's dive boat had been a far better platform for this operation, and Rasha looked around, wondering how she could access the body without getting wet.

She looked at me wearing a rash guard and dive shorts. "How about you jump in and I'll direct you?"

I wasn't particularly eager to be handling another dead body, but it made sense as I'd already been in there. Rasha handed me a GoPro camera.

"Here, start by filming the scene," she instructed. "Swim slowly 360 degrees around the body a few times at different depths, please. Then film the rope and how it's tied to the anchorage and to the body. We'll need to ascertain whether the body should be untied or the line cut free."

I wished I'd borrowed a set of dive gear from AJ's boat, but at least I'd kept the mask, and I freedived a lot, so I'd be able to get the film she needed on breath-hold. I stepped over the big rubber gunwales and slid into the warm water, pulling myself around to the stern.

"Film the sea floor all around the mooring. Oh, and carefully check his pockets, please," Rasha added. "The GoPro is set on video and ready to go; just press the top button to record."

Putting the mask in place, I nodded and quickly ducked under before she came up with a longer laundry list of things to do.

Jason Fraser's appearance had not improved since the last time I'd seen his corpse up close. The fish had begun picking at his lips and eyes, with small nicks from both. I forced my gaze away from the ghoulish vision of his face and pressed the record button on the little camera. Starting by his feet, tethered just above a sturdy chain looped through the rusty engine block and shackled, I began making spiralling laps around the body.

The knots tied in the mooring line were expertly made. From the chain, the line ran to Fraser's ankles where it bound them before returning through the chain where a knot had been used to perfectly set the depth. The remaining line had several wraps around his torso, securing his arms to his sides, leaving the buoy under his chin, keeping the body afloat and his nose clear of the surface… until it wasn't.

I surfaced for another breath, then swam down, filmed all around the sea floor and the small growths of coral attached to the top of the metal. Not seeing anything of interest, I moved up to the man's trouser pockets and hesitated a moment. The thought of diving a hand into the fabric and potentially touching body parts I wouldn't have wanted to have anything to do with when he'd been alive gave me the chills. Gliding to the surface, I bought some time taking a few deep breaths.

"No other signs of trauma I assume?" Rasha asked, standing next to Whittaker with their faces leant over the outboards.

"*Nei*," I said, then drew in a long breath and ducked under.

Holding the camera in my right hand, I filmed my other hand foraging in the dead man's trouser pocket. Nothing in his left pocket. I repeated the process for his right pocket, my hand flinching as it found what I assumed was a wallet. Carefully pulling it free in front of the camera, I rose to the surface and kicked to the side of the police boat. Ben leaned over and took the wallet from me, handing it to Rasha.

Swimming back to the stern, I heard her voice above me. "Driver's licence is Jason Melvin Fraser."

The victim was wearing a dark-coloured, lightweight hooded T-shirt which had kangaroo pockets, so I slipped below and repeated the procedure of filming and searching. They were empty. I was about to surface when I realised I hadn't checked the back pockets of the trousers. The idea of playing grab-arse with a corpse made me shiver all over again. But I sunk my hand in the snug pocket and my fingers touched something metallic. Still filming, I pulled out a key.

After checking the other back pocket and finding nothing, I happily surfaced and scaled the ladder Ben had dropped over the starboard side for me to clamber back aboard. Holding the key by either end, I showed it to Rasha and Whittaker. The brand name 'Master' was engraved on one side of the head, and on the other side, someone had scratched '115 THR'.

"The etching looks fresh," Whittaker remarked. "The salt water wouldn't do that, would it?"

Rasha shook her head. "No, the inscription is new. What could it mean?"

"It's an address," I said, looking towards the shoreline. If I hadn't just driven the street an hour or so earlier, I doubt I ever would've guessed it. "Town Hall Road."

"Huh," Whittaker grunted. "You might be right."

His mobile rang in his pocket and he glanced at the caller ID. "Were you picking O'Neill up this morning?" he asked me.

"Oh shit. What time is it?"

"8:15," he replied, and answered the call.

30

JUSTICE FOR ALL

Realising my uniform, Jeep keys, and mobile were all about to leave on AJ's morning dive trip, I persuaded Whittaker to let me be the one to go in search of the address on the key. If my guess was even right. It could be code for anything. The man in the skiff ran me to the dock where AJ and Thomas were just leaving.

"Your stuff is in the hut," she yelled from the fly-bridge.

I should have known AJ would have taken care of me. At the hut, I ran into Reg who was gathering his dive gear together.

"You've got a lot of cheek showing your face in 'ere," he groaned.

I accidentally smiled, and he shook his head. Whittaker had only agreed to me searching for the address as Reg was available to help pull the body out. The detective's reasoning was they needed someone in scuba gear for safety reasons. Whittaker had omitted the part about me leaving until the end of the phone call.

I squeezed past him and saw my uniform sitting on a stack of merchandise boxes. I peeled off the rash guard which was already dry and began putting my bra on.

"Oi! Could have given me some warning before you start stripping," Reg grumbled in his deep voice.

"Just look the other way," I replied, buttoning my shirt, which hung low enough that I could drop the Lycra shorts without flashing too much.

"Bloody Scandinavians," he muttered, now outside the hut, holding the door closed.

"*Takk*, Reg," I said with another smile as I walked out, tying my hair into a ponytail. "Better get that body out — the fish were starting to pick him apart."

"Sod you," he snapped back, but I could tell he was trying not to laugh. "Just remember you owe me for this."

I spun around and walked backwards up the hill. "I just paid you back. Not my fault if you didn't bother to look."

Reg spluttered a mouthful of expletives and insults, mixed with laughter. I wished his wife, Pearl, had been here, as she would have enjoyed seeing her husband flustered and lost for words. It didn't happen often.

While the Jeep warmed up, I punched the address into the map function on my mobile. It couldn't find 115. Some of the island's street numbers were a little haphazard, but if I drove the road, I figured I could narrow it down. A police patrol car turned into the car park, and I saw Officer Lisa O'Neill sitting bolt upright in the passenger seat with her satchel-like purse thing on her lap. She thanked the constable for the taxi ride and walked over to the Jeep.

"Good morning, ma'am," I said, determined to restart my day in the hope it would improve.

"I'm told you have a decent excuse for leaving me standing in the lobby of the hotel," O'Neill said, swinging herself into the Jeep with what was now practised ease.

"I think we have the *drittsekk* who drugged Elín," I replied, reversing out of the spot to leave.

"To be fair, it sounds like someone handed you the bloke, but if it is the right fella, she won't have to worry about him anymore."

I handed O'Neill the evidence bag with the key in it. "We're looking for the lock this opens."

She took the bag and looked at me instead of the evidence in her hand. "We starting at one end of the island and working our way across until we find a door that opens, pet?"

"*Ja*," I replied. "Island's not that big."

We both chuckled.

"115 T-H-R is scratched on the key. I think it means Town Hall Road, which is the street we're about to turn on. Jason Fraser was seen in this area yesterday, and he was executed in the nearest stretch of water."

O'Neill looked at the key through the clear plastic bag. "Are there storage units around here?"

I turned right on North West Point Road, then left at the stop sign onto Town Hall. An older single-storey apartment building was the first thing on the right, and I pulled in.

"Where are the house numbers?" O'Neill asked.

"Most places don't bother," I explained. "There's no postal delivery on the island, and you pick up residential shipping from the carrier's office. The locals all figure their family already knows where they live so why put a number on their front gate."

My map wasn't recognising any of the homes along the street until a newer condo building farther up near where it ended at a T-junction. It was number 336. Behind us, around the curve which then followed the waterfront, a guest house called Calypso Cove was number 80. That gave us less than a kilometre of road to search. If the numbering followed the logic used by most systems, the location would be on the opposite side to the two reference places, as it was an odd number.

I hopped from the Jeep and knocked on the first apartment door, marked by a faded chrome 'A' screwed to the front. After a few moments and excited shouting from kids inside, the door opened. A young boy pushed his way past his mother's legs and stared up at me.

"It's da police," he announced.

"I can see dat for myself, DeShaun, now stop pushing me," the young woman said before looking at me. "Are you here wit bad news?"

"Probably not," I replied, hoping this wasn't number 115. "What's the address of this building, ma'am?"

"100 Town Hall Road!" DeShaun informed me.

"Thanks," I said and turned to leave.

"Dat's it?" the mother asked, sounding surprised.

"*Ja*," I confirmed and got back in the Jeep.

The mother tried closing her front door, but her boy was far too curious to let her do it, wedging himself in the way. I pulled away to give the lady some peace.

"100," I told O'Neill, and drove to the next building, which was a house on the right, just past a side street.

A dog came running across the front garden and rattled the fence beside where I'd pulled over, barking loudly. It was what we called a Cayman brown hound, one of the mutts evolved from a handful of breeds melding together over the years. Part pit bull, part German shepherd, and part a dozen other breeds. Labrador being another major contributor, which probably accounted for the tail wagging.

I stood up and looked towards the house. An older dark-skinned man stared back at me with a paint can and brush in his hand.

"What's your address here, sir?" I shouted.

The man cocked his head to one side and touched a hand to his ear, letting me know he couldn't hear me. No shit he couldn't hear me. His dog was going to hyperventilate or give itself a heart attack if it didn't ease up on the barking. Its tail was wagging frantically, but I wasn't about to rush through the gate. The man whistled and the dog immediately stopped barking and ran to his side, where the old fellow rested a hand on his dog's head.

"What's your address, sir?" I asked.

"45 Jefferson Road," he called back.

I looked at the sign for the side street, figuring his address had to be that, but the cul-de-sac was Farrington Lane.

"This isn't your home, is it, sir?" I asked as the thought hit me.

"No ma'am. Dis is my mudda's house."

"What's your mother's street address please, sir?"

"120 Town Hall," he said, and waved a hand at me as he made his way back to whatever he planned to paint.

I jumped from the Jeep and looked across the street. Thick shrubs and low trees filled the area between two homes a few hundred metres apart in each direction. A break in the old waist-high chain-link fence opened to a sandy dirt trail curving into the woods. Both sides of the narrow lane were heavily overgrown, but two tracks were clear from a vehicle going in and out with some regularity.

"I should have brought me trainers for this malarkey," O'Neill said from the passenger seat. "Bit creepy looking, isn't it?"

"We can drive in," I suggested.

"Aye. This contraption has a reverse gear if we need it."

I got back in, turned hard left and started down the trail, branches and leaves scraping down the side of the Jeep. I drove slowly, easing around the curve until I saw a building ahead.

"Yer best stop here, pet," O'Neill said, so I braked, put the Jeep in neutral, and set the foot brake.

"I don't think there's anyone here, ma'am. I took the key from the pocket of a corpse."

O'Neill turned and looked at me. "Do you know what's in there?"

"*Nei,*" I admitted.

"But you're assuming it's safe?" she asked.

"*Ja.*"

"What if you're wrong?" she pointed out.

I didn't have a sensible answer to the point she was making, so there wasn't much I could say without sounding like an idiot. The truth was I didn't place much value on my own life as I'd spent too long not caring whether I lived or died. But things were different now. What would happen to Jazzy if I walked into a bullet? By the end of today, that question might be answered if she liked the family she'd be visiting, but as of this moment, I was still responsible for the kid. The feeling was equal parts beautiful and terrifying.

"I'll check the perimeter first," I conceded, turning off the Jeep, grabbing a pair of nitrile gloves from the dashboard cubby, and jumping out.

The building looked like an old concrete block garage or storage unit of some sort, except it didn't have a big swing or roll-up door. The steel roof was rusty but intact, and a metal entry door with peeling, faded red paint appeared to be the only way in. I noticed it was secured by a padlock. I moved around the left side of the building, where the brush had been cleared underneath overhanging tree branches.

There sat a car, covered by an old green tarp which was tied to the wheels. I pulled the dirty cover away from the front bumper and revealed the beige Kia. Moving on, the brush and shrubs became thicker as I turned around the back of the structure. A small, grubby but functioning air conditioner hummed from its opening in the block work, supported by metal stays. Pushing branches aside, and trying not to think about all the bugs getting caught in my damp hair, I stepped over fallen debris and discarded crap to complete a lap, finding no other entrance, window, or signs of human life.

When I shoved my way free of the brush and dusted myself off by the front of the building, I stared at the open metal door.

"I'm beginning to have trust issues with you, ma'am," I said, stepping into the building behind O'Neill who'd found a light switch.

"I didn't say you were wrong, I just asked *what if you were*, pet," she replied as we both looked around at the almost immaculate interior. "Better safe than sorry."

The rough unkept exterior belied the clean, tidy, well-maintained photographic studio hidden inside. Multiple lights on stands surrounded a twin bed, draped in a thick duvet, and a small desk sat to the left of the door. The only thing obviously out of place was a camera tripod knocked over in the middle of the room.

I slipped on the nitrile gloves and moved to the desk. Fallen to the floor was a receipt, which I knelt down and studied. It was from The Fox and Hare pub, which was not far from here. I guessed that weird thermal paper would be good for fingerprints and carefully avoided touching or moving the receipt, leaving it for the Scene of Crime unit.

On the desk, a laptop computer was open and powered up, but displayed the password login screen when I moved the mouse.

"I think they can stop looking for anything on the laptop we took from Fraser's house," I said, looking at the photography lights pointed towards the bed. "This one will have..." I stopped talking. I didn't want to imagine what pictures Fraser had taken of the girls in this room.

"Elín wasn't raped, so who knows how he was posing the girls, pet," O'Neill said. "Might not have been sexual at all."

I gave her a look of disbelief.

"I know, unlikely, but let's wait and see what's on there."

I went back to studying the desk. It had a single file drawer on one side, which I opened. Inside were neatly coiled and tied cables and wires, but when I lifted them out, I found several bottles of pills.

O'Neill walked over and looked down at the drawer. "Rohypnol?"

I picked up one of the unmarked pill bottles and unscrewed the top, tipping a round white pill out into my hand. One side had a single groove across the face, and flipping it over the other side had R-O-C-H-E in a semicircle and the number one inside a circle just below it.

"*Ja*," I confirmed, recognising the markings from the research I'd done.

"What was your lass wearing when she went missing?" O'Neill asked, using her foot to nudge a wicker basket sitting on the floor next to the bed.

"A light-coloured summer dress. I think she told me it was yellow."

O'Neill pointed in the basket. "Doubt she'll want it back now, but I'd say that's it."

I joined her and we both stared at a pile of clothes in the basket. Elín's dress was on top of a mixture of women's blouses, leggings, underwear, and other dresses.

"I think we know where the T-shirt came from," I said. "The one they found her in."

"He's either been shopping in the women's department of the thrift shop, or you're looking for a lot more victims, pet," O'Neill said, shaking her head. "But, if Fraser's fingerprints are all over this place," she added, stepping back and surveying the little room. "Then you've closed the first half of this case."

"Like you said earlier, whoever murdered Fraser and scratched this address on the key solved the case," I pointed out. "He probably grabbed Fraser from here last night, judging by the tripod tipped over. He marked the key, knowing we'd find it on the body. Now we're supposed to track down the killer and bring him to justice despite him doing the world a favour and executing this *drittsekk*."

O'Neill looked at me and nodded. "Aye, pet. Justice for all. Even shitheads like Fraser."

31

LEWIS BLOODY HAMILTON

The dried salt water on my skin was itchy and my hair was matted in tangles, but there was no time for a shower. As always, and especially with two crucial crime scenes in the same morning, it took forever to get the garage secured and Rasha's people on site. First priority was the computer, and second, processing finger-prints. By tonight, I was hoping to be able to tell Elín exactly what had happened during her missing hours. There would be pictures of her, that much was obvious, but whether they'd been posted online and the exact nature of the shots were still to be determined.

I drove us to West Bay station where I switched to the same police SUV we'd used before. Jacob wasn't on duty today, so Whittaker said he was happy with O'Neill partnering with me — or me chauffeuring her, depending on your perspective.

Our priority now was putting pressure on Jonas Richards. We might not have a warrant, but that didn't stop us questioning him again, so I drove us to the Grand Caymanian on North Sound. O'Neill was keen to meet Richards in person as we'd interviewed the prick just before she'd arrived.

As I rode over the endless series of sleeping policemen along

Safehaven Drive, I handed my mobile for O'Neill to read an email I'd been sent earlier in the morning.

"Louise Middleton goes back and forth to Miami every few weeks," she relayed, waiting until I cleared the next bump before continuing. "Looks like she was there the day of the murder, but only just."

"Only just?" I questioned, thinking she was either in Miami or not.

"Flew in that morning, so the timing would be tight," O'Neill clarified.

"What about Winskell?"

"He was in America, but not in Florida. Looks like he stayed in North Carolina for two months before coming here. Flew out of Charlotte with a connection in Miami. Whoever did this search for us went back six months and found flights for them all. Winskell has been jet-setting around since he got out of prison. He came to Miami almost a year ago for a few weeks. Australia for a month at the end of last year."

I turned right into the hotel entrance, then wound around their curving driveway which doubled back on the road we'd just been on.

"Where's he getting the money?" I asked. "I didn't think prison paid that well."

"Navy pension?" O'Neill suggested. "I think he did twenty years, so that would earn him a pension. Hard to spend that money behind bars."

I found an empty spot outside the hotel and parked the SUV. "What about the Loudermilks? Is their travel in there too?"

"Aye. The husband flies to the States most months, varies which city. Looks like Rhea tags along when he stays in Miami."

"Six weeks ago?" I asked.

"They flew to Orlando and stayed there for three days."

"Not hard to drive from Orlando to Miami," I pointed out, as I switched off the SUV and opened the door.

"I was hoping the flights would narrow down our suspects,"

O'Neill complained as we walked into the lobby. "Technically, we haven't eliminated anyone yet."

I continued past the front desk, skipping the room number request the receptionist would be obliged to refuse, and walked towards the restaurant building.

"Odds favour the killer being male, younger, and previous history of violence, right?" I said as we entered the front and looked out the all-glass rear facing the pool area.

"They do," O'Neill agreed.

"Then this *drittsekk* is our best bet," I responded, scanning the deck chairs for Richards.

"I don't see him," I said, and continued through the restaurant and out the back door, once again causing turned heads and excitement amongst the kids. "That's his room," I added, pointing to the shaded patio on the ground floor.

As we walked around the end of the curved pool, I caught movement inside the room and broke into a jog. By the time I reached the sliding door, I could see through the suite to where the front door was closing. I tried the slider, which of course was locked.

"He's running," I shouted as I sprinted past O'Neill who was just arriving.

Dodging holidaymakers in bathing suits, I ran around the paths of the neatly landscaped area between the restaurant and the reception. The automatic sliding door didn't open fast enough, and I ran into the glass, making the whole thing shudder, and for a moment I thought it might shatter. Shoving the doors apart, I slipped through and ran across the lobby, timing the main entrance doors a little better, stopping in time, then racing through the gap that opened.

Outside, the bright sun reflected off of every car and I squinted, looking for movement. I hoped to see Richards running, but instead a car screeched its tyres backing out of a spot, then shot away down the far row. I swung around and was surprised to see O'Neill running across the lobby. I'd been about to leave her behind, but she was on my heels as I ran to the SUV.

We were only thirty seconds behind Richards, but if he was driving like a maniac, that put him well ahead of us, and if he took the shorter route, he'd already be halfway to Esterly Tibbetts Highway. O'Neill swore under her breath as I took off in reverse while she was still trying to close the passenger door. When I braked and slammed the vehicle into drive, the door snapped shut and she moved on to fighting the seatbelt as I sped away, scattering a handful of tourists who abandoned their suitcases.

"Call it in," I ordered, and cut across the grass and scrub avoiding the winding driveway.

O'Neill finally secured her seatbelt and reached for the radio mic. "I don't know where the bloody hell we are or any of your call codes," she spluttered as the SUV bounced through a rut and back onto tarmac.

She held the mic my way and pressed the button. "Bravo Three in pursuit of suspect in a white hire car rented and driven by Jonas Richards. Leaving Crystal Harbour towards Esterly Tibbetts. Send cars to both exits. Over."

O'Neill released the button and I studied the road ahead. I had two choices. Turn left along the south side of the golf course, which was the way we'd come in, or go past and drive off-road through the hedge, dodging the security gate in front of us.

"Nora!" O'Neill groaned from the passenger seat.

"Hold on," I muttered back and brushed the brakes before swerving onto the grass.

Fortunately, there was no kerb to jump, so the transition onto the dirt wasn't too bad, but the ruts and holes once we were off the road were a lot bigger than they looked. The SUV compressed the front springs before lurching off the backside of a large gulley as we crashed through a footpath-sized gap in the hedge. I fought to keep control with pieces of shrub flying through the air and water splashing from puddles. Easing the SUV right, we made it back to the road and I accelerated hard towards the next left. My guess had been correct, and as we'd come back on the road I'd noticed wet tyre marks preceding us, which had to be Richards.

"I'm never getting in a bloody vehicle with you again!" O'Neill squealed as I braked hard and swung the big SUV left, facing the other security gate.

I ran wide, into the right-hand lane, where a yellow barrier blocked the road, which was lined with a kerb. I slowed a little more before slamming the right wheels over the concrete step, praying it wouldn't peel the tyres off the rims. Once the rights were on the pavement, I turned hard right and jumped the whole vehicle onto the pavement, smashing the left-side mirror off on the tip of the barrier. O'Neill reeled back as the mirror slammed against her window then flailed in the air like a wounded bird.

I veered back onto the road and moved over to the left lane, just as the radio blasted to life. "Bravo Three, this is Control. We have two cars en route. ETA four minutes. Over."

"*Fy faen,*" I moaned under my breath. "We have to catch him. They'll be too late."

"We'll be bloody dead so it won't matter much," O'Neill mumbled, hanging onto her door handle as the tyres squealed their complaints in the next right-hand turn.

I already had the lights going but now flicked the siren on as the next few curves were blind around trees lining the north side of the golf course. The one thing we now had on our side was the fact that Pinehurst, the lane we were now on, met the dual carriageway with only the option of turning left. There was no gap in the centre divider.

"Radio, ma'am," I ordered, and O'Neill snatched up the mic.

"Don't worry about ma'aming me, pet, just stay on the bloody road."

"Central, this is Bravo Three. He has to turn left on Esterly Tibbetts. Redirect intercept to the roundabout north of Camana Bay. Over."

We were doing 60 miles per hour as I exited the final curve onto a straight run to the highway. The white hire car was nowhere in sight. I thought I had to be catching him, but maybe his lead was too much. I hit 80 before jumping on the brakes as we approached the T-junction. The SUV skidded on loose, dusty gravel kicked over the road from a small car park as I looked for oncoming traffic from the right. The road looked clear, so I was about to release the brake and shoot out onto Esterly Tibbetts heading south, when I spotted a white car in the roundabout to the north.

Swinging the wheel the opposite way, the SUV lurched into a slide, and I heard O'Neill thud against the passenger door, letting out a sound halfway between a yelp and a deep moan. Steering into the skid, I squeezed the throttle but all that happened was a weird vibration and juddering through the whole vehicle.

"Find the traction control button and turn the fucking thing off!" I shouted, impatiently waiting for the SUV to settle enough for the computer to decide it was okay to proceed.

"The hell I will, pet," O'Neill snapped back. "Last thing I need is you unrestrained by modern science."

"*Faen!*"

I searched the dash for a button while accelerating down the wrong side of the dual carriageway. Fortunately, I had the advantage of the other cars being pre-freaked-out by Richards flying at them the wrong way. With sirens blaring, they all stayed to the sides.

"All right, all right!" O'Neill barked. "I'll find the bloody button if you'll watch where you're going."

I'd been busy trying my best not to crash when I'd spotted the white car in the roundabout, and now I wasn't sure which way he'd gone. Braking hard, I turned sharply left to join the correct flow for the roundabout and made a tyre-squealing lap. Squeezing into the throttle the skid control kicked in again and the SUV shuddered and vibrated instead of accelerating.

"You didn't take it off!" I bitched at my superior officer.

"It's kinda hard when I'm pinned against the bloody door!"

I risked a glance to the passenger side where O'Neill was indeed wedged against her door with a hand flailing towards the dashboard, unable to reach anything. Her satchel thing was in the footwell with its contents scattered around O'Neill's feet.

Traffic was beginning to flow again, and as Richards had probably left the roundabout in the correct lane, no cars were pulled aside down any of the other three exits. I smacked the steering wheel with my fist and slowed, silencing the tyre noise. I snatched up the radio mic and called in my position and the three possible directions Richards could have gone.

I exited on Lime Tree Avenue to the east which was a cul-de-sac ending at Governor's Creek. On both sides were condo complexes with car parks and we spent the next few minutes driving around, searching for the white hire car. There were several, but none were the make or registration plate of the one Jonas Richards had rented. Finally, I pulled to a stop by the side of the short road.

"Are you okay, ma'am," I asked as O'Neill gathered up her stuff and repacked her bag.

"Who do you think you are, pet, Lewis bloody Hamilton?" she replied without looking at me. "I need a good cuppa tea and a few months of therapy, but I'll survive,"

"I'm sorry," I said, although I wasn't sure what she expected me to have done differently. "I thought you'd be used to this sort of thing."

"We have trained people for that malarkey," she said, sitting back and trying to straighten her hair, which had turned into a bird's nest. "I let the silly buggers knock down doors and fly about in cars and boats. I'm one of the sensible few who comes in afterwards and sorts it all out."

"Oh," I said, somewhat surprised. Not that I could picture her kicking down a door.

My mobile had been vibrating in my pocket for several minutes, so I dug it out to see what could be more urgent than a murderer slipping through my fingers. I also needed to call Whittaker and fill him in. My heart skipped a few beats when I saw it was Jazzy messaging me. 'Are you coming with me?'

I looked at the clock on the dash. It was 11:41am. Raylene from the Department of Children & Family Services was picking her up at noon. This day was relentless, one hit after another. I stared out the windscreen, mud splattered around the edges to remind me I'd let another criminal escape.

I typed 'no' and hit send.

What I wanted to say was that my heart ached at the idea of losing her to a sensible, loving, and stable home, but it would be the best thing for her, and she should embrace the opportunity if she likes the family. But I didn't, because I'm shit at all these things.

Instead, I called Detective Whittaker and buried my head in the case.

32

WHICH WAY TO DIE

Every police officer on Grand Cayman was on the lookout for Jonas Richards and his white hire car. Despite the island only being 22 miles long, picking out a singular white four-door saloon car amongst a sea of similar white hire cars was harder than it appeared.

Whittaker had no problem getting a search warrant now, and he joined O'Neill and me at the hotel, where the staff let us into Richards's room. Everything appeared much the same as I'd remembered from two days before, except the screwdriver was nowhere to be found. A stack of freshly laundered clothes was folded neatly on the bedroom dresser, waiting to be hung in the wardrobe, and I gave them a careful sniff. The detergent and dryer sheet odours overpowered any possible lingering smoky smells I'd hoped to find.

We bagged a laptop computer he hadn't had time to grab and found a phone charger but no mobile. Whittaker would start the process of tracking the mobile number Richards had given at registration, but it was an overseas number and service, so it would be days before we'd get a response from the US service provider.

"If I hadn't just witnessed this bloke running from the police, and walked into this room, I'd say we were looking at a regular old tourist on holiday," O'Neill said, closing the final kitchen cupboard after searching them all.

"I don't understand why he's still here," I said, because the thought kept coming back to me.

Whittaker tucked the evidence bag under his arm and opened the door for us to leave. "I'm worried about that too," he said as we filed by. "Only three reasons I can think of."

"He's not the arsonist," I suggested as we walked down the hall, which smelled of cleaning solvents.

"That's one," Whittaker agreed. "Which raises the counter of why did he run?"

"Because he's guilty of something else," I replied, having thought he was up to something from the first time we'd met.

"He doesn't care if he gets caught is number two," Whittaker offered. "But then, again, why did he run?"

"Wants to finish up his holiday," I said, more in jest than as a plausible argument.

"And the third reason?" Whittaker asked, holding the hall door leading outside.

"He's not done," O'Neill and I both answered in unison.

"Exactly," Whittaker said, letting the door swing closed behind us with a thud.

A handful of thick, dark clouds gave us momentary relief from the intense sun, but not the humidity. It was early for an afternoon shower, the kind which often wetted down the island for ten or fifteen minutes, and I glanced at my watch. It was 12:20. I unlocked the SUV and climbed into the driver's seat. Jazzy was probably just being introduced to the family who Raylene had deemed suitable, and who were interested in bringing a teenage girl into their lives.

An older couple, I guessed, who couldn't see raising a baby with all the nappies, mess, and sleepless nights. A kid who'd graduate from secondary school as their adoptive parents were turning senile. The couple were probably childless, or with grown children who'd already left their home.

"Sierra One, Control. Sierra One, this is Control. Suspect vehicle sighting at the north end of the old West Bay Road. Over."

The call instantly brought me out of my overactive imagination.

"Control, this is Sierra One responding. ETA three minutes. Over," Whittaker responded. "Warn other units to observe and report only."

I looked over at the detective in his Range Rover and he signalled for me to follow.

"Oh, heaven's above," O'Neill groaned. "Here we go again."

I waited for Whittaker to pull past me before backing out and following.

"Don't worry, he'll take it easy," I assured her, although I knew he was more than capable behind the wheel.

I'd been sitting in the passenger seat when he'd chased a suspect the year before. It had ended badly. Fortunately, no one else was seriously hurt, but the suspect was killed in the wreck. Since then, Whittaker had become a proponent of refraining from high-speed chases out of concern for the public. I figured I had a bollocking coming for this morning's episode, especially when the Crystal Harbour Strata — Cayman's version of a Home Owners Association — complained about their hedge and landscaped grass.

At a brisk but controlled pace, the detective led us alongside the golf course on the longer south side, using Safehaven Road. We sped over the sleeping policemen with jarring thumps, but otherwise maintained a moderate speed, even on the straight sections, and finally O'Neill released her death grip on the door handle.

Forced to turn left at the dual carriageway, Whittaker put his lights on and picked up the pace, looping 180 degrees around the next roundabout to head north. I followed suit and ran the lights, but we both kept the sirens off so as not to forewarn our suspect. The radio chatter had gone silent and I began to wonder if we'd be the first on scene. If he was moving when spotted, he was probably long gone by now unless the patrol car was able to follow.

Two roundabouts later, Whittaker called my mobile. "Sir?" I answered.

"Stay on the bypass. I'll turn at Seafire and drive up the old West Bay Road."

"Yes sir," I responded over the SUV's hands-free system.

"Keep the line open so we stay off the radio," he ordered.

We passed him as he slowed and turned left, while we continued on the dual carriageway, which gently climbed to an elevated section. Raised at least by Grand Cayman standards, as the island was mostly pancake flat. I picked up the speed to 60 mph, passing a few cars with a large, cleared area on our left, and mainly woods and mangroves to our right.

"What's that place?" O'Neill asked, pointing to the 500-metre-long dirt lot with lanes and a big semicircle marked.

"It was cleared for the KAABOO Music Festival they held a few years back, but now it's going to be more hotels and condos, I think."

We were nearing the next roundabout where we'd converge with Whittaker if we took West Bay Road when I noticed something amongst a group of shipping containers to our left. A thin stream of grey smoke rose before being whisked away in the breeze.

"Anything, sir?" I asked, slowing for the roundabout.

"Not yet," he replied. "Control texted me the location. A constable was responding to an incident at White Sands when he spotted the car. He wasn't able to pursue, but said Richards was heading south. We didn't pass him, so he must..." The detective paused and I heard the engine note die down as he slowed. "I think I see him."

"I'll cut through the new road that comes out by Sundowner," I told him, taking the first left off the roundabout.

"Come in easy. Let's not spook him," Whittaker warned me.

I was about to respond, when the smoke caught my eye once more. It was most likely workmen burning rubbish or trimmings, but the location was odd. I slowed at an entrance to the dirt lot.

"I'm one minute away, sir," I blurted, and turned left, accelerating across the bumpy dirt towards the containers.

"Where the bloody hell are you going now?" O'Neill asked, grabbing the door handle once more.

"Nora?" Whittaker asked over the open phone line.

"Just a minute, sir," I replied, and skidded to a stop as I reached the space between the big metal shipping containers.

"Oh, bloody hell!" O'Neill shouted, and whatever else she or Whittaker said was lost to me.

I had the door open as I slammed the SUV in park and bolted to the back, where I lifted the tailgate and wrenched the fire extinguisher from its mount. Sprinting, I could hear the screams coming from the dark grey Audi long before I reached the vehicle. Smoke was beginning to fill the interior as it fought to vent from the window tops.

Ripping the security strap from the top of the bottle, I pulled the pin and shoved the nozzle through the gap, squeezing the trigger. I aimed at the footwell where orange flames enveloped the man's legs. The rush of powder mixed with the smoke and the screams turned to deep hacking coughs. If I didn't get him out, he'd die of asphyxiation long before the flames killed him.

I knew the door would be locked, so I smashed against the glass with the base of the fire bottle. I couldn't believe it took three or four hits before the tempered glass shattered into a million little pieces, and a wave of heat and smoke drove me backwards. Coughing and spluttering, I ducked low and gave the footwell another blast of powder as the flames found fresh oxygen and leapt around the dashboard and steering wheel.

In the rear, flames were rising up the back of the driver's seat and I smashed at the rear side window until it shattered. I doused the flames and staggered back a few steps trying to draw clean air into my lungs. From inside the car, the man groaned and coughed, and I knew if I couldn't breathe, he certainly couldn't. Running around the other side, I smashed the passenger windows, which helped vent the interior but also allowed the flames to rekindle themselves.

The heat inside the car was overbearing, but I leaned in though the broken window and used well-aimed short bursts to extinguish the little spots of fire still burning. Moving back to the driver's side I reached in and yanked the interior handle. Melted plastic broke away, burning the shit out of my fingers, but the lock released and I swung the door open.

The man was unconscious, his head slumped against his outstretched arms, and his wrists strapped to the steering wheel with same type of metal clamps. I blasted one more small fire by his legs, which I could see were badly burned, and a vision of Osgood's scalp shot through my mind.

"Here!" shouted O'Neill, and I turned to see her holding a toolkit in a zippered folding pouch.

I grabbed a flat-blade screwdriver and leaned in, trying not to touch the man or the still roasting-hot car. The hose clamps were blackened and it was hard to see the slot against the dark steering wheel and the man's scorched flesh. I slipped and the blade scraped his wrist, gouging a piece of flesh away, and he jolted in the seat.

At least he was still alive, but I needed to work faster. "Hold up his head so his airway is clear," I said and felt O'Neill brush against me as she went to work.

Carefully fitting the blade into the slot, I started undoing the nearest clamp, and once I'd made a few turns, the metal glimmered where I'd scratched the soot away, making it easier for me to see what I was doing. I kept going until his hand dropped free and fell to his lap. He was making a disgusting wheezing sound now, but it meant he was breathing, which was all I could hope for.

Running around the other side, I opened the passenger door and sat in the singed passenger seat. This time I scraped the slot first so I could see better and made quick work of the hose clamp, letting his right arm fall to his lap. With O'Neill's help, we dragged his limp body from the driver's seat and laid him on the ground.

I'd been completely oblivious to the world around me as I'd fought to put the fire out without killing the man in the process, and now I sat on the ground, coughing, with my ears full of wailing sirens. Within a minute, we were surrounded by people, and a paramedic was asking me all the questions they're supposed to ask me which I had no interest in answering. I snatched the water bottle from her hand and took a mouthful, swilled it around, and spat it out next to me. It felt like it would take a million times more of the same to get the foul taste of burning from my mouth.

Malky was quick to the scene as the fire station wasn't far away, and once he had his crew organised, he checked on me.

"We have application forms at the station if you want to be a firefighter this badly, you know," he joked, once he saw I was fine.

"Someone has to pick up your slack," I wheezed.

He laughed and re-joined his men.

"Nora, are you okay?" I heard Whittaker ask, and his hand gently squeezed my shoulder.

I nodded. "Did you get him?" I asked in a husky voice that sounded like I'd smoked a pack an hour for my twenty years.

"We have him," he said. "He was hiding by the beach, just across the road. Found a stash of pills in his glovebox too."

I pointed towards the man a few metres away being frantically worked on by the paramedics. "You remember Dalton Loudermilk, sir. If he lives, we might finally have a witness."

33

IT'S A SMALL WORLD

I showered at West Bay station, where I had a spare blue RCIPS T-shirt I could put on as my white uniform shirt was toast. Literally. My right hand hurt like hell. The paramedic had put burn cream on my fingers and palm which of course I'd just washed off in the shower. I didn't think the burn was bad enough to blister but I should probably get something more to put on it. Whittaker had agreed with the paramedics and urged me to go to the hospital, but I slipped away when he was busy. I'd had enough of the hospital over the past few days.

At least the SUV was an automatic, so I drove one-handed to Central where they'd taken Jonas Richards for questioning. I didn't know whether Whittaker would let me in the room, but I certainly had questions for the *drittsekk*. I had no idea what connection the Florida case had to ours, beyond the similar methods, but the Loudermilk house had clearly been targeted on the island. I guessed we now knew why Richards hadn't left after the first murder, as he indeed had more planned as we'd suspected.

"How's your hand, pet?" O'Neill asked when I arrived at Whittaker's office.

"It's okay," I lied, happy she didn't want to shake my hand.

"Good timing," Whittaker said, rising from his chair. "We were just about to interview Richards. He's been processed and Hadley's taking him to an interview room now."

I followed them both downstairs and borrowed a third chair from another room, dragging it awkwardly with my left hand. Whittaker informed the suspect of his rights and notified him that the interview was being recorded.

Richards sat back in his chair, as far as the restraints would allow, and tried his best to look bored. "Lawyer," he said.

"Do you have counsel here on the island?" Whittaker asked.

"Nope."

"I expect you'd like us to appoint someone then?"

"I've no idea how you do things here," Richards replied in a condescending tone. "But I'm not saying a word until I have a lawyer."

"No problem," Whittaker responded, maintaining a friendly and obliging voice. "We'll see who's available. Of course, it's Saturday afternoon so I doubt anyone can be here until Monday morning. We'll be back to see you then."

Whittaker rose, so O'Neill and I followed suit. Richards quickly sat up.

"You can't hold me all weekend on a simple possession charge!"

Whittaker smiled. "Actually, we can, Mr Richards. We can also hold you a lot longer on the murder and attempted murder charges we'll be bringing against you. Not to mention that the quantity of pills elevates to possession with intent to distribute."

"Is Loudermilk still alive?" I asked, partly to help Whittaker's tactic, and partly because I wanted to know.

"So far," he answered as we made to leave. "He's on a ventilator."

"Murder?" Richards yelled, his handcuffs rattling as he tried to stand. "What the fuck are you talking about?"

"Ian Osgood," Whittaker replied.

"I like him for Jason Fraser too," I threw in. "Although he

doesn't seem smart enough to have figured out how to do that one."

Richards glared at me and I saw a flash of something else in his eyes beyond anger and panic.

"When was the last time you saw Jason Fraser?" I asked, and there it was again, a slight twitch and sudden blink.

"Who?"

I laughed. "I think we're wasting our time, sir. Perhaps by Monday he'll be more interested in getting out from under one of these charges."

"I didn't kill anyone!" Richards shouted. "Tell me what the fuck is going on. I had a few pills on me, sure, but I've no idea about this murder shit you're talking about."

"Tell us about Fraser, and we'll start there," Whittaker said, remaining standing.

"Are you telling me the guy's dead?"

"Are you finally admitting you knew him?" Whittaker snapped back. "If you are, we can talk. If you're sticking to your 'I don't know anyone or anything line', we'll see you Monday."

Richards let out a long breath. This wasn't his first time in a police interview room, but I doubted he'd ever been accused of murder before. He should have been, for killing the dogs in the warehouse, but he'd walked the last time he set fire to something with a heartbeat.

"I met Fraser a couple of times," he admitted.

"And sold him Rohypnol," Whittaker said.

Richards nodded. "And some oxy. I was supposed to meet him again this afternoon. I think he'd found a local buyer and was playing middle man."

"When was the last time you saw or spoke with him?" Whittaker continued, as we all took our seats again.

"I met with him Tuesday. That was the last time I saw the guy. He texted me a few times since then. This morning he told me he wanted to meet and buy more stuff."

"We'll find these texts on your mobile?" Whittaker asked.

The suspect shook his head. "I deleted them each time."

We could retrieve those texts through the cell provider, but we'd be waiting a while. The request had already been sent earlier in the day. My scratchy throat reminded me to get back to the subject of the arsons, but I was in the room as an observer and needed to let the detective direct the interview in his own way. Which I'd discovered over time was usually very effective.

"Where were you last night, Mr Richards?"

"In the room. I ate dinner at the hotel restaurant, sat at the bar for an hour or so, then watched a little TV and crashed."

"What did you watch on TV?"

Richards scoffed. "Some *Law and Order* bullshit where they ask a stupid question like that to check against the programming schedule."

Whittaker smiled. "How did you know Ian Osgood?"

Richards shook his head. "I have no fucking idea who you're talking about!"

"He's the man you set alight on Wednesday."

"The arson thing!" Richards shouted, trying to jump up but pulled back down by his restraints. "You've gotta be kidding, man! Why the fuck would I set fire to some dude I've never met?"

"Had you met the two dogs you burnt alive?" I snapped.

Richards froze for a moment before his face contorted into a disgusted look. "That's what's going on here?" he said, shaking his head. "You saw the bullshit arson charges they tried to pin on me and figured you'd stitch me up for this one. Well, I had nothing to do with that warehouse fire, and I sure as fuck had nothing to do with whatever shit you have going on here. You'd better get back out there, 'cos you got the wrong guy."

He sat back in his chair as though his outburst had cleared up the whole matter. Because criminals never lie. Whittaker switched tactics again.

"What was your argument about with Fraser?"

Richards looked at the detective and frowned. "What the fuck are you talking about now?"

"You don't expect us to believe you were tucked up cosy in your bed last night while Fraser was being murdered, do you?"

"Fuck this," Richards blurted.

"Enough with the dramatics and foul language, Mr Richards. Neither are helping your cause," Whittaker interjected before the suspect could continue. "Give us the truth, or we'll try again Monday morning."

"I'm giving you the damn truth — you're not listening!"

"We're listening, sir. We're not believing. How do you know Osgood and Loudermilk?"

Richards's eyes flicked up for a second.

"Loudermilk," I challenged. "You know Loudermilk."

He looked at me, then back at Whittaker. O'Neill had stayed quiet the whole time and he seemed to ignore her. "Loudermilk? You mentioned that name before. Are you saying Rhea Loudermilk has been murdered?"

"So you know the Loudermilks?" Whittaker pushed without answering the question.

"I met Rhea at a gym. You're saying she's dead?"

"Did you know her husband?"

Richards looked confused. "I didn't even know she was married. We worked out at the same gym where I bought a guest pass for a few weeks. I talked to her a couple of times."

"And…" Whittaker pressed.

"And nothing. She's hot, I chatted with her some, she was friendly, but not interested. That's it. Someone murdered her? Shit, she was really hot."

"With her husband out of the way, I suppose you figured you'd have a better chance," Whittaker said, and we all watched carefully for a reaction.

Richards slapped his hands on the table. "You know what? I'll wait until Monday. You idiots aren't pinning murder on me. Get me my lawyer."

Whittaker stood and casually tucked the file under his arm. "Have a pleasant weekend, Mr Richards."

. . .

It was late in the day for coffee, but I made a cup anyway, then stood in Whittaker's office, holding it in my left hand. It was surprising how awkward it felt sipping from a cup held in my non-dominant hand.

"Thoughts?" Whittaker asked, and O'Neill looked to me first.

"We have him on the pills, but there's nothing concrete tying him to either murder. It's all circumstantial. He knew Fraser, he knew Rhea, and he ran to the location where Loudermilk was set on fire. Beyond that, we don't have anything."

"Agreed," O'Neill added. "The timing is tight for him to have attempted the murder on Loudermilk, but doable. The others he could have committed from what we know at the moment. Richards is the only suspect who could have been at all three."

"I must say, I was starting to gain interest in Fraser for the Osgood murder, but he was in our morgue when Loudermilk was attacked using the same MO," Whittaker said, pacing behind his desk. "Richards has too many links to all the victims for it just to be a coincidence. I'll put a priority on tracking his movements from CCTV and have someone ask witnesses in the restaurant from last night. We need actual evidence placing him at the scene of the murders before Monday morning. Sergeant Hadley has assigned a constable to be with Mrs Loudermilk around the clock for the time being, which also limits her movements and gives us an opportunity to monitor her. I'll leave Rhea alone this evening, but tomorrow morning I'll question her about Richards and their paths crossing at the gym,"

"Maybe it's just a small world," O'Neill offered, but the look on her face told us she didn't believe that.

"We know she was already having one affair," I pointed out. "Maybe she was having two."

Whittaker stopped pacing. "That's true, and perhaps she likes to have options based on her fancy that day." He paused and let out a long sigh. "TSU have unlocked both of Fraser's computers."

He looked at me, knowing I'd been waiting to hear what our Technical Support Unit had come up with. Dreading, but waiting.

"Nothing of interest on the one we seized from the house, but the other was full of photographs which appear to have been taken in his makeshift studio."

"How bad are they?" O'Neill asked.

Whittaker shrugged his shoulders. "Not great, but not as bad as I'd feared. The women are nude or partially dressed, posed in a variety of positions. To be honest, the shots are more artistic than pornographic, but that'll be little comfort to the women he drugged."

"Were they distributed?" I asked, knowing what the answer would be.

"I'm afraid so," Whittaker confirmed. "The tech guys will have to explain the details to you as they lost me with their jargon, but the gist is Fraser was uploading them to a site hosted somewhere in an Eastern Bloc country. They're online, but they think they're on pay sites, so maybe the pictures will stay somewhat contained."

"They might for a while," I responded. "But not forever."

"Those sites will sell them on or use them as clickbait to the site after a while," O'Neill agreed. "And there's nothing the victims can do to stop it."

A silence fell over the room. Fraser had already paid for his crime, but that wouldn't stop the women suffering for the rest of their lives. Pictures and words stay on the internet forever. Copied, reposted here, there, and everywhere, their naked bodies would be available to anyone keen enough to search with the right keywords.

Whittaker picked his mobile up from his desk. "I don't think there's much more we can do for now, so why don't you both head out. We'll convene again first thing in the morning."

O'Neill rose from her chair and we both stepped towards the door. She stopped and turned back to Whittaker.

"Does it really take that long to get a public defender here?" she asked. "I'm surprised you don't have someone on call over the weekends."

"We do," Whittaker replied, his lips curling into a grin. "But this weekend it just so happens they're tied up and can't make it here until Monday."

O'Neill laughed, and it felt good to hear after all the madness of the day.

"Drop me at my hotel?" she asked as we walked down the stairs.

"Sure," I replied, and for the first time in hours, my mind leapt to what might be waiting for me at home.

I didn't know if O'Neill needed a quiet evening to herself or sensed that I did, but she was happy to be dropped at the Marriott with a plan to pick her up at 7:45 in the morning. I drove home, keeping the SUV instead of switching to my Jeep, as I didn't need the extra challenge of changing gears one handed.

A pharmacy would have been a good stop to make on the way, but I had a tube of aloe at the shack I'd used on sunburns, and it would have to do. There was a part of me that needed to be home as soon as possible, and another part that was keen to hide in denial for as long as possible. When I walked through the door, neither half was satisfied.

"Hey," I greeted Elín. "Where's Jazzy?"

"She's not home yet," she replied, and my heart stopped beating.

Jazzy wasn't one for sticking around in environments she didn't care for. No way would she spend a whole afternoon with the family unless she liked what she saw. The lump in my throat felt like it would cut off my air supply if I tried to breathe, which I hadn't done since Elín spoke.

"How was your day?" she asked me and I looked at her in confusion.

Of course, she had no way of knowing all that had taken place in the past ten hours. I relaxed and thought about which pieces of the puzzle concerned her.

"We caught the guy who drugged you," I said. "Actually, we found him rather than caught him. Someone murdered him last night."

Elín looked at me with her mouth slightly open as though she wasn't sure what emotion she was allowed to express.

"Good riddance to the *drittsekk*," I said, helping her out.

"Who killed him?" she managed to ask.

"We're not sure. We have a man in custody who sold him the pills, and he's our prime suspect, but we don't have enough evidence yet."

As I thought about how much to tell her in regard to the photo studio and the computer, my mind fell upon the receipt I'd picked up from the floor. I wondered if it had been dusted for prints yet. With the multiple crime scenes we had piling up, Rasha and her small group had to be overwhelmed, and I was sure priority had been placed on the fires.

"Where was he killed?" Elín asked, which I took to mean, 'How was he killed?'

"Someone tied him to a dive mooring so he drowned as the tide came in. Pretty clever really."

Elín looked horrified. If I was her, I'd be hoping the bastard suffered plenty, but she wasn't like me, and that was a good thing. I thought over what I'd just said, which was something I should probably do more often when people look at me as she'd just done. In actuality, I should do the analysis before speaking my thoughts aloud, but I doubt that would happen.

As I replayed my own words, I quickly forgot about my lack of tact, and an idea began forming. Rather than hit me in one blow, the seed steadily grew, and with each step that I searched looking for reasons to be wrong, I couldn't find any. The skill it had taken to tie the knots to set the perfect height. The Fox and Hare receipt. The convenient alibi. People often lied for their close friends and loved ones.

The door opened, and Jazzy walked in, just as my mobile rang. I looked from her nervous expression to the screen. It was O'Neill.

"Hey," I answered, and Jazzy walked past me, across the room, and closed the door to the bathroom behind her.

"You won't believe what my people have dug up back home, pet."

I stared at the bathroom door and gritted my teeth. I wasn't cut out to deal with this home life shit, but I was certain I knew who O'Neill was calling to tell me about.

"Can you be ready in ten minutes?" I replied.

"Meet you by the front door," she said, and we hung up.

"What now?" Elín asked.

"Now," I replied, taking a deep breath. "I have to find and arrest the person who did us a favour and really killed that prick, Fraser."

34

SPRING BREAK

2009

Something wasn't right. Maybe the crowds, or maybe the heat? Although the temperature had dropped to a comfortable level since the sun had gone down. Allie felt like the world was shifting around her. Nothing would stay still or remain in focus.

"Are you okay?" she heard Alfred ask, his voice close to her ear.

Why was she thinking he was Alfred? What a stupid name. The whole Batman theme was childish.

"Allie?"

His voice was strangely attractive, which was also weird. She wasn't interested in him; she never had been. They both knew that. Other voices came and went like trains passing through a station. They were in a hallway which never ended, then stairs, with bodies scattered about the place. Allie dropped the water bottle and watched it glide slowly to the floor as though she was floating in a spaceship. Maybe she was an astronaut. Maybe Batman was here too.

"Why don't you lie down?" came her friend's voice, and now they were in a room.

That was good. She'd wanted to go to the room, but she had no idea why anymore. Falling to the bed, she felt him next to her, and pulled him closer. Her skin felt alive, tingling and begging to be touched as his hands slid her clothing aside. Somewhere deep inside she knew it was her childhood friend, the man she'd shared so many memories with, yet never sought his embrace. But none of that mattered anymore.

"I've waited too long for this," his voice breathed into her ear, desperate and eager.

In her hazy, chemically confused state, Allie had no will to resist. After so many years in which she'd never considered this moment with the man who used to be her best friend, she was powerless to resist Ian Osgood.

Rafa saw them leave but was caught up in his argument with Garcia. He hated the man. Rafa was no angel, and made no pretence to be one. He did what he did to feed his mother and two sisters, but he had a line in the sand he wouldn't cross. It was partly driven by the fact he'd rather deal with rich assholes than addicted lowlifes, but it also had to do with a distinction between recreational narcotics and hardcore drugs. Garcia had no such line in the sand or moral compass of any degree.

By the time Rafa had made it clear these were his clients, and not to be messed with, Allie and the English guy had vanished into the crowd. He knew she'd wanted to get back to the room, so he presumed that's where they'd gone, but he instinctively knew something wasn't right. Garcia swore he hadn't sold anything to the group, which meant about as much as the bullshit falling from the lips of a Florida politician. Rafa had noticed Allie drinking from a water bottle she hadn't had with her when they'd arrived. Most probably it was simply that, a thirst-quenching bottle of water, but he knew the tricks people played... and the products Garcia sold.

Rafa looked around for Dalton, or Bruce as he insisted on being called, but he and his girlfriend had moved on too. He could text him again, but what was the point? They hadn't left with Allie, and it was the English girl that Rafa was concerned about. She'd seemed genuinely freaked out. He was also honest enough to admit that he found her attractive, which was partly fuelling his unease. Spring Break had a way of consuming people. He didn't want to see her become another victim of the biggest party in America.

His phone had grown quiet lately as most of his clients were happily stoned with more in their pockets for later. The texts he was getting now were drunken blabbering he could ignore, knowing they were a wild goose chase without a payday. Rafa slid through the crowd, keeping an eye out for Dalton and his wild girlfriend. That girl was built South Beach style all the way, a stark contrast to Allie. Why he found the pale-skinned English girl so interesting, he had no idea. Perhaps for the simple reason she was different? Sure, she was pretty with a slender figure, and she had the cool accent, but there was something more he couldn't put his finger on.

Feeling a buzz in his pocket, Rafa glanced at his phone. It was Dalton. He was out back of the hotel and had run across some friends who needed a hook-up. Rafa thought about it a moment. He didn't know the English guy very well. Ian had bought some Molly from him at parties over the past few months, but Rafa had got the impression he was using something more. Still, the man was Allie's best friend from what Dalton had told him. Surely he'd look after her?

Winding through the lobby and hallways of the hotel, Rafa came out in a two-storey parking structure. He found Dalton on the upper level, with a small crowd off to the side. After brief introductions and the usual banter, making everyone feel like they were super cool, especially Dalton as he had a drug dealer at his beck and call, Rafa made his sales.

"Where are your English friends?" he asked Dalton.

A shrug of the shoulders was his only response.

"They left, for the room," his girlfriend chimed in. "Remember? You gave Alfred a key," she added, rubbing up against her boyfriend. "I think they were finally getting over their platonic friendship crap."

Dalton laughed. "That's right! Well, I texted him a few minutes ago and told him we were here getting a reload."

Rafa had figured he'd leave the parking garage and head to the hotel room, but if Ian or Alfred or whatever he wanted to be called was coming here, there didn't seem much point. The thought that he'd missed his last opportunity to see Allie was disappointing. He'd been conjuring up ideas about inviting her to stay in Miami instead of going home early. His plan was full of holes, such as where she could stay, as he lived with his mother and sisters, but he'd figure all that out if she said yes.

A group had gathered at the top of the ramp leading down to the lower parking, and beyond that the street. Traffic had died down considerably, but the city still throbbed with a mixture of voices, music, and police sirens. Rafa walked to where Dalton and Rhea had joined the crowd surrounding a beaten-up looking old car. Encouraged by the onlookers, several guys were using spray cans to write 'Spring Break 2009' all over the sun-faded and rusty red paint. More and more people converged on the scene as cheers and chants grew louder.

"We should get out of here," Rafa shouted to Dalton.

"No fucking way, man," Rhea yelled in response. "This is going to be epic."

Rafa shook his head. "This is the kinda shit that ends badly. We should leave."

Rhea reached over and draped her hand around Rafa's neck. "Come on, baby, we gotta see the car go zoom!"

Dalton climbed on top of a concrete wall to see over the four-deep crowd of bodies surrounding the ill-fated car. He offered a hand to his girlfriend, who accepted, and the two wobbled and fought to keep their balance as she joined him. People were slapping and banging on every panel of the car and then something else happened, which Rafa couldn't see, sending the drunken horde into a cheering frenzy.

"You go, girl!" Rhea yelled, waving her arms in the air.

"That's crazy!" Dalton screamed.

Rafa had no idea what was going on, but a knot formed in his stomach telling him it wasn't good. He jumped up to the wall, careful to keep out of reach of Dalton and Rhea's windmilling arms. When he turned, it took him a moment to realise what was happening.

The first thing he saw was Ian, standing next to the car, having just closed the driver's door. Rafa searched for Allie, before remembering her plan was to leave, so she wouldn't still be with him. He watched as Ian bent over and waved through the driver's side window before the crowd began pushing the car to the edge of the ramp.

"What the fuck is going on?" Rafa muttered to himself.

To a chorus of deafening cheers, the faded red car was pushed over the lip of the ramp where gravity took over and it gathered speed down the steep slope. Veering left, the car glanced the back of a parked SUV, sending a shower of plastic through the air as it ricocheted right towards the entrance barrier.

Rafa winced when the errant car hit the kerb, whipping the steering left, which kept the front wheels aimed at the barrier. The right rear wheel rode up the kerb, bouncing the back end into the air before striking the hefty steel stand for the barrier mechanism. The violent impact brought the car to an immediate stop in a shower of electrical sparks which quickly ignited the ruptured fuel tank.

Petrol, which had sprayed in the air, landed in an arc across the car park, and more fuel now gushed to the ground underneath. The crowd switched to a mixture of cheers and gasps as the whole car became engulfed in flame. People ran in different directions, stumbling, falling, and bumping into each other.

Rafa noticed that one man stood still, paralysed by the sight at the bottom of the ramp.

"Fuck! Ian! We gotta go, man," Dalton screamed, leaping from the wall and catching Rhea, who followed.

Rafa jumped down and ran to where Ian stood as the other two joined them. They all stared at the little red car which had become an inferno.

Dalton grabbed Ian's T-shirt and pulled him away. "We gotta get out of here."

Rafa was about to turn and leave with them, when through the thick black smoke now filling the interior, he saw something move. Allie's face pressed against the driver's window with a mixture of disbelief and confusion, before the smoke and flames consumed her.

35

SETTLING A SCORE

O'Neill was standing outside as I pulled in faster than I should have been going in the Marriott car park. She'd always waited in the air-conditioned lobby before, but I'd barely brought the SUV to a stop before she already had the door open.

"Did you call Whittaker?" I greeted her as she hopped into the passenger seat.

"Aye, he said to meet him down the road from the guest house at the football pitch. He said you'd know where that was."

I nodded, and sharply pulled away, causing O'Neill to wrestle her seatbelt.

"Steady on, pet," she fussed. "There's no reason to drive like a silly bugger. We'll be waiting on the detective anyhow."

She was right, but I was keen to get this over with. I joined the traffic on West Bay Road and drove more sedately.

"Okay, so tell me about Winskell," I said, and her reply confused me.

"He had an estranged daughter, who was raised by her mother," she said, as though that should mean something to me.

"So?"

"His daughter died in a car fire in Miami while she was visiting a friend."

Now she had my attention. I'd been solely focused on Elín's case.

"Didn't the Loudermilks go to university in Miami?

"Yup, at the same time Alice Mason died. And get this… Ian Osgood was the friend she was visiting. He was spending a year there, but dropped out after the accident and returned to the UK. It was all very suspicious, but no one was ever charged with any wrongdoing. The case was never officially closed, but the comments in the file I read suggested the whole thing was a Spring Break accident. You know, all those kids going berserk by the beach."

"Then why would Winskell have murdered Jason Fraser?" I asked, trying to process the shift in focus.

"Who said he did?" she replied, and looked at me.

"That's what I thought you'd called to tell me," I admitted. "I'd just pieced together the receipt we found and the clever knots in the rope. I saw Winskell with his landlady at The Fox and Hare the other night, and he was a Navy guy. It took some skill to tie Fraser up that way."

"Bloody hell," O'Neill muttered, and took her computer tablet out of her satchel. After a few moments of logging in and clicking around, she slapped her knee. "I'd read that his kid had alcohol and drugs in her system, but I didn't look at the tox screen to see exactly what. She was doped with Rohypnol."

"*Fy faen*," I swore under by breath. "You think the Fraser thing was spur of the moment? Sounds like he carefully planned to kill the people I guess he's blaming for his daughter's death, so why the different MO and added risk with killing Fraser?"

I pulled into the car park for the football pitch in West Bay, just down the road from the guest house. Whittaker wasn't there yet, but two patrol cars were.

"Maybe he saw it on the news and the Rohypnol angle tipped him over," O'Neill offered in response.

"We didn't release any details about the crime or why we were looking for Fraser," I corrected her. "He couldn't have known."

I parked by the patrol cars and groaned. This time it did hit me like a slap in the face.

"He overheard me talking to Elín in The Fox and Hare."

I smacked the steering wheel with my burnt hand and yelped when it stung like crazy. "I didn't know he was there until we saw them outside. They had to have been sitting right behind us. Though I've no idea how he tracked Fraser down at his studio."

"Seems a pretty resourceful chap, our Sonny Winskell," O'Neill replied. "He had a long time to plan all this, too."

"Not the Fraser part."

"True. Maybe that's why he was sloppy and dropped a receipt on the floor."

I looked up at the sound of a vehicle and watched Whittaker pull in and park next to us. Everyone got out of their cars and congregated behind the detective's Range Rover.

"I'd like one patrol car on Star Close to the north and one on Bramble Close to the south," Whittaker began. "I'll approach through the reception off Birch Tree Hill Road. Keep the cars out of sight but nearby and cover the exits on foot. We're interested in interviewing Mr Winskell as a suspect in the arson cases. Our evidence is circumstantial at this stage, so we'll be polite, but if he runs, use whatever means necessary to prevent his escape." He turned to O'Neill and me. "You two with me. We'll take my car."

"Sir?" I asked, before we dispersed. "Have you heard from Rhea Loudermilk's guard lately?

"They were still at the hospital last time I checked. She may have planned to spend the night there with her husband. I'm not sure."

I stood still, lost in thought for a moment. I'd been dreading arresting Winskell for the murder of Jason Fraser, as I liked Sonny, and the world was better off without a doping *dritt* like Fraser. Shame he hadn't tied Jonas Richards to the same mooring. But the arsons were altogether different. I wasn't sure why, and maybe it was simply me struggling to come to grips with the new information, but I still didn't want to be a part of Winskell's arrest. The man had hung on to the loss of his estranged daughter for how many years?

"Something wrong?" Whittaker was asking me.

"I'd like to interview Rhea Loudermilk tonight, sir," I said, although I hadn't truly formed a plan. "Our best chance of knowing what happened fourteen years ago in Miami is while Rhea is still scared she might be next."

My own words made me realise what was eating away at me now was the fact that Alice Mason's case was unresolved. Winskell was obviously convinced he'd found those guilty of her death, but unless he had new evidence, nothing could legally be done.

"Let me talk to her before she knows we've arrested Winskell, sir."

Whittaker thought for a moment and looked at O'Neill.

"She'd probably end up sticking that Taser somewhere it doesn't belong if she comes with us," O'Neill said, winking at me. "Maybe she'll get something useful out of the Loudermilk woman."

The detective nodded. "Okay. But remember, to the best of our knowledge, the Loudermilks are victims of what's taken place here. Don't go Viking on the lady."

"I'll be respectful, sir," I assured him, and got in the SUV before he changed his mind.

I went left while I watched the others in my mirror turn right towards the guest house. They'd be arresting a man who'd waited all those years to settle a score. That was a long time to carry that much hate and pain around inside.

I wound my way through the labyrinth of West Bay streets to the bypass and headed south. I began formulating questions in my mind, preparing myself to politely interview a woman whose husband was lying in intensive care. Although I didn't care for the Loudermilks, I didn't envy the rehabilitation and scarring the man would have to endure. If he lived. Of course, if he'd actually been responsible for whatever happened to Alice Mason, then maybe that pain and daily reminder would be just reward for his crime.

Passing Seafire on the right, I went through the next roundabout and realised I was about to pass by the Loudermilks' house on the left. I'd waste a ton of time driving to the hospital in George Town if she'd already come home. Checking the rear-view mirror, I saw I had no one close, so I braked, slowing the SUV before rumbling across the grassy divider between the highway and the frontage road.

Leaving a plume of dust behind me, I turned left onto Cook Quay and drove slowly down the cul-de-sac to the fish tank house. There in the driveway sat Rhea's bloated-looking Mercedes and a RCIPS patrol car. I was glad I hadn't spent ages driving to the hospital and back. Not to mention the house would be a better place to talk. I parked outside their gravel driveway and walked to the front door.

I expected to see the constable sitting in his car, figuring Rhea wouldn't want him inside the house, but both cars were empty. I banged on the door and waited, peering through the glass beside the entrance, not seeing anyone. I rang the bell and knocked again. Still nothing.

Taking the radio from my duty belt, I was about to key the mic and call for back-up, when Rhea's voice came over a speaker.

"I'll be right there, just one moment."

I looked at the doorbell. It was one of the fancy kind, wirelessly connected with a built-in camera. She was probably watching me on her mobile, which meant she could be anywhere. Not even in the house. Her voice sounded strained. I looked back at the two cars in the driveway and took a step towards them.

"Hold on, I'm on my way," came her voice again, but I kept walking.

I tried the driver's door of the police car. It was unlocked, and I looked around inside. Nothing appeared amiss beyond the fact the constable hadn't locked the car. We were taught to always leave the car running and door open during a traffic stop or situation where we might need quick access to the onboard computer or to leave in a hurry. But always lock the cars if we're stepping away for any length of time.

The car jolted and a thud came from the back. I glanced back to the house, where no one had come to the door, and Rhea had given up telling me to wait a while. I reached down and pulled the boot release, before moving to the back of the car with my Taser ready. Zip tied and gagged, the constable looked up at me with a faraway gaze, his large frame crammed into the small space.

My mobile rang in my pocket, which I answered with my left hand while I flicked open my knife and cut the plastic zip ties binding the constable's wrists with my right. I winced at the pain from my burns.

"He's not here," Whittaker told me over the phone.

"I know," I replied, "and he has Rhea Loudermilk."

36

SUNSET

The constable leaned against his car, rubbing his wrists, and if I had to guess, drugged with some form of sedative. I paced back and forth, talking to Whittaker on the phone.

"She was still alive one minute ago," I assured the detective. "But now he knows we're after him, she won't have long."

Whittaker took a moment to respond. "He's rushed. The question is where would he take her? To one of the two spots he's already used, or somewhere new?"

I walked to the SUV and started the engine, switching the call over to the hands-free system. "He would have had a third spot already chosen. He's planned everything in detail to date." Except the Fraser part, but even that was incredibly well thought through, all things considered.

"Agreed," Whittaker replied. "But now I think he's having to improvise. We need to cover the two locations he's used and knows."

I sat in the car, watching the constable stare at his hands in a stoned haze, knowing I needed to get moving. "Is O'Neill with you, sir?"

"That's Officer O'Neill," Whittaker reminded me before

handing his mobile over. In the background I heard him barking orders over the radio, which echoed from the handheld on my belt. I turned it down after hearing him order units to both prior arson locations.

"Nora?" O'Neill asked.

"Who was mentioned in the report?" I asked.

"In Alice Mason's police report?"

"*Ja.*"

"Osgood was interviewed, and so were the Loudermilks," O'Neill replied. "That wasn't her surname back then, but they talked to her."

"Any others, or just them?"

"No, there were quite a few more interviews. Witnesses who saw the car on fire. They found a few people who remembered seeing Alice that evening at various parties and what-have-you. One policeman said he talked to her on the beach."

"So, how does Winskell know who caused his daughter's death?" I asked. "He's picked certain people from all the names in the report."

"Right," O'Neill said while she pondered the notion. "I mean, this is the crowd she was there at Spring Break with. They all shared a room apparently."

"And the Florida guy was the drug dealer who sold them or gave her the Rohypnol?"

"That was never proven, and he wasn't charged, but yes, that would be my assumption. It appears Winskell figured he was the drug dealer involved."

"So Rhea is the last one he's after..." I pointed out.

"Aye, that might be."

"*Takk,*" I said. "Tell Whittaker I'm checking a third location."

I think O'Neill was trying to say something else, but I'd hung up the call having already slammed the SUV in drive and steered away from the house, wincing once more from the burns I couldn't seem to remember until it was too late. I had an idea, but it was a wild guess more than a hunch, based on an even more marginal theory that Winskell knew he was going back to jail. When he was done seeking vengeance, he'd want the world to know what had happened to his daughter. For that, he needed a bigger stage.

We were minutes away from sunset, and as I sped south on the bypass with lights and siren blazing, the sky was beginning to dim. I thought about calling it in, but I was so unsure that it seemed a waste of resources. I half expected someone to call in a car fire from another location, but I pressed on. I was committed to my theory and one more constable at the other two locations wouldn't make a difference.

There's a hundred ways to get from the bypass to the waterfront in George Town, and none of them are direct. They all twist and turn through a maze of streets whose patterns had evolved over the centuries from trails established to avoid a big tree or a low spot of ground. Saturday evening traffic was busy but moving, with most folks already in place to watch the sunset.

I chose Shedden Road, which brought me out by the historic building housing the Cayman Islands Museum. I paused at the stop sign with my siren off but lights still throwing red and blue flashes across the surrounding buildings. Pedestrians stood still, staring at me, which was all I needed to tell me I'd been wrong. If Sonny Winskell was staging his finale in downtown, my police lights would not be the star of the show.

My theory had been based on his enthusiastic talk of the sunset from downtown, which I'd known was thin, but now seemed ridiculous. The other two attacks had been staged in remote locations, the absolute opposite of where I'd guessed the third would be.

"*Fy faen,*" I muttered to myself, deciding what to do next.

I remembered I'd turned down my radio, and quickly twisted the volume knob. Reports were streaming in from the two previous attack locations, all saying they were clear. Whittaker was right, we'd surprised Winskell, and now he was probably improvising and perhaps even changing his method. I glanced in the rear-view mirror to see a line of cars disappearing around the corner behind me. No one had honked, but only because I had the lights going. I switched them off and turned right, not knowing where to go next, but feeling I should move.

To the west, the bottom of the sun was about to touch the horizon, and the sky above the water was a vivid fade from orange through yellow before blending into the deepening blue overhead. A white compact car drove slowly towards me, the tourists no doubt wishing they'd found a place to park by now. I slowed behind the cars in my lane waiting for pedestrians on the zebra crossing by the cruise ship terminal, then glanced at the white car passing by.

In the passenger seat, Rhea Loudermilk was screaming. At least I assumed she was by the terrified look on her face and her wide-open mouth. I couldn't hear her over the police radio and music from Sharkeez Bar which I sat alongside. Behind the wheel, Sonny Winskell's bright blue eyes met mine for a moment as he rolled by.

Selecting reverse, I looked over my shoulder and saw I was penned in by several cars behind me. I thought about ramming them to make myself room, but then I noticed the white compact turning across the road and stopping. Leaping out of the SUV, I ran towards where Winskell had found a gap in the traffic and stopped, straddling both lanes, bringing the narrow road to a standstill in both directions.

Inside the car, Rhea was shaking and screaming, with tears running down her face. I couldn't see the restraints, but by her odd position I could tell she was tethered in some manner, probably to the seat rails. Winskell sat still in the driver's seat, looking at me as I reached the front of his white hire car. He lifted a hand in which he held a lighter with a flame flickering.

It all became clear. I'd beaten him here because he'd stopped to prepare the car, knowing he wouldn't have time when he arrived at his chosen spot. The windows were all cranked down a few inches, and now I could hear Rhea's screams and sobs. I wasn't certain whether Sonny intended on staying in the car when he set it ablaze or if he'd jump out, but he had to know it was over for him. His eyes glanced past me and I turned. The sun was halfway below the horizon.

That was his fuse. When the sun was gone, he'd light up the petrol I was sure he'd already doused on the carpets of the car. If I waited, she'd be torched. If I tried something, he'd drop the lighter. Horns were now honking at the car blocking the road and people stood along the balconies of the upstairs bars and restaurants wondering what was disturbing their peaceful sunset.

I walked to Rhea's side and continued past the passenger door. Her face flickered hope until I kept going, causing her to scream even louder. Winskell watched me, lowering the lighter closer to the floor to let me know any false moves and he'd let it drop. I snatched open the back door and slid inside, slamming it closed behind me.

Sonny looked at me with a stunned expression, but the lighter was still in his hand. Holding the knurled wheel open must be killing his thumb. Rhea had fallen quiet as I'd leapt in but now burst into hysterical blabbering.

"Shut the fuck up or I'll set you on fire myself," I snapped, and she fell into stunned silence except for the odd sniffle.

The inside of the car reeked of petrol, burning my eyes and stinging the inside of my nostrils. For the first time, I noticed Sonny's left hand was cuffed and connected to the driver's seat rail by a hose clamp. I guessed he needed the extra length to reach the automatic transmission shifter.

"What the bloody hell are you doing?" Sonny asked, "I'm sure you know by now why I have to do this."

I nodded. "I do. But I have some questions first, and then you can barbecue yourself. And this one," I added, nodding at Rhea.

He risked a glance out of the windscreen, where the sun had dipped below the horizon. "Bugger it," he snorted and turned back to me.

"Sorry, I screwed up your dramatic timing, huh?"

His face broke into an acquiescent smile, and for a moment I saw the tired man who'd carried the heartbreak and rage of his loss for so many years. If I'd doubted his conviction for setting himself alight, that look told me otherwise. He was at the end of his personal road and comfortable with leaving this life. Even by the excruciating method of burning to death.

"I wish you'd been there when these twats murdered my little girl," he said. "You're just determined and mad enough to have stopped them."

"But you hardly knew your little girl," I said, hoping I wasn't pushing too far.

He shrugged his shoulders. "The missus couldn't take the Navy wife gig. She'd had enough by the time Allie was only two. After that, she met another bloke and didn't want me dropping in and out of the girl's life."

"But you killed the man who attacked her?"

He shook his head. "That was my second wife. Police were bloody useless on that one too. He was getting away with it, but I wasn't having any of that."

I looked at the back of Rhea's head, bobbing gently as she cried. "How do you know it was them?" I asked, partly because I really wanted to know, and partly to buy time. "They were all cleared at the time."

Sonny's face tightened into a frown. "It was them. Starting with that piece of shit drug dealer."

"I didn't meet Osgood, or the Miami guy, but the Loudermilks are pretty worthless based on the time I've spent around them," I said. "But that doesn't make them guilty of what happened to your daughter, Mr Winskell."

Rhea began protesting in incoherent sobs. I reached over and slapped the side of her head. "Shut the hell up unless you have something useful to say. I'm trying to have a conversation with Mr Winskell."

Rhea feebly whimpered and he grinned at me.

"Call me Sonny. I think the setting deserves a more familiar tone," he said before his expression became resolute once more. "I found a retired copper in Miami. The bloke worked the case in the first few days, until he was moved onto something different for no good reason. He shared all his notes with me. Retired less than a year later, so it was still fresh in his mind after all this time."

"Hey, what's going on?" a man shouted, having got out of his car, he stood a few metres away.

I lowered the rear window and flashed my badge. "Stay back and make sure everyone else does too."

The man looked unsure but waved at a few other onlookers and began telling them a policewoman was in the car.

"Sorry, so what's his name?" I asked, leaving the window down. "The copper you found."

"That's not important. I don't want trouble for him."

As I thought about tracking down the retired cop, another piece of the puzzle came to me. "You drove down to Miami from North Carolina, didn't you?"

Sonny smiled again, but ignored the question. "This copper told me they were about to arrest the four of them, when all of a sudden they were told to back off. He said he made a fuss about it and that's when they shifted him off the case."

"He told you they had evidence?"

"According to him they did," Sonny replied. "The drug dealer swore he had nothing to do with it and was going to squeal on the others. Then Loudermilk's old man rolls in — who's some rich bastard from Georgia — and next minute the case falls apart and they all walk. My Allie deserved better than that. I may not have been there for her growing up, and I can't make up for that, but no way could I let these arseholes get away with murdering her."

Rhea's sobs rose a touch louder as though the guilt couldn't stay contained. I was in a unique situation, sitting next to a man who felt he had nothing to lose by being completely truthful. As law enforcement, that was a rare opportunity, but I also knew we couldn't sit here forever.

"You were sitting behind me at the pub, weren't you?" I asked.

Sonny nodded.

"That was clever how you tied Fraser to the mooring."

"Thank you," he said. "I guessed he was the one when you ran the alert looking for him. I was taking my daily swim and happened to see the piece of shit. Followed him to his lock-up. I take it you found it?"

"Yeah, thanks for the address."

"Bloody hard with these old eyes scratching it so small, so I had to abbreviate I'm afraid," he replied. "You seemed smart. I knew you'd figure it out."

"All right," I said. "That's what I wanted to know. I'll let you get to it, Sonny."

He laughed. "Are you sure? Nothing more you want to know?"

I thought for a moment. "You got the landlady to lie for you. You charmed the pants off her, so getting her to give you an alibi probably wasn't hard. We covered the Fraser stuff..." I drummed my fingers on the seat. "I think that's about it. I mean, I'm not sure on the drug dealer part. If he was willing to tell the whole story, maybe he was innocent, but we'll likely never know. Unless Rhea wants to fess up," I said, thumping the back of her seat.

"Ian gave her the roofie. He told us," she blubbed. "Rafa didn't sell those kinds of drugs. They came from another dealer."

"Oops," I said. "I think you torched the wrong drug dealer."

Sonny shrugged his shoulders again. "Still a drug dealer."

"Dalton and I didn't do anything," Rhea wailed. "It was Ian!"

"No, but you stood there and watched it bloody happen!" Sonny shouted, spittle flying from his lips. "The copper told me you confessed. You stood by while Osgood shoved her in the car."

"All right," I said loudly, holding up my left hand. "It was nice talking to you, Sonny, but I'm sure you want to get on with things, and I don't want to be in here if you drop that lighter."

Winskell stopped shouting and looked at me as though I was mad. Rhea wailed like she was already on fire. My right arm reached around the side of Sonny's seat where I jammed my Taser into his shoulder, ignoring the pain in my sore hand. His body convulsed and with no muscle control, the lighter popped up in the air for a moment before falling. My cobbled-together plan after climbing into the back seat was to catch the lighter before it hit the carpet. Unfortunately, I underestimated gravity, and my hand grazed the plastic Bic, knocking it into the footwell.

I held my breath, but nothing happened. My fallback was based on the knurled wheel snapping closed so there'd be no flame to ignite the carpet, and I was about to shout with joy when orange flames appeared. Part of the lighter must have been stinking hot from being held on for so long, and ignited the petrol-soaked carpet. The fire quickly began to spread.

Rhea screamed from the depths of her soul, and I couldn't blame her now. I reached over and hit the unlock button on the door before scrambling out of the back and pulling the front passenger door open. The footwell was alive with flames which were rapidly spreading around the perimeter of the seat. I took the screwdriver I'd kept on my duty belt after Dalton's fire, and leaned over Rhea's lap, grabbing for the hose clamp I hoped held the handcuffs to the seat rail. If Sonny hadn't utilised the same items he'd used to anchor himself, Rhea was in big trouble.

I yelped as the fire began singeing the fine hairs on my arm, and Rhea kicked me as she flung her feet around trying to escape the heat. Sonny was moaning from the passenger side as he came around from the zap I'd given him, and someone was shouting from behind me.

"Get a fire extinguisher!" I yelled. "And keep still, Rhea!"

She was now screaming at the top of her lungs and wildly thrashing her feet, making it impossible for me to get to her restraints. I was draped over her lap, pinning her cuffed hands, and trying to free her while she bucked like a wild horse. The fire had spread along the sides to the back of the seat and I could feel flames roasting my stomach. I leapt back, took out the Taser again and hit Rhea with a shock. Her body twitched for a few moments before falling still.

"What are you doing?" Winskell mumbled as I went back to work.

Without her thrashing, I quickly found the hose clamp and began turning the screw.

"Don't," Sonny spluttered. "Don't let her go. She murdered my baby girl."

I had no idea if the flames had reached him yet, but I was certain my hand was getting scorched. Working the end of the screwdriver put my already stinging right hand so close to the fire it felt like my skin was melting away. Just when I didn't think I could stand it anymore, the hose clamp came loose and I dropped the screwdriver.

I rolled backwards out of the car and scrambled to my feet. I'd freed Rhea's binding but by tasing her, I'd turned her into a sack of potatoes. Her feet had slumped into the footwell fire and I needed to pull her clear. I leaned in and scooped my arms under her shoulders, dragging as hard as I could. She was coming around but her head still flopped and her body weight was limp in my arms. I pulled with all my strength and she slipped from the burning car and dropped to the tarmac with a thud.

Onlookers rushed forward and helped move her clear while I looked across the inside of the car to where Sonny stared at me, shaking his head.

"How could you do this?" he said as flames began enveloping his seat.

He'd poured petrol around the edge of Rhea's seat, as he'd done with the others to make sure the fire took it's time killing them, but he'd completely doused his own. Once the fire spread to the driver's side, it quickly engulfed the man and I heard his spluttering groans as the flames roasted his flesh. The awful smell was one I'd hoped to never encounter again.

"Here, here!" a man yelled and thrust a fire bottle into my hands.

I stripped the safety pin and pointed the nozzle at the base of the fire.

"No!" Sonny screamed, and behind the licking flames and billowing smoke I saw the look on his face. The same look at I'd seen earlier, although he was no longer smiling. Resolute. Committed. Ready.

I lifted the nozzle, and sprayed the powder at his chest and neck, smothering him in a whitish grey cloud which covered his face, smothering the fire, and the man. Slowly, I worked the nozzle down and killed the fire around him. Someone yanked the driver's door open and as the fire bottle ran dry and the smoke wafted from the interior, I heard Sonny Winskell's final wheezing gasp.

37

RAT BRAINS, MAYONNAISE AND BRUSSELS SPROUTS

I stared from the bandaging around my right hand to the turquoise water I was not allowed to dive in. Two weeks, the doctor had told me, before I could fully immerse my hand in water. Why I was sitting on the deck looking at the one thing I was barred from doing — the one thing I longed to do more than anything else on my days off — I had no idea, but there I sat.

The house was strangely quiet. The silence I had enjoyed for so long now seemed like a void waiting for someone to come home. Which Jazzy would, for a little longer. Right now she was visiting the family again, spending more time with them to see how it would go. After I'd finally made it home last night, her effervescent mood told me how the first visit had gone. They had a dog, three TVs, her own room…

O'Neill and Elín had been on the same flight to Miami, which would be taking off shortly. I'd driven Elín to the Marriott where the hotel shuttle took them to the airport. I still had the police SUV, so I was able to drive one handed. As the three of us were all reserved and non-mushy types, the goodbyes were brief, awkward, and over without anything much being said. Elín hugged me.

O'Neill didn't. But she did throw out an 'if you're ever in the UK' vague invitation.

We would undoubtedly be in touch, as she was stopping in Miami for a few days to pursue Allie Mason's cold case. Maybe, if O'Neill could track down the retired detective, the case could be revisited, but we all knew that was a long shot. Evidence swept under the rug in 2009 was probably gone forever. Two of the suspects were now dead, and two were being flown to Atlanta, Georgia, later today to be treated in a specialised burns unit. None of them had got off lightly. Regardless, O'Neill had gone from pain-in-my-arse to respected officer in just a few short days. I'd learnt a lot working with her.

Elín said she would keep in touch, but there was no way she was coming back to the island. I'd like to see her again as we got along well, but why put herself through the memories by returning? Perhaps it was because she didn't talk too much and kept her questions to the important ones, but we enjoyed being around each other. She would email a few times, until she realised I rarely checked mine and only replied if it was something worth discussing. Slowly, they'd peter out and she'd become another person lost to my past.

I was used to the occasional acquaintance brushing by my life, so while O'Neill and Elín might give me pause to think every once in a while, their absence wouldn't greatly affect me. But their presence had added to the social activity and interaction over the past week which made the sudden silence harder to resolve in my mind. I should feel relieved and unburdened, yet I didn't.

As much as I told myself Jazzy would be better off with a stable, normal family, the emptiness was far too reminiscent of the loss I felt over Ridley. Sonny Winskell had spent fourteen years unable to move past his loss… was I destined for the same fate? I'd killed the man who'd shot Ridley, so would that give me a chance? Some days it felt like it did, but other days, like today, seemed like I was chained to the tragedies of my past.

The situations and the feelings with Ridley and Jazzy were

different in many ways, but the hole I felt inside was remarkably similar. He was gone forever and she would be living just a few miles away, but she was a teenager with a new world opening up for her. It would be like the emails. A visit every week or two would become an occasional meeting for dinner, then pretty soon a dinner would be postponed, and somehow our paths would diverge forever.

I would be her fading memory of the weird chick who had something to do with her leaving the streets and beginning a new life as a functioning part of society. The last thing I wanted or needed was recognition for the part I played in her transition. I just wished I hadn't let the little shit mean so much to me.

Movement at the other end of the deck caught my eye, where Edvard had boldly waddled half the distance towards me. He tilted his head to one side and stared. I took a piece of lettuce from the table beside me, leaned over, and held it just above the wood planking. I used my left hand so the mixed stench of ointment and burnt skin didn't scare him away forever. The lizard moved closer and stopped as he always did, a metre from me.

"Not this time, leather face," I told him, and we locked eyes in a staring contest.

He raised a foot as though he was about to come closer, but left it suspended in the air like he'd been freeze-framed.

"Listen, you prehistoric rat, we've played this game for how long now?"

His head tilted to the other side.

"I can't remember either, but it's been a long time."

The raised foot lowered to the wood.

"At any point during the time we've known each other, have I ever tried to eat you?"

His head turned to one side as though he was listening intently.

"Exactly. So make both our lives easier, and take the fucking lettuce from my hand."

Edvard stood perfectly still, then turned his head the other way, looking out over the water.

"Fine. If you're not interested, then neither am I."

I sat back in the chair and dropped the lettuce leaf on the table. The intense midday sun was high overhead, its arc constantly moving the brightly lit portion of the deck from the east side to the west. Feeling the heat on my right foot as the shade was chased away, I quickly moved my leg. I'd had enough of burning skin to last me a lifetime.

The lizard moved forward and to his left, seeking the very thing I was trying to avoid. I picked up the lettuce leaf once more and leaned down, holding it in the sun-drenched spot where my foot had been. Edvard walked straight over, tore away a big piece of lettuce, looked up at me, and chewed.

"*Fy faen,*" I groaned. "The only one who wants to live with me is an old, wrinkly, endangered lizard with trust issues."

I heard rustling from the woods, and voices grew louder. Edvard looked up at me as though I'd betrayed him to the lizard mafia, snatched as much lettuce as he could grab in his mouth, and scurried off the side of the deck.

"Hey there," AJ said cheerily as she rounded the corner, followed closely by Jazzy. "Look who I found wandering aimlessly around West Bay."

Jazzy laughed and rolled her eyes.

AJ held up a shopping bag. "Brought you lunch, what with you being a one-armed bandit and all."

She reached in the bag and pulled out a Strongbow cider, which was her favourite drink when she indulged. They were refreshing, and as someone who only drank alcohol occasionally, I decided a cider was more acceptable than wine at midday. AJ put the bag on the table and pulled out a sandwich wrapped in paper.

"Here," she said, taking the cider bottle back and handing me the sandwich instead. She then popped the top off the cider and set it down.

"What did you bring me?" Jazzy asked with a cheeky grin, dropping into one of the other chairs.

AJ pulled another sandwich from the bag and handed it to her.

"I brought you rat brains with mayonnaise and Brussels sprouts. I hope you like it."

"Umm, my fave," Jazzy said, playing along and unwrapping her lunch.

I found my lips curling into a smile until I reminded myself why Jazzy was in such a great mood. She and AJ bantered back and forth a little more as AJ sat, opened her own cider, and unwrapped her sandwich. AJ was happy, because that was her nature, and it was typical she'd think of me on her one day off in the week. She was also unaware of Jazzy's impending departure.

As much as I was trying to be happy for Jazzy and her new opportunity, it was hard to swallow how someone else could step in so easily and become the centre of her world. Perhaps that was the problem? The kid had become the centre of my world, but not the other way around. My thoughts were purely selfish, which made me even more angry and disappointed in myself.

I was about to ask Jazzy about the next move, and probably not in the mature adult way I should, when I heard more noise coming from the woods.

"Who could that be?" AJ asked quietly, knowing my only visitors currently on the island were already seated on the deck.

Jazzy curled into her chair and focused on her sandwich as Raylene appeared, looking like she'd managed to snag herself on every branch along the narrow trail.

"I thought I'd find you here," she said, and it took me a moment to realise she was talking to Jazzy.

"What's going on?" I asked, sitting up.

"She didn't tell you?" Raylene asked, clearly aggravated.

I shook my head.

"She just up and disappeared," the social worker explained. "Everything seemed fine and I was about to leave them to spend the afternoon, and next minute, Jasmine has run off."

"I told you I found her walking along the road," AJ added. "She said she was coming home from a friend's house."

"I thought you were kidding around," I mumbled, trying to

fathom what was happening.

"Well?" Raylene asked sharply, looking at the teenager.

Jazzy sighed. A long exhalation and anguished look on her face that teenagers everywhere perfect at the age of thirteen and a half.

"I'm fine here."

"Fine isn't the point, young lady," Raylene responded in frustration. "Nora has been kind enough to make this work on a temporary basis, but we all knew that's exactly what this always was. Temporary. We've found a couple who are a perfect situation for you with a lovely home, and they already think the world of you. Now we need to…"

"Wait," I interrupted.

Raylene had gone above and beyond to help with Jazzy, and I admired her for truly caring in an often unrewarding and frustrating job, but I had to stop her. She was missing the point. I stood and walked over, crouching next to Jazzy's chair.

"Why?"

The kid looked at me with her big brown eyes which had been full of laughter just moments ago. They were now full of what I interpreted as sadness.

"I have everything I need right here. I'm fine."

I rested my good hand on her arm. "Did something happen?"

Jazzy shook her head, and her crazy mop of hair tried to keep up, shaking from side to side. "No. They're really nice."

"Then you should go, Jazzy. They can offer you so much more. This is your chance at a normal life with all the stuff normal kids get to do."

She shook her head again. "I'm fine here."

"Just because this feels safe to you now doesn't mean you won't feel that way, and more, with these people."

Jazzy looked at me with resignation. "I'm not going."

"You need to tell me why, and 'I'm fine here' isn't good enough."

She tilted her head to one side like a damned lizard. "Because you need me as much as I need you."

ACKNOWLEDGMENTS

My sincere thanks to:

My incredible wife Cheryl, for her unwavering support, love, and encouragement.

My family and friends for always being there.

My marvellous editor Andrew Chapman at Prepare to Publish for his diligent work and wise suggestions.

Gretchen Douglas, who always catches a few key items with her fine proofreading skills.

Lily at Orkidedatter for her Norwegian advice.

Casey Keller, Craig Robinson, and Alain Belanger for their help with all things Cayman Islands related.

Lisa (O'Neill) and Richard Preskenis for their hospitality and being our Cayman dive buddies… and for letting me borrow her name for a cool character!

Shearwater dive computers for their friendship and support.

The Tropical Authors group for their advice, support, and humour. Visit and subscribe at www.TropicalAuthors.com for deals and info on a plethora of books by talented authors in the Sea Adventure genre.

My beta reader group has grown to include an amazing cross section of folks from different walks of life. Their suggestions, feedback and keen eyes are invaluable, for which I am eternally grateful.

Above all, I thank you, the readers: none of this happens without the choice you make to spend your precious time with my stories. I am truly in your debt.

LET'S STAY IN TOUCH!

To buy merchandise, find more info or join my newsletter, visit my website at
www.HarveyBooks.com

If you enjoyed this novel I'd be incredibly grateful if you'd consider leaving a review on Amazon.com
Find eBook deals and follow me on BookBub.com

Catch my podcast, The Two Authors' Chat Show with co-host Douglas Pratt

Find more great authors in the genre at TropicalAuthors.com

Visit Amazon.com for more books in the
Nora Sommer Caribbean Suspense Series,
AJ Bailey Adventure Series,
and collaborative works;
The Greene Wolfe Thriller Series
Tropical Authors Adventure Series

ABOUT THE AUTHOR

A *USA Today* Bestselling author, Nicholas Harvey's life has been anything but ordinary. Race car driver, adventurer, divemaster, and since 2020, a full-time novelist. Raised in England, Nick has dual US and British citizenship and now lives wherever he and his amazing wife, Cheryl, park their motorhome, or an aeroplane takes them. Warm oceans and tall mountains are their favourite places.

For more information, visit his website at HarveyBooks.com.

Printed in Great Britain
by Amazon